SUMMER'S LIST

SUMMER'S LIST

ANITA HIGMAN

MOODY PUBLISHERS
CHICAGO

The author is represented by MacGregor Literary, Inc.

Interior Design: Design Corps
Cover Design: Dean H. Renninger
Cover photo of woman copyright © 2013 by Nabi Tang/Stocksy 21449. All rights reserved.
Author photo: Circle R Studios Photography

Library of Congress Cataloging-in-Publication Data

Higman, Anita.
    Summer's list / Anita Higman.
      pages ; cm
    ISBN 978-0-8024-1232-4
    I. Title.
      PS3558.I374S86 2015
      813'.54—dc23

                                    2015001168

This is a work of fiction. Names, characters, places, and incidents either are the product of the author's imagination or are used fictitiously, and any resemblance to actual persons, living or dead, businesses, companies, events, or locales is entirely coincidental.

We hope you enjoy this book from River North Fiction by Moody Publishers. Our goal is to provide high-quality, thought-provoking books and products that connect truth to your real needs and challenges. For more information on other books and products written and produced from a biblical perspective, go to www.moodypublishers.com or write to:

River North Fiction
Imprint of Moody Publishers
820 N. LaSalle Boulevard
Chicago, IL 60610

1 3 5 7 9 10 8 6 4 2

Printed in the United States of America

In sweet memory of Laney—
*the beloved dog who brought my
daughter-in-law, Danielle Higman,
much love and comfort through the years
and who can still bring tears of joy
every time she is remembered.*

"The value of life lies not in the length of days,
but in the use we make of them;
a man may live long yet live very little."

❧

Montaigne

"See! The winter is past; the rains are over and gone.
Flowers appear on the earth; the season of singing has come,
the cooing of doves is heard in our land."

❧

Song of Songs 2:11–12

PART ONE

shadows

CHAPTER
one

The engagement ring was stuck—just like her life. Summer glanced toward the heavens and sighed the sigh of love gone awry. Again.

Here she was, thirty-three years old, and still floundering in every part of life that mattered. And so went the mental ramblings of Summer Snow as she continued to twist Elliot's engagement ring on her finger, trying to pull it off. She was impatient with herself for delaying what she knew she should do: follow through and finally let him go. After all, Elliot Whitfield was famous for taking smooth talking to epic levels.

Summer straightened her spine, looked across the table at her fiancé, and said, "Honestly, Elliot, you don't need a wife. What you need is a good PR consultant."

Elliot smoothed a crimp in the linen tablecloth. "You'd think a five-star restaurant could have wrinkle-free linens." He emitted a slow breath that strangled itself into a groan. "Now, no more talk of leaving me, my pearl. You're going to make the perfect senator's wife. You're articulate. You're beautiful. You can hold a smile for hours." He grinned. "With a few tweaks, you could be my Summer Eleanor Roosevelt. And with you by my side, I now have an eight-point lead over my opponent," he added in his pretend British accent, the one he used when he was kidding around. "Come on. You know I'm joking."

"Right." Summer's wry expression made him laugh.

A waiter came by—bristling with pomp—and refilled Elliot's goblet with Pellegrino.

Then he whirled off amidst the live harp music, which floated around them as did the scents of fine cuisine and expensive perfume, and the smell of money.

Elliot turned his attention back to her. "Seriously now, you *will* be part of this noble endeavor to represent the great state of Texas." He raised his hands as if addressing the masses. "It gives me the chills to think about it. I can almost hear the theme music from *Chariots of Fire* revving up in the background. Don't you hear it too?" He tilted his Harvard-educated head to dramatize his point.

No matter how green-eyed and Greek-angled Elliot was or how much he could make her laugh, the hour of reckoning had come. "As much as I care about you," Summer said, "I don't have the chills, and I'm sorry to say that I don't hear the music."

Her fiancé's eyes dimmed, and he placed his hand over his heart as if she'd pierced him through.

"Please, Elliot, anything but that look . . . that Bambi's-mother-has-been-shot-in-the-meadow look."

"Good one," he conceded.

The ring finally loosened its hold on Summer's finger, and it sailed upward and then plopped into Elliot's personal patty of Lone Star–shaped butter. "Sorry." Invariably, when she got nervous, crazy stuff happened. Today it was merely the butter, but if she married Elliot, it would mean embarrassing herself—and Elliot—in front of the media. It could happen. It *would* happen. But that wasn't really the reason she had to give his ring back. She curled up her toes in her high heels. "And I'm sorry I can't be everything you and your voters want me to be. Truly."

He retrieved the diamond ring and wiped it off. "I just want what every man wants, my sweets . . . a woman who looks like you do, and a woman who's also so totally into me that she's willing to give up her whole life to meet all my needs." Elliot's twinkle was back.

"Cute, but I refuse to be moved this time by your sense of humor *or* your silver tongue."

"Ouch." He squeezed his wedge of lime into his Pellegrino.

A spray of juice hit her eye, which made her twitch for a moment.

Elliot didn't seem to notice, so he bulldozed forth. "You think I'm trying to change you, but I'm not. Well, I just made that *one* tiny demand."

"It's not tiny to me. I can't sell my grandmother's bookshop." Summer ate a spoonful of her lobster bisque, but a droplet escaped and landed on her dress. *Great.* Why was she such a messy eater?

"But how long can you keep her store running when it's making so little money? How far can you take this sentimentality? Your grandmother is retired now, and maybe it's time to retire her shop too." He sat back in his chair, glimmering with enough pomposity to propel him right into the mirrored halls of political life.

Summer wet a napkin and dabbed up the stain on her only spring gown. "Her bookshop was always about making kids happy, not about making a lot of money. You used to think these dreams were admirable."

"I did. And I still do, but being a public servant is serious business. We both need to look successful. *Be* successful. No room for error. You can't even misspell potato in this business without the media jumping on you faster than you can say au gratin." He ran his hand along the silk tie that coordinated perfectly with his navy Armani jacket. "So I just felt that if you sold the shop, you'd have more time for me."

Summer arched her brows at him.

"More time to devote to this gallant effort. We'd be a team. Don't you see? A force to be reckoned with, you and me. Hey, some women would see sharing my life as a dazzling adventure." Elliot set the diamond ring in the middle of the table and slid it back toward Summer as if it were an addendum to a contract. "I mean I'm being flexible for you."

"How?"

"Well, I'm overlooking the fact that you don't have a college education. That's going to make a difference. It's expected of a senator's wife, but that's okay."

"I *am* sorry, but what I chose to do with my time back then when I had the chance to go was more important."

"Yes, that was noble of you, actually, what you did for your parents, but—"

"But?" When it came to political life, she guessed that doing the decent thing didn't weigh in as heavily as doing what looked right. "Why were you ever attracted to me in the first place if you knew I wasn't going to make a suitable wife?"

"Because I found you irresistible. I couldn't help myself. I guess I was letting my heart rule over my common sense."

"Well, I do appreciate the honesty." Summer slid the ring right back to him. "Look, Elliot, you should let your common sense win this time . . . for both of our sakes. Okay?

"You're truly cruel."

"I'm cruel?" Summer teased him with a smile.

Elliot grinned and then stared at her as if seeing her for the first time. "You really are an incurable romantic, aren't you? Just a child, really," he murmured.

"You're right. I was a child to think I loved you enough to make this work." Summer picked up her beaded bag from the table—the one she'd fished out of a cardboard box at a garage sale.

"My jewel, sit down. Please. People are watching." Panic flashed across his fine features.

"I'm sitting back down, but only because the hem of my dress is caught under the leg of my chair."

"I'm just saying, if you're going to be the wife of a—"

"But I'm not going to be the wife of a senator. We're no longer engaged." Why was it that the people who were the best talkers were the worst listeners? Then she lifted the chair, freed the hem of her dress, and rose.

As Summer stepped away from the table, Elliot reached over and latched onto her wrist. "I honestly can't live without you."

"And this is honestly going to put a crimp in your agenda. Right?"

He sighed. "Yes, that too."

"I'm sorry. Truly." Summer leaned down and planted a tender kiss on his cheek.

"What if I can't win the election without you? Don't you see? I doubt my constituents will fancy the idea of my fiancée dumping me for another man."

"You don't have to worry. There's no other man."

"There's always another man." Elliot stared at what was left of his vichyssoise. He always did love cold soup. "My prediction?" He looked up at her. "Before another week is over, your heart will already be attached to another man."

"How can that be?"

Elliot pressed a kiss to Summer's hand as if it were made of hand-blown glass. "While we were sitting here, you didn't see the dozen or so men who were glancing your way. Because no man can resist you. Eyes the color of sapphires, auburn hair, and that graceful way of yours. All that is missing, Summer, is your crown. And I could have bought you a thousand of them."

Everything sounded like a speech. "Ah, well. Such is life." At that moment Summer realized how it was she'd fallen for Elliot. She'd been so hungry for attention she'd gobbled up his every word, even though it was mostly baloney. She had to admit, though, it was the best gourmet baloney she'd ever eaten. "I wouldn't worry about the bad press over this. Your speech writers are good at putting a spin on things. They'll remind everyone how faithful you were and how I was the ungrateful one, the disloyal fiancée. That should quiet my exit."

"So this is goodbye then? Really?"

Poor Elliot. He really couldn't imagine a world where people said no to him. "I pray your life goes well." Summer leaned down and whispered, "I may even vote for you."

"But where will you go without me?"

"I have no idea."

Summer walked away as the waiter arrived with a big question mark on his face, which looked very similar to the one scrawled all over her life. Mist stung her eyes then, not because of regret but because saying goodbye was always hard, even when it was right.

Partway out the restaurant Summer paused and looked back at Elliot to make sure he'd be all right. Elliot readjusted the small American flag pin on his lapel and then dug into his next course. He was even eating with his fork upside down like a Brit, so that meant he was in a pretty good mood and had already moved on. *Boy, that was quick.* But this was good, really. Now she wouldn't have to worry that she'd hurt him. And Elliot's parents would be relieved about the breakup rather than disappointed, since after first blush, they too had sensed she wasn't cut out to be the wife of a senator.

Yes, Elliot Whitfield would be fine. He'd most likely succeed in everything he touched, and maybe even someday he'd be nominated for the presidency. Summer could already see the red, white, and blue placards—Whitfield for President. And as far as finding a wife, half of the women at their church would be eager to marry the name and the hair and the entitlements that came with him. And well, the other half of the women were already married. Summer didn't linger there, since Elliot was right, people were watching.

Minutes later Summer settled into her car, relieved they'd come in separate vehicles. Her old Chevy was much more comfortable than the hard seats in Elliot's coupe. In fact, her whole life suddenly felt more comfortable—more real—like in *The Velveteen Rabbit.* Maybe she really was an incurable romantic.

Summer pulled down the rearview mirror and gave herself an assessing gaze. Her hair had blown up in the Houston humidity like an umbrella suddenly popping open. Even though it wasn't summer yet, the heat was already creeping in. But beyond her rowdy hair, she looked more than a little off. There was something else playing in her expression. Was it a glint of regret that went beyond the breakup?

She let the window roll down as she turned her attention to the swirling firmament. The slightest puff of air tickled her cheek, and a pleasant but unfamiliar fragrance came in on the breeze. *Lord, when will I ever hear the music? God, do You still love me after all my wrong turns and semi-disastrous choices?*

She opened her beaded purse and pulled out a trinket she'd kept for many years—a wooden carving of two tiny robins in a nest. The gift had been from Martin, a childhood friend. He'd said the pair of birds were created especially for her and said they were really two friends that could never be parted, for their wings were carved as one.

Such a beautiful sentiment.

What had ever become of Martin? Summer gazed up at the stars—at the beauty and the breathless wonder of it all—and wondered what Martin was up to this very moment.

CHAPTER
two

Summer closed her fingers around the tiny carved birds. Turning the page of life would be scary. That is, turning the engine on and driving away. But where would she go? Home? Fine, but after that? It would take care of the logistics, her movements from point A to point B, but what would happen to her insides—her heart? Would she just muddle through with life until there was none of it left to fritter away? But why did she always feel that if she weren't in a meaningful relationship about to tie the knot then she was squandering her time? That she was idling instead of setting forth on some worthy and adventurous endeavor?

Not a healthy mindset.

Summer turned on the engine, and then turned it off, not feeling quite ready to see what was on the next page. In a novel it was easy to read chapter after chapter. And no matter how bleak the plot, there was sweet safety in the cozy armchair, that hot cup of chamomile tea, that yawn that said it was time to set the story aside and go to bed.

But in real life, well, there was no safety in trying to make one's way in love. Or in one's career. Or anything for that matter. Oh, the perils of being earthbound. The fears of choice. The doubts and dangers of every crossroad's moment.

Life suddenly didn't feel as decisive and confident as it had minutes before, when she had sashayed away from Elliot's table, chin up, knowing she had done a right and noble thing.

All the past disasters in love came back to her in one big haunting tidal wave—the painful words, the lonely feelings, and the empty seat when dining out. And she'd be forced to go back to the singles' group at church instead of the young marrieds and soon-to-be-marrieds. When she walked back into church, she might as well wear one of those sandwich board signs, proclaiming to the world that Summer Snow was officially a mess. Would men bolt from her, thinking she would be on the hunt again? Would women flee because they might worry that her singleness was like an incurable disease? And catching?

Summer rolled up the window and pressed her head against the glass. Maybe she'd make use of the tear ducts that God had given her. That thought seemed to give her permission to let go of her emotions, and so her eyes pooled with tears until they spilled over. She swiped them away and slapped her hands against the steering wheel.

With every breakup she experienced, the more it rubbed a little more of the shine off the silver until the whole of life appeared tarnished if not a hunk of bare, rusty metal.

Summer stuck a few tissues over her mouth and let out a scream. The muffled holler did nothing to ease her confusion and sadness. She glanced around, hoping no one had seen or heard her outburst. She laughed then. Right in the midst of the tears. Maybe she *was* a little nuts.

After much pondering, the lone word "twilight" slipped from her lips. For a long time she'd been living in a sort of half-light—that strange twilight hour when one couldn't see things clearly, especially a road. But then all her roads seemed to lead to a dead end.

Summer turned the key, and her granny came to mind. She looked at her watch. Seven-thirty. Still not too late to drop by. Her house wasn't far away. Maybe she'd stay just for a few minutes so she could get her bearings.

Of course, she knew her granny would see her splotchy cheeks and red-rimmed eyes and insist she stay the night. Granny had the best guest bedroom of any house she'd ever been to—with enough pillows piled mile-high on the bed to soften at least a few blows of the weary traveler.

The next day would be Saturday. There was help at the bookshop. Amelia Landers was there, faithful as always, and just as much in love with kids and books as she herself was and enough to make Summer feel at ease to let her run the shop. It would be nice to take the day off. Except for Sundays, she mostly worked. It was a shame the Once Upon a Time Bookshop didn't make more money for her to live on, but the last thing she wanted to do was close the store that Granny had spent the bulk of her life building. Or closing down the one place that had changed the lives of countless children through the decades, including her own.

Summer pulled out of the parking lot, already feeling a mite better, thinking of Granny's soft things—her mattresses, her chocolate chip muffins, and her hugs. They were the best. Yes, when one was at Granny's house, it was always a muffin-top experience.

She goosed the gas pedal on her jalopy, trying to get to Granny's just a little faster. After pulling up to her stone house—which was quaint in every way with its arched windows and gingerbread cuteness—Summer made haste getting to the front entrance.

She tapped on the front door. Nothing. She rang the bell. No answer. Could she be ill? Granny did suffer from a few heart problems but nothing too serious. In general, Granny was as sturdy as the live oaks that lined her yard.

Maybe she was out back. Summer headed around the side path to the backyard and looked up to the upper open balcony. "Granny? You up there?"

"Is that you, little love?" Granny yoo-hooed down to her.

"It's me, Granny."

"Come on up."

Summer grabbed the bulk of her evening gown into her hand and hoofed it up the spiral metal steps to the balcony.

Granny Snow met her with a big hug. "Oh sweet child, what a surprise tonight. I didn't expect you. I knew you were on a date with that fancy boyfriend of yours. Oh, and how pretty you look, just like a fairy princess in that turquoise evening dress."

"And you look pretty too."

"With my hair looking like a dust broom?"

"No, your snow white hair befits your namesake, and you look huggable in that dress."

"Sounds like a big fib to me, but thank you." Granny pulled her away from the edge of the stairs and looked at her face more closely. "You don't look so chipper. What happened? Did Elliot ask you to coordinate your hairstyle with his?"

Summer snorted.

"I'm sorry. That wasn't funny." Granny rubbed her back. "It was mean."

"Not really that mean." She grinned. "It's a lot truer than it should be. I think Elliot would do anything. And I mean *anything* short of illegal, to win that election."

"Including making you his puppet?"

"Yes."

Granny motioned for her to sit down on one of the chaise lounges chairs. "It's sad to think that a man would marry a woman who was never meant for him."

"Yeah, it is sad. And yes, I guess he would." They both sat down and rested back on the chaise lounges chairs as they always did, getting comfortable with each other like soft comfy shoes. "I broke it off tonight, Granny. It's over between us."

"Oh? Do you want to tell me about it?"

"Maybe." They both stared up at the night sky until Summer said, "My friends at church will think I'm foolish to walk away from the chance to be a senator's wife."

"Do you think you're foolish?"

"I don't right now," Summer said, "but I might in the morning."

Granny smiled. "I do think Elliot loves you. In his own way. And you could have been a fine senator's wife. You could have done some good in Texas. But you would have strained to live the life he wanted from you. And knowing your level of loyalty to folks, you would have even sacrificed your health to do it."

"Why didn't you tell me this a few months ago?" Summer held up her hand. "Never mind that. I know. I wasn't listening. No matter what you would have said, I would have followed my own path. I only saw the glow of Elliot, and he's quite the beacon, isn't he?"

"You could light a city with the flashes that young man could put off."

Summer laughed. "Yeah. Isn't that the truth?" Bits and pieces of Elliot's speeches came to her—as well as his lofty dreams and his amazing perseverance. But also she remembered his arrogant pontifications as well as his scoldings. And, of course, there was his schmooze. Elliot took schmooze to a new level. He could talk the spots right off a leopard, as her granny liked to say. He could smile his way into the good graces of almost anyone, even some of his opponents. Elliot was an ambassador of goodwill, yes, absolutely. But he was also the headmaster of charm. And Summer had always had trouble figuring out which mode he was in, since those two qualities were often as close as a neck and neck election.

Summer heaved a sigh. "Oh, Granny, I keep picking all the wrong guys. I mean they're all men of God, but they never seem to be the *right* ones. Not for me anyway. Something's always missing."

Granny looked over at her. "And what do you think that is?"

She thought, then said, "Well, it's like they see me, but not the real me. They're looking right past that. I guess they think I'm attractive. But I'm hoping there is more to me than the way I look."

"There always was. Always will be, little love."

Summer placed her hand over her heart, wishing she could heal the brokenness with just a touch. "What's wrong with me, Granny? Except that I'm not like other women. I don't fit in, and I never have."

Granny looked at her then. Really looked at her the way that Summer loved—like she was being understood as well as being seen. "Do you remember one time when you asked some of the school girls over for a slumber party, and that very night we had an ice storm?"

"How could I forget?" Summer said. "Ice storms are rare in Houston."

Granny smiled and rolled her head back and forth as if allowing the whole scene to unfold. "Well, those little gals were all upset the next morning because the roads were slippery, and I wouldn't drive them to the mall to buy some trinkets . . . trinkets those girls would have thrown away by the end of the month. But you?"

"What about me, Granny?"

"Well, you looked at all of them curiously and said, 'Can't you see it?' But they couldn't see anything. Just the cold, cold wetness of the day that kept them from the mall. But you saw splendor in that day. You said we were covered in this silvery white wedding veil, and as the breeze blew through the trees it rained diamonds on the grass. Those are your words, not mine. That's the difference, my little love. You're a woman who looks beyond the cold to see a miracle."

"That's sweet. I can't believe you remembered all that. But I never felt that way."

"Oh?"

Summer grinned. "I never could flip my ponytail like the other girls. Or ride horses. Or do cartwheels. Or giggle without sounding horsey. Or have smooth hair that didn't turn into a ball of frizz-fuzz like a dandelion gone to seed."

Granny laughed.

"Those high school girls did have a way about them."

"It was called arrogance." Granny winked at her. "You just need to find a man who sees the miracle too. He's out there. And by the way, if you don't mind me saying so, his name might be Martin."

"Martin Langtree?" Summer remembered the tiny wooden birds she'd left on the dash of the car. What a coincidence that they would both think about Martin at the same time. Or perhaps that word didn't allow for the stirring hand of providence.

"That's the one."

A tingling rush swept through Summer. "I can't believe you remembered him right now at this moment."

"I do remember him, much more than you know."

Summer leaned forward. "What do you mean, Granny? You have another story coming on, don't you? I can always tell."

"I do have a story. Before I explain myself, I want to share something with you."

"Oh?" Whenever her granny wanted to share something it was always a time for surprise. "What amazing thing have you been up to?"

"Be right back." Granny went inside for a moment and then came back out with a small copper-bottom sauce pan. And two spoons.

"What do you have there? Something delicious?" Summer swung her legs around and rose up to see inside the pan.

"Creamy, decadent, homemade chocolate. *The* best fondue." Granny handed her a spoon.

"Ohhh. That sounds good." Summer waved her spoon around, ready to taste.

"Careful of your pretty dress." Granny wiggled her eyebrows. "But why not have a big bite."

"I can smell the calories." But since she had no intention of arguing with Granny on matters of chocolate, Summer took the pan in hand, dipped her spoon into the thick goo and took a big gloppy bite. "Oh wow," she mumbled with her mouth full. "Wicked stuff." She licked her lips and then took another bite. "Swoon worthy."

"Indeed."

"I mean, I can feel all the butterfat being slathered onto my hips, and somehow I don't care. It's *that* good, Granny."

"I've been perfecting it over the last few days. I've been eating my weight in chocolate. I've been dipping everything in these little vats of sweetness. Strawberries. Cheese. My protein bars. My blood pressure medicine. My—"

"What?"

"Kidding about that last one."

"But you've always been so health conscious with your eating. What's up?"

"Well, I've been trying to find the right time and the right way to tell you."

"Tell me what?" Summer took another bite of the chocolate and licked on the spoon some more, but when Granny didn't answer her, she looked at her again, this time studying her face. "Granny? Tell me what?"

"Well, little love . . . the doctors have some not so good news for me."

"And what is that?"

"They tell me I'm dying."

CHAPTER
three

"Oh, Granny." Summer dropped the pan onto her lap, and the chocolate spattered all over her dress.

"Child, your beautiful gown!" Granny took a wad of napkins and started to wipe off her dress.

"I don't care about that. Granny, please tell me you were just joking around. I know you're such a kidder sometimes."

Granny closed her eyes briefly as she shook her head. "No, little love."

"I guess I didn't really think you'd joke about such an awful topic, but . . ." Summer took Granny's hands in hers. "But I thought the doctors said you were just tired. You know, nothing some good food and rest wouldn't take care of."

"They did say that, months ago, and for a while it worked. But in these last few weeks I've been declining in my health."

"Why didn't you tell me right away?"

"I didn't want to worry you."

Summer tried to absorb the news. It was too much to take in. The tragedy of it. The injustice. And the loneliness. *Oh, dear Lord, help me.* "But you're my family. I would want to know. Surely you know that."

Granny stared at the smears on the gossamer fabric. "If you let me put that to soak now I think I can get the stains out."

"Stains don't matter in the least to me now. Don't you see? *You* are all that matters."

Granny reached out and caressed her granddaughter's cheek with the back of her hand—the way she used to do when Summer was a young girl.

"Surely they have it wrong," Summer said. "Doctors misdiagnose ailments all the time. Just like with me and that hypothyroid scare I had several years ago. It wasn't that at all. Remember?"

"I know. But I did get a second opinion. And a third."

Silence settled between them for a moment. Summer knew her granny must be praying—hoping there was a way she could accept it. Finally she asked softly, "It's your heart, isn't it?"

Granny nodded. "Yes, the congestive heart failure is getting worse, and there's nothing they can do."

"You mean, the doctor actually used those words? That you were going to—not get better?"

"You can say it," Granny said. "I'm going to die. And so must we all, eventually. I've had some time to think about it. I'm at peace with it."

"Well, I'm not at peace with it. Not at all." Summer rose off the chaise lounge. "Granny, you can't go. I love you. You're my life. I rely on you for so much. You can't go. The doctors will have to come up with something. I won't let you die." Her voice rose nearly an octave.

Granny rested back on the lounge and looked up at the night sky. "It's not our decision to make, little love. Sometimes I wish it were. I do. I admit it. I wish that life wasn't so hard. Or I sometimes wish that we had more control of the good things and the bad that come to us. But what kind of thinking is that? Surely the One who created me and loves me best could plan my life and my home-going better than I can."

"But even if you're okay with it, and you've made your peace, I'm not okay with it. And I don't have one speck of peace."

"You will. Eventually."

Summer knelt in front of her grandmother on the rough-cut planks, the delicate fabric of her gown now tearing along with her heart. "But what would I do without you?" Tears stung her eyes. "I wish this were just a terrible dream. I'd wake up, and I'd make you coffee. I'd tell you all about it, and we'd have a good laugh about it. We'd . . ." her voice failed her. She rested her head on the lounge by her grandmother. "This makes me feel small again."

Granny laid her hand on Summer's head. "Then it's a very good thing that God is so big."

She looked up at her granny, her face stained with tears.

"I wish I could be with you always. And someday we will be. Never to be parted again. Won't that be lovely?"

"Yes, but this earth will grow colder and darker without you. I can already feel it."

"Well, that makes me feel loved."

"You are loved." Summer raised her head. "Granny?"

"Hmm?"

"How long did the doctors say, you know, that you'd be with us . . . with me?"

"I knew we'd get to that." Granny sighed. "Not long."

"How long?"

"Six months. Maybe more. Maybe less. They don't really know, do they?"

"Six months," Summer repeated numbly. "That's no time at all. Not nearly enough."

"Not nearly enough for what, my dear?" Granny asked.

"I don't know. Just not enough."

"I suppose when you think about it, we never think we have enough time here."

How sad and true—when it came to her grandmother—there would never be enough time. Summer's chin quivered and the trickle of tears turned into deep cries of sorrow.

Unbearable was the one word that kept playing over and over in Summer's head. *No, please, God. I lost my mom and dad. Not Granny. Not the one person I need more than anyone on earth. Why does it have to be this way? Granny has been such a godly woman. Always the first to volunteer at her church. She did anything and everything, from nursery care to tending the grounds. Always the first to open her home to anyone in need. Always there, loving You, God. Why not take someone who's evil? Not someone so good and fine. So full of love in a world that knows more cruelty than kindness.*

Granny began humming an Irish cradlesong she'd heard as child. So soothing. So Granny. Slowly, Summer stopped her weeping and sat back down on a chair. "What can I do Granny? I have to do something for you, or I'll lose my mind."

"You will not lose your mind. With God's help you will cope with this unhappy news as I am dealing with it."

"But how *are* you coping?" Summer asked. "Tell me, honestly."

"There were days when I begged God for a different outcome. Some nights when I felt fear nipping at my spirit. When that happened, I got up and prayed. Read some of the psalms. But now, most of the time I'm fine. I keep thinking about where I'm headed. There are such amazing things to think about. I'll be able to hug your mom and dad. And *my* mother and father. It will be good to see so many of my friends and family that have blazed the trail to heaven before me. I miss Ralph, of course, so it will be heaven to see my hubby again." She smiled. "And I will be in the presence of my Lord. That will be beyond any joy we know here. My heart will be made new as well as the rest of me. I will be able to run again like I did when I was your age. Really breathe deeply, and oh, my goodness, that first big breath will be the fragrant air of heaven. Imagine!"

"Yes, I know it must be wonderful, but it's hard to imagine." Summer paused, thinking about all that her grandmother had said. "Come to think of it, I have noticed that your breathing was getting more belabored. And that you seemed more fatigued. Maybe I didn't want to admit that there could be a problem. Couldn't even stand to think about it. But I'm also guilty of being tuned in to my own problems."

"I disagree."

"But I wish I'd paid more attention. Forgive me, Granny."

"Nothing to forgive. I'm so happy you decided to drop by tonight. It makes the end of the day so much better."

"I need to know, though, you mean you really don't have any bad days concerning this illness, this news? You can be real with me, Granny. You know that. Mom and Dad were at peace before they died, but they had some days when they struggled."

"I remember. Your parents talked to me about it too. Okay, I admit I have an occasional rough moment. When the medicine seems to stop working, and when I struggle to breathe, I get a little scared and angry. Not so much at God, but mad at this old world, that it's been so difficult. And before I am released from this old body it's certainly not going to get any easier. If I do have a rough moment or two, well, I throw one of my dishes over the railing."

Summer looked at her grandmother, thinking she really was joking now. "If you're trying to make me laugh, I just don't feel like it. I'm sorry."

Her grandmother got a sheepish expression.

"You weren't kidding?"

"Go have a gander." Her grandmother gestured toward the porch railing.

Summer went over to the wooden banister and took a look below. Sure enough. There was a pile of broken dishes on the concrete patio. "Wow. You weren't kidding. Does it make you feel better?"

"When I feel overpowered by some dark angle on this illness, I watch the plate fall below and smash into pieces. It is a vivid reminder that this life is broken. My body is worn out. All of us are shattered like glass. And where I'm going there will be no more brokenness. All will be mended and made right. The remembrance of that helps me get through that valley, that shadow of death."

"It's a good thing you don't have the rest of those dishes here now," Summer said, and tried to smile. "I'd probably want to dump them all over the edge."

Her grandmother joined her at the porch railing. "I have a good supply in case you want to. But do know, I've kept the heirloom ones in safekeeping. I want you to have all the ones we found together in our treasure hunting days. Those are the ones I want you to give your daughter someday."

"Without you, what do I care about heirlooms?" Summer asked. "You might as well smash those too."

"You will care someday when you settle down with the right man." Granny took her hand. "You'll want to set a pretty table like I always did. It's such a blessing. Such a joy to do that for people. Nobody seems to entertain anymore. Or have the gift of hospitality."

"You always did. You were good at it. People loved coming over here."

"Thanks."

"You said I'd one day settle down and marry the right man." She let out a snorting little chortle. "Seems kind of unlikely now, doesn't it?"

Granny smiled. "Maybe he's closer than you think. Like a beautiful garment put away in the closet. Forgotten, but still within reach."

"You're not talking about Martin again, are you?" Summer asked, wishing her grandmother would stop changing the subject. "I have no idea whatever happened to him. We lost track of each other ages ago."

"Yes—I remember as if it were yesterday." Granny leaned on the railing and locked her fingers together. "You asked me a moment ago if you could do something for me."

"Yes, I meant it. Anything, Granny."

"Well, that's good, since I really do have something in mind for you."

"Oh? Okay. Is it something about the bookshop?"

"Yes, it is about the bookshop." Granny looked over at her. "For starters, I'm asking you to quit your job. Right away."

CHAPTER
four

"*What?" Summer thought she might* have heard Granny wrong. "Did you say quit my job?'"

"Maybe I should call it a short leave of absence."

"But why? This little bookshop is your dream."

"Yes, I do believe that's the problem. It's *my* dream. Not yours. It never was your dream . . . or at least one you chose."

"I don't know what you mean. I wish now I hadn't said it was merely *your* dream. It's mine too, of course." Summer looked up at the evening sky, so full of beauty. But also mystery—way too far away to touch or even fathom. "Listen. I know I've been a disappointment. I know the shop has not done well, but—"

"Please stop." Granny turned to her, her brows furrowed in concern. "The shop never did well when I had it either. And please never say that again, that you've been a disappointment. Never could you be a disappointment to me."

"Then why do you want me to leave it behind . . . for a while?"

"Because this illness has changed me some," Granny said. "This knowledge that I don't have a lot of time has made me see things I've never seen before."

"Like what?"

"That no one gave you the time or chance to do a few of the things you talked about when you were younger."

Summer pondered that, but she already knew where Granny was going with her comment. "As you well know, there were more important things to attend to."

"I know. After the accident, you took care of your mom and dad better than any young woman could have done. But my dear, when all the other young women were going off to college you stayed home with your parents."

"I wouldn't have done anything else."

"And yet many young people would have gone on to college anyway, and left their mother and father to fend for themselves." Granny looked at her. "Or they would have allowed a government service of some kind to come in and give them assistance."

"Maybe. But I couldn't have done that. It wouldn't have felt right."

"And that's one of the many things that separate you from other young women."

"Thanks, Granny. But in spite of what you think, I did fall in love with that bookstore growing up. So many kids who, for one reason or another, didn't feel loved at home or school could come to your shop after school and receive the love and attention they never found anywhere else. And I know those kids surely did better in life because of your loving affections. The books you read to them and the books they read to you. The way you allowed them to be whoever they were meant to be. They learned the art of play under your tutelage as well as the gift of kindness. It changed their lives. I know it changed mine. What kind of price can you put on that? It was the noblest thing. I was honored to take over the store and continue that legacy."

Summer gazed at her granny, into those blue eyes, which were the color of a cloudless sky. But those eyes of her beloved granny had gone misty.

"What you're saying isn't without truth," Granny said, "but I still say that you gave up so much for your parents and for the store that I think you might have forgotten those dreams . . . the ones I remember you talking about years ago. I want you to let your assistant, Amelia, take over the shop for now. Just a little while. And

I have been saving some money. I will be paying your salary for you to do something for me."

"You certainly don't need to pay me. I have some money saved. But what is it you need me to do?"

Granny slapped the railing. "I want you to go out and find Summer Snow and who she would have been had life taken a different turn—in life and in love."

Summer smiled. That idea did have a stamp of Granny on it. "Oh?"

"I have a made a list of things. A list of adventures that I hope will change your life." She raised her chin.

"But I don't want to leave you right now," Summer said. "I'll stay here at the house and take care of you."

"No. That's not what I want. You've given up enough of your life in the care of others. I have a good friend from church who will help me if and when I need more help, and then later hospice will take over when things get closer to the end."

At Granny's words, a floodgate of tears almost opened again, but Summer kept them at bay for now. "But I want to spend this time with you. As much as I can." Her chin quivered and she turned away.

"And you shall." With her fingers, Granny combed out the wild tangles in her long hair and then put it into a loose braid. "But my little love, I also want joy, and doing something for Summer will bring me that joy. I know Amelia loves the shop, and she'll take good care of it while you take some time off."

"How much time?" Summer asked.

"As long as it takes to do this list, but I would think no more than a few weeks. Look, think of it as all the vacations you never took all rolled into one." Granny shook her finger. "I know you have rarely taken time off, which isn't right."

"The shop needs me. The kids need me."

"Now, now. Everybody needs a rest. Even Jesus took a break from the crowds. Am I right?" Granny gave her one of those over-the-reading-glasses kind of stares.

"Okay. I suppose a vacation does sound good."

"That's the spirit. Now I also know the other reason you haven't taken a vacation, and it's because the shop isn't making you much money. Well, a check will arrive each week, and it will cover your salary as well as the items on this list."

"But how can I take your money? I won't."

"You will." Granny sighed. "Please?"

Summer was silent for a moment as she looked across the yard. She turned back to Granny. "All right. I guess. If it makes you that happy to do this."

"You'll have most of my money soon anyway," Granny said. "I'm leaving everything to you."

Summer shook her head. The tears came now, and she didn't think they would stop anytime soon.

"Oh, Summer. I love you so."

"What does any of it mean without you? I don't want you to go."

"I know." Granny wrapped her arms around her in a tight hug. "I will make you this promise. I'll do my best to stay as well as I can to see you through this list and on to a new life."

"Then I'll make sure I never finish the list." Summer sniffled like a child.

Granny gave her a little shake. "Now, Summer."

"I know. That's like something I would have said when I was five. Okay. I'll do it right. I'll agree to anything to bring you some joy."

"Thanks." Granny released her. "But I want to add this: If you've gotten to the end of the list and you still want to run the bookshop then you should go back to it with my blessing. Okay? Deal?"

"Deal."

"And if in the process of fulfilling this list you don't find the love of your life, then I'll understand. No more suggestions or lists. No looking back. Deal?"

"Deal. But what do you mean, the love of my life?" Summer leaned down and caught her grandmother's guilty gaze. "What exactly is on this list anyway?"

Granny went over to a patio table, picked up a large white envelope, and handed it to her.

Summer's hand trembled a bit as she slid her finger through the seal and pulled out the list, which was handwritten on golden parchment, no less. "This paper looks like it's part of the Dead Sea Scrolls."

"I found the paper in the attic when I was cleaning it out. I thought it would make the list official." Granny grinned.

"It does. Enough to give me the chills." Summer glanced over the list, and read from it. "Number one: Find your childhood friend Martin Langtree, and convince him to fulfill the life-list with you." What a flood of emotions came with that name. Should she mention to her grandmother that she'd just been thinking about Martin this very night? Or would it give her false hope? Maybe she should let it go. "I know what you're up to, Granny dear." Summer waved the list in the air. "You must have had quite a bit of confidence that I was going to break up with Elliot if you've already made this list."

"Well, let's say that I did have quite a bit of *hope* that you would."

Summer smiled. "I will say this: I do remember Martin. Very well."

"Who could forget or not love that sweet gangly little lad? He was one-of-a-kind. No boy could have been so thoughtful or so full of imagination."

"Mom and Dad liked him too, although I guess they didn't know him like you did." Summer tugged on her granny's sleeve. "Martin sure did love being in the bookshop."

"When was it . . . those early years of Martin after school? How old were you two?"

"Let's see. He started coming to the bookshop when he was maybe ten. Then after his mom died and he was adopted into the Langtree family, he moved across town, which was probably around age fourteen. We never saw him again after that." Summer saddened at the thought.

"Those Martin years were good years. Happy times." In all honesty to herself, those were the best years of her life. And she never had a friend since Martin who was as loyal and kind to her. Or as much fun. "This idea of yours to find Martin is a good one I admit. To at least find him and reconnect with him as a friend. That sounds good. I think the chances of anything romantic happening are slim, though. I mean, you have to admit, life has moved on in a big way here. So many years have gone by. Almost twenty."

"You're right. I know it's been a long time. But you do admit that it's interesting we both remember him with such fondness."

"Absolutely. Great fondness. No doubt about that." And even as a child, she had secretly dreamed of growing up and marrying Martin. Such a lost dream. So long ago. And yet when she was breaking up with Elliot, Martin had soon come to mind. "But I can think of a dozen scenarios that will make doing this list with Martin impossible."

"I'm all ears."

"Okay. He's got a wife and five kids. *Or*, he's been through a bitter divorce, and the last thing on his mind is another romantic entanglement. *Or*, he's moved to who-knows-where, and I'll have to hire a private investigator to find him. *Or*, he's busy with a full-time job, and he doesn't want to waste his valuable vacation time traipsing around town trying to help me find myself." Summer looked at Granny. "Sorry, that sounded harsh. It's just that the chances aren't in our favor that this will work out. I hope you haven't gotten your hopes up too high. The last thing I want for you right now is to have you stressed over this. I want you to get well."

"My darling girl, haven't you been listening to me?" Granny asked.

"But what if God works a miracle and you recover?"

"Then I will thank Him most profoundly. But until then I want you to have a vacation on me and to work on this list. Okay?"

"Okay."

"I really did bathe this list in prayer as I wrote it. And too, I looked Martin up online." Granny winked at her.

"You did?" *Perhaps I should have looked him up years ago.*

"He still lives in the Houston area. In Bellaire to be exact. His address is on a slip of paper at the bottom of the large envelope."

"Oh, wow. You really have done your homework."

"Well, I am retired, and I'm on a mission here."

Summer smiled.

"You may read the rest of the list when you get home. Oh, and you don't have to do it in order or anything like that." Granny sighed. "Listen, I think I'll head to bed. I need—"

"Are you feeling ill? Do you need to go to the hospital?"

"No, I was about to say that I need my beauty sleep." Granny smiled as she placed her shoulder to her chin in a demure shrug.

"Oh, I see. Okay. Well, know that I'm calling Amelia tonight, and I'm going to ask her to cover for me for a while. I think she's been itching for more work. So this might work out just fine. And tomorrow morning, *after* my coffee, I'm going to try to find a man named Martin Langtree."

Granny chuckled. "So good to hear his name in our presence in such a casual way again, almost as if we'd never lost touch with him."

"True." Oh, how she wished it really was true. A sudden breeze fluttered the chimes just below them. They jingled, but the sound of it seemed melancholy instead of merry. "That breeze feels cold now." She rubbed her arms to warm herself. "I'm glad you're headed in for the night."

Summer leaned down and kissed her grandmother on the cheek. She lingered there in a cloud of sweet lilac powder—a scent she'd grown so accustomed to, since it was Granny's favorite. But while she was close to her face, she could hear the shallow breathing, the slight struggle for air. *Oh, Granny.* But what could she say that hadn't already been said? She settled on, "Please take it easy. For me. Don't overdo anything." But telling her grandmother not to overdo life was pretty close to impossible.

"Okay, girly. I promise. I'll try." Granny planted a kiss on her hand. "I love you big and high—"

"As the Texas sky," Summer finished. If she didn't go right now, she would start crying again, and it would only make her grandmother worse. So Summer kept up her smile until her grandmother was out of sight, but then her expression drooped. Maybe she could stop at a local Starbucks for a double espresso and drive around Houston all night, praying for her grandmother. But she needed to follow through with her granny's request by working things out with Amelia.

Summer climbed into her car and headed toward home, but two subjects weighed heavily on her mind. First, and most importantly, how on earth would she ever get along without her granny? It seemed impossible. Too many people had died in her life. And now one more. It was hard to imagine the light of Granny Snow being extinguished on this side of eternity.

And secondly, how would it go with Granny's list—this journey of the heart? What would happen in the morning when she showed up on the porch of her old friend? Most likely he would be out for some reason, even though it would be a Saturday. What a relief that would be. But she would have to return to Martin's house in the evening to try again, since she would never disappoint her granny.

But one scenario hadn't crossed her mind until that moment. She tightened her grip on the steering wheel. What if she really did find Martin Langtree in the morning—and what if he had forgotten all about her?

CHAPTER
five

Summer woke in the morning with a start. *What was that noise? A jet flying low? Or a car backfiring out in the parking lot?*

And what in the world had she been dreaming? Something awful. Yes, she'd been tormented all night by a woman who was shrouded in some kind of disturbing mystery—a woman who was dressed in a turquoise evening gown and dancing inside an engagement ring the size of an inner tube. *Oh dear.* She'd been chasing herself.

As Summer moaned and rubbed her aching head, the sudden remembrance concerning her granny's condition washed over her like a black flood. *Granny is dying.* No doubt that had fed her nightmares. That and her final farewell to Elliot.

She felt her pillow. Still damp from crying on and off in the night. "Oh, Granny. I'm so sorry life has given you this dreadful news," she whispered. If anyone didn't deserve it, it was Granny Snow. She was seventy-five and yet Summer always hoped she'd live to at least ninety. Or more.

Summer picked up the parchment off her nightstand and looked at the life-list Granny had created. Some of the items on the list made her squirm emotionally but none as much as the one at the top of the list—which was to locate her childhood friend Martin Langtree and convince him to help her with the life-list. Tall order.

But doable.

Maybe.

Or not.

The part about knocking on his front door, well, that would be easy. Then she could always sprint back to her car like the coward she was. She tried to laugh but couldn't quite get it out. She'd need some caffeine to clear the pipes.

After two mugs of French roast brew, a yogurt parfait, and a shower, she dressed in a nice outfit—navy blue with a white vest. She gazed in a long mirror. Not bad. The color enhanced her blue eyes. Good. No sense in scaring the man out of his giblets—as Granny might say—by showing up in jeans and her hair in its natural state of ferocity.

After one more spritz of hairspray and a quickie glimpse in the mirror, she headed toward Bellaire in her little red Chevy—a car she'd had since forever. It was like a faithful friend, yes, but to say her car was the color of red was meant in the loosest sense of the word. Her vehicle hadn't known true red for ages—the poor thing was only pretending. Elliot had jokingly called her transportation a moving blight on the freeway, and he vowed to buy her a new sports car as a wedding present. But even though the gesture showed Elliot's generous nature, it was a gift she'd hadn't really wanted.

She glanced in the rearview mirror. Too much makeup? Maybe like her car, she too was pretending with her ultra-painted face. What was she afraid of—that Martin would be shocked that she'd aged?

But then she hadn't seen or talked to Martin in almost twenty years. People really did change and sometimes a lot. The chances of him being the doting darling that Granny remembered with affection was as likely as Elliot giving up politics to become a lumberjack. Not happening.

Yes, Summer had thought Elliot was a saint too, until she saw that he loved her more for the way she looked on his arm than merely for being Summer Snow.

She scooted down in her seat as she sped along the 610 loop. Then Summer jacked up the volume on her music. For some reason the men who'd worked on her car had changed her station to country—a music style that made her feel more like scrubbing off the bottom of her shoes than singing along. But this time the song was Tammy Wynette's "Stand By Your Man." She laughed at the absurdity of thinking about Elliot while hearing that song. Of course, the gals at church would think that she was out of her gourd to have broken things off. They'd say, "Won't you feel silly if he someday becomes president and you could have been First Lady?"

Maybe she would feel silly then. Or maybe she'd feel nothing but relief, since if there were ever a pressure cooker kind of pot for a marriage it would be inside the confines of the White House.

Summer snapped off the radio, took the Bellaire exit, and cruised along the boulevard until she came to the street name Granny had written on the slip of paper. After making a slow turn, she soon found the correct house number. In a matter of seconds she pulled up to the front of the Langtree home.

Martin's house. How easy was that? Almost too easy.

And just look at Martin's house. Austere and enormous were the first adjectives that came to mind—obscenely so. But it didn't seem like anything Martin would have bought. Maybe it was his wife's taste. But what did he do for a living that he could afford such luxury? Rob banks? You know, she wasn't all that far from the freeway. Maybe she could just run some errands on this side of town and then head home. Her granny was a wise woman, but this idea suddenly seemed nuts. But then on the other hand—a promise was a promise.

Summer didn't pull in Martin's driveway but just parked along the curb. That felt safer in case she had to make a quick getaway. With anxiousness bubbling up inside her, she finally opened the car door.

Then her stomach lurched. *You're fine, Summer.* But still she didn't move.

Get out of the car.

Was she that much of a chicken? Had she really become so pathetic and gutless over the years that she couldn't even go to the home of an old friend?

But there was more wriggling around in her hesitation than ordinary spineless behavior. Martin wasn't just an old friend. Had his family not moved him away to Bellaire all those years ago, he might have become more than that. Even at that tender age it was easy to sense that they'd forged something rare. Something that might only happen to two people once in a lifetime.

Sweat beaded up all over her body, tickling her unmercifully as she waiting for her courage to kick in. Then she made herself open the car door.

Okay. Let's do this thing. She got out and slammed the door shut, which made the poor thing creak and shudder as if it was going to fall off.

Concerned she might change her mind, Summer ran up the walk without stopping. Martin's house of brick and stone and turrets and leaded glass and iron balconies—oh, my—became so looming it was almost overpowering. Such grandeur. There were manicured beds. Lush flowers of every color. Hollywood Boulevard–style palm trees. Big fountains. Giant stone lions on either side of the entry. Big Texas everything. Elliot would have loved it.

But it was so not Martin, the Martin she remembered. Had he changed that much?

She rang the bell and stood in place, tapping her heels together like Dorothy trying to get out of Oz. She squirmed, rang the bell again, and waited.

Martin wasn't home. Was that feeling a clear sign of disappointment or relief?

It was both.

Then, without ceremony, the door unlocked and swung open.

Summer's insides tightened. The man standing before her was this sleek, hazel-eyed, smart-alecky-looking guy one might find on a movie set.·

Summer's lips moved, but her brain didn't feel fully engaged when she said, "You're not Martin."

CHAPTER
six

"No, I'm not Martin," the stranger said. "And I couldn't be more grateful for that fact." He grinned. "I'm his brother Ivan. And you are?"

"I'm Summer Snow." *Oh, my.* Ivan was now a man. He looked so different. So seriously grown-up. But what else had she expected?

"What a lyrical name." He leaned leisurely against the door-frame, his whole demeanor suggesting smugness.

"Thanks."

"Your name sounds familiar." His eyes widened.

Perhaps he recognized her now. Maybe she should get down to business. "Actually, I'm searching for Martin. I thought he lived here."

"My brother Desmond and I live in the big house, but Martin lives in his own private abode in the back." He gestured with his thumb.

"Oh?"

"Yes, it's the guesthouse. He prefers it that way. To be alone. It used to be quite an amazing little showplace of a house—a Realtor's dream—but I'm afraid Martin has turned it into a junk heap with those infernal projects of his."

"Projects?" Now that *did* sound like Martin.

"Yes, well, that's what he calls them. I think his projects border on flights of insanity." Ivan frowned. "Do you mind if I ask what you want with him? He rarely gets visitors."

"Really?" Summer asked. "I'm surprised at that."

"Why?" Ivan tilted his head just so, gazing at her as if she were something to be studied inside a cage.

Summer clasped her hands behind her to keep from fidgeting. "Because when I knew Martin he had the kindest personality of anyone I'd ever known. I assumed he had lots of friends. And really I assumed he'd be married with kids by now." Her heart sped up, thinking she'd dug herself pretty deeply with that big shovel that was really her mouth. She took one more spadeful and asked, "So, he's not, uh, married then?"

"No."

"Oh?" The word made a little croak as it came out. Summer's face went hot. In fact, a slice of her granny's jalapeño cornbread couldn't have given off any more heat.

Ivan shattered the silence with laughter. "Martin will never marry." Ivan shook his finger at her. "You think I don't remember you, but I do. Your grandmother had a bookshop as I recall."

"Yes, the Once Upon a Time." Summer smiled, and that smile felt like a good bubble soak in her tub, since it was bathed in the new knowledge that Martin never chose to marry.

"Sounds like Martin, since he lives in never-never land. But you never did answer my question. Why do you want to see him?"

Not sure that's any of your business. "Well, for one thing, I'd like to say hello to him."

"You skirted around that question pretty well. All right. You may pass go." He chuckled at his own joke.

"Do you think he's at home?"

"Probably." Ivan looked past her at something on the street. "He doesn't go out much."

"So it's all right if I go on back?"

Ivan shrugged. "Sure, why not?"

"Is there a path to the back?"

"It's on the right side of the house, and the iron gate on that side is kept unlocked."

"Thank you."

"But do beware. Martin's not used to company, so he might be hanging from a tree or making electricity from scratch. Approach with care or you might get electrocuted." He smirked.

Ivan's voice, while tolerable at first, seemed to take on a metallic quality that gradually grated on her nerves. Or maybe it was just his not-so-subtle insults aimed at his brother. "I'm not scared."

"You should be." He laughed.

What did *that* mean? She gave him a curious nod and said without her usual enthusiasm, "Nice to see you again."

"Same here." Ivan shut the door a little too soundly.

Had he been agitated at her for some reason? Oh well, nothing was going to discourage her from her quest. Summer scuttled down the steps, eased through the rusty iron gate, and followed a pebble-lined path to the back of the property. Just as the guesthouse came into view she saw a man treading steadily across the lawn to the big house. The man—who looked a bit familiar—had to be his other brother, Desmond. Apparently he didn't see her, so she studied him for a moment. He had grown up to be an attractive man with confident strides. But Desmond could never be Martin. Not even close.

She turned her attention to the guesthouse. Martin's cottage was situated in a lovely spot in a small cluster of pine and oak and red cedar. Even a grove of eucalyptus adorned the little white house. Lovely. Perhaps Martin liked the peace of such a miniature dwelling.

Summer strolled up the path to the front door—which was greenish and round at the top—and reminded her of the entrance to a hobbit hole. How utterly quaint, and so much like the Martin she remembered. She stepped up onto the munchkin porch, lifted the brass knocker, and gave it two solid raps.

Would Martin be at home? Would he recognize her after all these years and with so much makeup? Maybe she looked like a floozy instead of an old friend. In a moment of panic, she quickly lifted her arm to her lips and wiped off her lipstick, lip liner, and lip gloss. That's better. Maybe.

The door suddenly opened and there stood a grown man—yes, a sprouted version of Martin Langtree. It was him all right. Same dark inquisitive eyes and brown hair that stood up in amusing directions as if combing it was the last thing on his mind. Nice. It reminded her of someone—oh, yeah—her own hair that could go wild at any moment. Then, of course, there was that unmistakable Jimmy Stewart–lankiness in his frame, same friendly facial features, and guilelessness in his smile. She knew the actor well from watching a lot of old films with her granny. Yes. Martin was like Jimmy all right. She said, "Hi. I'm—"

"I know just who you are," he said. "You're Summer Snow."

He remembered me. "Yes. It's me."

"It's been a very long time. Too long." He smiled.

Summer clutched the handle on her purse.

Then they held a little smiling jubilee, and she basked in his presence.

A bee emerged from a patch of ivy and buzzed by her head, waking her up from their reverie.

"I like your front door," Summer said. "It's like a hobbit dwelling."

"I'm kind of a Tolkien fan."

"Isn't everyone?"

"Not my brothers. They think I'm—well, the nice version of their word is eccentric."

Guess that was what Ivan meant by scary—Martin's brother apparently couldn't understand anyone who was unconventional. Summer raised her chin. "Eccentric certainly isn't boring." She looked at one of the urns that sat by the front door, and for a brief moment while she gathered her wits, she admired the sweet William that was blooming in the pots.

"True." Martin leaned forward, picked a blossom, and handed it to her. "Eccentricity is one of the seeds of surprise."

She accepted the flower and smiled.

"You might find it interesting to know that sweet William signifies gallantry." Martin went a bit red-faced.

Summer twirled the pink flower under her nose. She always did love the scent of sweet William. Yep, in all the ways that mattered, he was still pure Martin.

"Would you like to come in?" He opened the door wider. "I'm afraid I keep it in a colossal mess, but then I was in the middle of one of my projects."

"Yes, your brother Ivan said you might be."

"Oh, you saw him too then." He released a jovial sigh. "Of course. You had to stop at the big house to know where I was." He gestured for her to come inside. "Please, come in."

Summer stepped over his threshold, looking around, expecting Bilbo Baggins to pop out from around a corner at any moment and offer her a "second breakfast" or maybe some roasted taters in a rabbit stew. She grinned at the thought.

Summer followed Martin into the living room, which had been transformed into a sort of workroom, with tables here and there brimming with books and contraptions and oddities that she couldn't even explain with ordinary language. It reminded her of a biography she'd read once about Leonardo da Vinci and his voracious desire for experimentation and invention. Yes, she'd entered a curious new world, where the earth had tilted, but somehow she didn't feel ill at ease. Instead, she felt grounded. She felt at home. *Summer, don't fall too fast. You haven't even been asked to sit down yet.*

Martin turned to her and gazed at her arm. "You look—"

"I look? Yes, Martin?"

"You look like you're bleeding."

Summer glanced at her arm. "Oh, that. I'd forgotten. It's my lipstick. I smeared it all off before you answered the door."

"Did you think I wouldn't like lipstick?"

Always the authentic and direct Martin. He deserved no less than the same candid reply. "Yes. I thought you might think it was too unnatural looking."

"Well, I wouldn't wear lipstick," he said, "but I think you might look nice in it."

Summer laughed.

"You laughed." Surprise lit Martin's features.

"It was funny."

"I never really know when I'm funny. It always seems like an experiment that usually goes awry. It used to be worse, but maybe I'm improving. Although technically, it's not improvement if I made you laugh by accident." He smoothed his wrinkled flannel shirt and slacks as if he wished he'd taken a little more care with his appearance, but when the wrinkles seemed hopeless, he merely shrugged and grinned.

Even as a kid Martin always was a casual dresser. She knew most young boys were. But he seemed so busy living life. Enjoying the natural world around him to worry about his appearance. Elliot was just the opposite, of course, touting that in politics, appearance was the despot ruler of every waking moment. Goodness gracious. Why had she ever agreed to marry him in the first place? Ahh, life was a mystery. She'd almost forgotten what he'd said. Oh, yes. He'd made her laugh by accident. "Nope. It still counts in my book. What's your secret for improvement in humor?"

"Sometimes I watch old reruns of the *Andy Griffith Show*."

"My granny always loved that program."

"Ahh, yes. Your grandmother. I remember her well." Martin pointed toward a worktable. "Uh . . . I just made some cocoa. Do you want some? Then we could sit down awhile."

"Cocoa. That's my favorite." Cocoa was such a comforting elixir for loneliness, but unfortunately it wasn't a cure.

Martin nodded. "I know it's your favorite. And you like cocoa topped with whipped cream. The real stuff. Not the kind that tastes like plastic."

"That's right. How could you possibly remember that?"

"I remember what's important. And that's the way I like my cocoa too."

"Oh? Yes, I would love some. Thanks."

"Good. Two mugs coming up."

The music piped in from somewhere was the pan flute along with the gentle ebb and flow of ocean waves. Wow, it was so lullaby-like it could melt one's bones. "I like your music."

"It helps my mind wander when I'm working."

"That's funny, since most people want to focus when they're working."

He grinned at that but didn't reply.

Yes, Martin wasn't most people. Summer sniffed at the sweet William again. It seemed this tiny flower meant more to her than all the expensive bouquets of roses that Elliot had bought her. Somehow that realization made her feel sorry for Elliot, though, since it meant that even his best wasn't enough to win her back.

Summer studied Martin as he moved some papers on a nearby table, making a clear space.

Some halogen lights shone down on him from the ceiling, and she was able to get a clearer look of her childhood companion. Unfortunately, time had not been a friend to Martin, since he had more wrinkles than she would have imagined. Strange that Desmond was only one year younger than Martin and Ivan only two years his junior and yet they seemed significantly more youthful. Had life been tougher on Martin than on his brothers? The wrinkles didn't matter to her, but the thought of him suffering grieved her.

"By the way, you mentioned your grandmother. How is Mrs. Snow?" Martin stopped to look up at her.

Summer wished now she'd not mentioned Granny in the conversation. She hated to start their reunion with such dismal news. How would he take it? As a child he'd been very fond of her— seemed to even love her like his own grandmother. "I'm sorry to say that she's—" her voiced failed her.

"Yes?"

CHAPTER
seven

Martin stared at Summer as her face grew pale. She was about to share something dreadful. It was in the nuances of her gestures and the shadow that had fallen over her lovely eyes. "You okay?"

"Yes. What I'm trying to say is that Granny is not doing too well."

"I'm sorry to hear that. What's the matter, if you don't mind talking about it?"

Summer went silent.

"Listen. I'm pelting you with too many questions right off."

"No." Summer gave him a reassuring nod. "You're fine."

"I'll let you get settled with some cocoa." Martin took two cups off a little mug tree. "Oh, and please sit down anywhere you like."

Instead of sitting down, Summer tooled around the living room looking at his books and drawings and terrarium. She twirled a miniature windmill. "What's this?"

"Oh, it's just something I'm playing with. A new windmill design that has blades similar to the wings of a bird."

"How clever. Does it work better this way?"

"A bit. But I still have some tinkering to do on it."

"Tinkering. Pleasant word. Nobody uses that word anymore. You seem to have found your sweet spot in life."

"That's a nice way to put it. Yes, I guess I have."

She pointed to an old telephone he'd been toying with. "What is going on with this?"

"Oh, it's an antique hand crank telephone. I was merely study-ing the insides with no real goal in mind. Sometimes I think curios-ity comes first. Then purpose might show up later."

"I like that. I never really understand the insides of anything. I just *use* stuff." Summer laughed. "That didn't come off quite right. Where would you like me to sit?"

That's why Summer hadn't bothered to sit down, he realized. His chairs were overflowing with junk, and she probably didn't feel right shoving the stuff onto the floor. "I'm sorry. I'm a lousy host. It's just that I'm not used to having company. Please toss something on the floor. It'll be all right."

Summer gingerly moved a pile of papers and books to the floor and sat down.

Martin reluctantly refocused his attention to the beaker full of cocoa, which sat on a small Bunsen burner. How beautiful Summer had grown up to be. If she only knew how many times he'd thought about her over the years—wondered how her life was going. If she were happy or unhappy. Or married yet. Soon he would have those questions answered. What a miracle to have Summer suddenly ap-pear on his doorstep.

Summer glanced around the open room. "I like your Einstein poster. Good quote. 'Imagination is more important than knowl-edge.'"

"It was a quote your grandmother had displayed in her shop. I've never forgotten it. Just as I've never forgotten her either."

Summer smiled. "You're right, Granny is a very memorable woman."

"She's like one of the great clocks in the big house—a gold, Louis IV mantel clock. A rare find."

"Yes, that sounds like Granny."

Martin poured some of the thick brown liquid from the beaker into two glass mugs. He dumped big dollops of whipped cream into the mugs and then licked the spoon. He moved a pile of junk from a chair and they both settled in, sipping at their cocoa.

"You can never have too much whipped cream." Martin took a sip of his drink. "If you're able to tell me now, how ill is Mrs. Snow? I'm sorry if that's too forward, but I'd really like to know."

"It's very serious, Martin." Summer touched her nose. "You have a bit of cream on your nose."

"Oh? Thank you." He wiped the cream off on his flannel shirt and smiled. Then he took another sip of his cocoa. "When you said your grandmother was seriously ill, did you mean she's—" His voice faded.

"I need to just say it. Granny is going to die, Martin. I found out yesterday, and I'm not dealing with the news very well."

"You seem pretty calm."

"I'm not, though. I'm a train wreck on the inside. Granny has been like a mom to me since my mother and father passed away. I can't imagine doing life without her." She held the mug tightly in her palms. "I hate death."

Martin set his mug down on top of a coffee table. "What's wrong? Why is she so ill?"

"It's her heart, and she doesn't have long." Summer stared into her mug and said no more.

"I'm sorry."

Summer nodded as her eyes got misty.

Summer, I'm so sorry. "I still have the same shoulder to cry on. It's right here." Martin came over to her and knelt beside her chair. He pointed to her head and then to his shoulder.

"I'm so scared for Granny." Summer set her mug down. "I know how strong Granny tries to be for me. I doubt she'll tell me when things get really bad. The idea of her suffering so much is unbearable. Oh, Martin." Summer put her head on his shoulder, and the tears began to fall.

Martin placed one hand on her back. Then tentatively, he put his other hand on her shoulder. He held her for a while, wishing he could make the pain go away, but for now he simply made a sheltering place with his arms.

Summer wept quietly on his shoulder, and then she eased away and said, "Thank you. I'm a little embarrassed."

"Why?"

"Because I haven't seen you in a very long time. Now that I'm here, the first thing I do is come to your house and bawl like a baby."

"It really is okay," he said softly. "Your grandmother is worth the tears, and I'm honored that you would feel you could share those tears with me."

"Thank you."

"You're more than welcome." Martin slipped off his flannel shirt—which he always wore over his T-shirt—and offered it to her. "I'm sorry I don't have a handkerchief, but you're welcome to use this."

"I don't want to mess up your shirt."

"That's okay. It's already covered in tears anyway." Martin grinned and then sat down across from her.

She dabbed at the tears on her face with the shirt. Then she retrieved some tissues from her purse and blew her nose. "Martin, I want to tell you the real reason I came today. I have something I want to ask you. It has to do with—"

Before she could finish her sentence, Laney, Martin's brown and white Chihuahua came trotting up to his feet.

"And who is this?" she asked.

"This is a friend who showed up at the back door one day about a year ago." Martin turned to Laney and said, "Sit now."

The little dog obeyed and then looked up at Summer with earnest eyes.

"Good girl." Martin leaned down and scratched her behind the ears and then turned back to Summer. "I immediately started calling the dog Gizmo, but she would have none of it. She told me her name was Laney."

At the mention of her name, the dog ran around in circles excitedly.

"How adorable."

Martin grinned. "Laney is quite a dog. She's spunky, personable, even with cats, and if you're sick, she'll never leave your side."

"That's sweet, but wait a minute. *She* told you her name was Laney?" Summer gave him a teasing expression. "And do you often converse with dogs?"

"No, only this one. Actually she had a tag, and it had the name Laney on it. I tried for the longest time to find her owner, but no one came forward. But it seemed Laney had made up her mind to stay here, and I didn't have much to do with it either way."

"Maybe Laney was running away from something or someone."

"Yes, I think so. But I suppose everyone is running from something." Martin paused. "I don't know why I just said that. Anyway, I do think Laney had a bad owner before, since when I first tried to pet her, she flinched. But she knows now that she'll always have a friend here."

"Well, since good friends are sometimes hard to come by, I guess she knew what she had when she found you."

Martin smiled. Nice.

When the dog trotted over to Summer, she reached down and placed the back of her hand in front of Laney's mouth. "Hi there. My goodness, look at you. You are so perky and cute. And with those pointy ears and white and tan coat, you look just like a little fox. Don't you, girl?"

The dog gave her hand a few licks, and then Summer gingerly lifted the dog onto her lap.

Laney looked up at her.

Martin already knew how the dog was maneuvering to make Summer her friend. Her dark eyes would become pools of serious study as she offered the slightest whimper. Hard to resist.

Summer sighed and gave the dog a few strokes on her back and her furry ears. Laney curled up on her lap and rested her head on Summer's hand. "You are a sweetheart of a dog, I can tell. And your hair is so soft, it's like velvet."

"She's sweet tempered with you, but she growls at Ivan and Desmond."

"Oh?"

"Laney is not only my friend, but I owe her my life."

"How is that?"

Martin took a swig of his cocoa. "About six months ago I was ill with a cold, but it turned ugly. Anyway, I stayed in bed thinking I'd get over it if I just rested. But days later, it turned into pneumonia. It got serious enough that I no longer felt like getting up or even moving. My brothers were out of town at the time, so they weren't here to help me. But Laney, sensing how ill I was, went through her pet door in the kitchen, found a neighbor, and barked so frantically that he showed up here and called 911. The doctors told me that if Laney hadn't done what she did, I might even have died. So I feel I owe her my life."

"What an incredible story. So heartwarming." Summer gave the dog a hug.

"You never know what will come into our lives that might change us or rescue us." He smiled at her. "A moment ago, I think you were about to ask me something."

"Yes, I was." She reached over to her cocoa, took a sip, and then set it back down on the end table. "This is very good."

"Thank you." He pointed to her nose. "Now *you* have a bit of cream on your nose."

Summer grinned and dabbed it off with his flannel shirt. "What I wanted to ask you—"

They were interrupted by a sharp rap at the front door.

"I'm sorry." *Great. Who could that be?* Martin rose. "As I said, I rarely get company. Let me see who it is."

"Oh, no problem. Please go ahead."

Martin walked toward the entry and answered the door. Ivan stood on the welcome mat, shifting his feet, his usual impatience getting the better of him. He rarely came to his door unless he needed money. "Is everything all right?"

"No, it isn't."

"What's the matter?"

"The caterer is here," Ivan said, "and he wants to be paid now. You did promise to pay for this dinner, right?"

"Yes, I did," Martin said to Ivan. "I have company, but I can be there in a little while."

"Okay, but make it fast." Ivan marched off.

Martin closed the door and went back to Summer, but unfortunately, she was already getting up as if to leave.

"I think I should go." Summer placed Laney on the dog bed next to her chair. The dog rustled and whimpered but then snuggled down on the cushion.

"I wish you wouldn't go."

"But I hate to make your caterer wait."

"My brothers are always in urgent need; that is, when it comes to money." Martin shook his head, trying not to be thoroughly annoyed at Ivan for closing the door on such a fine moment. Maybe he could still salvage the day. "Would you do me a favor?"

"Yes, of course."

"I'd love for you to come to the dinner this evening at the big house. Please say yes."

"Are you sure you want me there?" Summer edged to the front door. "Seems like I'd be barging in."

"No. I want you to come. If you can."

"Well, okay. I will. Thanks. What time?"

"Time?"

"Tonight?"

"Oh, sorry. It's at six-thirty."

"And what should I wear?"

"Anything that would make you happy."

Summer smiled as Martin opened the front door again, and she stepped out onto the front porch. "Okay."

"And you may leave your lipstick on if you'd like." Maybe he shouldn't have said that. He did have a way of bungling his words.

She chuckled. "Okay. I will."

"But what did you want to ask me?" Martin asked. "It sounded important."

"It can wait. Go take care of the caterer. I'll ask you tonight."

"Good."

"Bye." Summer gazed at him. Then she turned to go and stepped off the porch.

"You will come, won't you? I'd hate to think that you'd go away, and it would be decades before I see you again." Martin took a step out onto the front step.

Summer seemed to study him. "But Martin, it was you who moved away all those years ago."

"Yes, but I didn't want to move. It was my parents' idea. It wasn't even necessary. We didn't need a bigger house or a better neighborhood. We were pretty close to heaven where we were. I wish you had come to visit. You would have been so welcome there. Anytime at all."

"What do you mean, Martin?" Summer asked. "I never heard from you, so I assumed you'd moved on with your life. Made new friends at your new school, and all that."

"No, I never did make any new friends. Not like you anyway. Nothing like that."

"Oh? But after you moved across the city, you never tried to get in touch with me. I called you a couple of times, but I never heard back from you. You never called back," Summer repeated in a whisper.

"Ivan and Desmond both told me you called," Martin said, "but they said you were only keeping up our friendship out of loyalty. That you didn't know how to break the news to me without hurting me. So I decided that the kindest thing to do was to let you go."

CHAPTER
eight

Summer closed her gaping mouth. "And you believed them?"

"I did. They said you were afraid to tell me the truth since you knew it would hurt my feelings. And since I knew you were a loyal person, I assumed it was true. In my childish mind, I thought I was being noble to let you go. Almost like Aragorn in The Lord of the Rings when he walked away from Arwen. But that parting was one of the hardest things I've known." His eyes glimmered with a hint of mist.

"Oh, dear." The sorrow in his face—even the lighter tone in his voice that tried to downplay the pain—tore at her heart. She wanted to rush into his arms and tell him she was so sorry that his brothers did such a terrible thing—that they would invent such a lie—but she stood still and simply said, "I had no idea they told you that. And what they said wasn't true. Your friendship meant the world to me. It still does."

"I have always felt the same way."

"Why would your brothers say such a thing to you?"

"I don't know. They can both be pretty bad-tempered sometimes. But I'm profoundly glad you came back. And I'd sure like to know what made you show up today after all this time."

"I promise I'll tell you tonight."

"Good. That means you will return. I'd hate for another twenty years to go by, but then this time around, I would come after you.

Or perhaps if you go missing again I would climb to the tallest spot in Houston and light a signal fire."

Summer smiled. "Like Pippin?"

"Yes, just like Pippin."

Oh, how she'd missed Martin's view through life's looking glass. And he still had that endearing crinkle around the eyes when he smiled.

Laney trotted up to the door, stared at her, and pawed at the floor.

"See?" Martin said. "Even Laney insists that you come back."

"I promise you, Laney," she said. "And I promise you too, Martin."

"All right then. See you tonight."

"Yes."

"One last word, just so you know." Martin paused and then said, "You'll discover at our dinner tonight that we're not like a typical family. Our interworkings haven't been like your family or other families you've known over the years. We're a bit, I guess the word might be, *impaired*. So prepare yourself."

"What family isn't dysfunctional in some way?" Summer said lightly. But she had to admit that it was an ominous statement.

"I'm afraid our family has been broken for some time, almost beyond repair. But not quite. I believe in miracles. After all, you showed up today."

"That's sweet, Martin. I assure you that I won't be scared off tonight." Summer tucked a curl of her hair behind her ear. "I promise."

"Good." He gave her a friendly wave and then lingered in the doorway.

Summer stared for a moment longer, waved, and then reluctantly turned to make her way back to her car. On the drive home, she mused over their connection and how it hadn't changed. They were grown-up, of course, but beyond that, nothing important had altered. But she'd certainly like to have a few sharp words with his brothers. What a mean-spirited trick they'd played on Martin, telling him such a lie—a falsehood that tore them apart, broke their hearts, and stole from them a most precious friendship that would surely have reached into their adulthood.

And then Martin's words came back to her. "Prepare yourself." Before he had moved away, Summer recalled that Martin had mentioned some trouble at home with his brothers—some sort of trickery and cruelty. It seemed that Martin had taken his role as the oldest brother to be a serious one, but it also seemed like Ivan and Desmond had taken advantage of his bigheartedness. She just hoped that Ivan and Desmond—now that they were adults—had grown out of their deceit and meanness.

Summer exited onto the Beltway toward northwest Houston. One thing was certain, her dear granny had been right about Martin. Of course, Granny had proven herself to be right about many things over the years. One more reason among a thousand that losing her would be agonizing.

Thinking about Granny's situation made her stomach tighten and twist. She wanted to keep praying for Granny's healing, but she knew well that the moment Granny passed from this life to the next she would step into paradise. She would not only be able to run without exhaustion but run into the arms of Jesus. What an eternal blessing. And yet—her summons to heaven seemed too soon. Too abrupt of an ending for a life so very well lived for God.

"Oh, Lord, I know You can heal Granny. Why couldn't she live, say, another twenty years, and *then* You give her Your heavenly reward? Or even ten years. Granny would love to see me get married. That is, if I *ever* marry. But having Granny recover surely wouldn't alter anything in the long scheme of things. Or some grand earthly plan. Would it? Except that it would bring Granny and a lot of other folks hope and joy? And it seems to me, Lord, if You don't mind me saying, sometimes this life feels like it's in short supply of those two things." She sighed. *Well, that was a shabby little prayer, but at least it was honest.*

Once home in her apartment, Summer picked up the phone and called Granny to give her the updates concerning her mission. "Granny?"

"It's me. Any news?"

"Yes. I found Martin. He was the same Martin, just grown-up. A delightful man, really."

"I knew it. Oh, that makes me so happy. Did he agree to do the list with you?"

"We got interrupted, but I'll ask him tonight. He invited me to dinner."

"My, my, my, things are progressing faster than I even imagined."

"Now, Granny. Please don't get your hopes up. It's obvious that we both are very glad to reconnect, and I feel that our friendship will continue, but I just don't know if it will turn into anything more."

"I understand, little love, but a granny can dream, can't she?"

"Yes, you certainly may. Your breathing sounds a little strained. Do you need me to come over?"

"No, not at all. I'm just excited because of your good news."

"Okay. If you're sure."

"I am." Granny wheezed a bit before she said, "How about I treat you to a new dress for this evening?"

"Thanks, but I've got one in mind I think will work. But I do appreciate the offer. Really."

"All right."

When they'd wound up their chat, Summer said, "Love you big and high—"

"As the Texas sky."

After they hung up, Summer went to her closet to make sure the dress she thought was a good one for the family dinner was indeed wearable and not moth-eaten. When she found it at the back of her closet, she noticed a small spot that looked like it might be a spaghetti stain. *Lovely.* Fortunately, Martin had never been impressed with outward appearances. At least not to the level of what she'd experienced with Elliot and his preoccupation with facades. But then, Martin was no longer a kid. He was a grown man, and perhaps she shouldn't be too nonchalant in her appearance. Martin did tease her, after all, saying that she was more than welcome to wear lipstick if she chose to.

As the day wore on, Summer became more intense with her appearance, since nothing seemed to look right. Five outfit changes later and then a quick run to a local dress shop—Summer emerged from her bathroom dressed in an ice pink dress and matching shoes and bag. Staring into the mirror, she felt like a superficial twit of a woman, preened to the max like some freshly sheared poodle. But alas, she had to admit the idea of dining with the adult version of her beloved friend gave her pleasure and a sense of adventure. *Wow, I really do need to get out more.* And that was part of what her dear Granny was trying to do for her.

Summer felt the back of her hair, which she'd swirled up off her shoulders. Guess she'd used enough gluey hair lacquer to endure hurricane force winds. Maybe she was so gummy, Martin's brothers would want to stick her up on the wall for dart practice. She smiled ruefully at the thought.

What would it be like to share a family meal with those two brothers? Unsettling perhaps?

Summer grabbed her purse and keys and headed to the apartment's parking garage, praying that whatever rocky feelings the brothers had for her would be kept where they belonged—in the past.

At seven sharp—Summer knocked on the door of the big house, waiting and speculating on who would answer the door. Would it be Mr. and Mrs. Langtree? Were they still living at the big house? *Please let it be Martin who comes to the door.*

Something unbolted inside the house, and the heavy oak door swung open.

Desmond—the middle son in the Langtree family—stood before her with a toothy grin. "Well, it's little Summer Snow all grown-up and looking as sweet as cotton candy."

Great. What had she been thinking to drench herself in pink like that?

Desmond leaned against the doorframe and gaped at her with the same wise-guy look that his brother Ivan had given her. But with Desmond, there seemed to be something darker lurking in his expression. Hard to tell what it was exactly. She let it go. When his cologne wafted out on a sudden breeze, Summer sneezed. "Hello."

CHAPTER
nine

Martin rushed up to the front door just in time to hear Desmond's inappropriate welcome to Summer, but before his younger brother could say a few more things that might embarrass her, Martin tapped Desmond on the shoulder and said, "Greetings, Summer. Please come in."

Honestly, sometimes his brothers were more socially awkward than he was, and that took some doing. He sent up a quick prayer to the Almighty, pleading to Him for help to make the evening pleasant, since dinner at the Langtree home could become as stable as uranium.

Desmond opened the door more fully and stepped aside for Summer to enter.

She walked into the entry hall with faltering steps.

Martin took hold of her elbow to steady her.

"Thanks." Summer smiled at him. "Sorry. I suddenly seem to be bumbley."

"I've been that way most of my life," Martin said.

"How true," Desmond replied. "In fact, sometimes we call him Martin Bumbley Langtree."

"Oh," Summer said, "that makes me think of the character Bunbury in Oscar Wilde's work *The Importance of Being Earnest.* I just *love* that comedy." Summer grinned back at them both.

Desmond stroked his chin. "Quaint."

Martin ignored his brother and released Summer's elbow. "We're very glad you're here." Could any words ever be truer? He gazed at Summer. "You look nice." He wanted to say more on that note—perhaps that tonight she looked as lovely as an antique rose. The kind that grows wild and beautiful and never needs pesticides or fertilizers, but then on second thought, he was glad he'd kept silent. That compliment needed some tweaking before he let it fly. He'd read in one of his how-to books that admiring comments were delicate things and needed forethought as well as a light touch.

Summer looked around the entry. "What a beautiful home. And that grand staircase is remarkable. Like it's spiraling up into heaven."

"Yes, well, thank you." Desmond raised his hand to the stairs as if presenting it to a large audience. "My parents had it designed by Lenard Klondike, a European designer. It's freestanding and one-of-a-kind. And the accents on the wrought iron are, of course, real gold." He swiped at a finial on the end of the balustrade as if to wipe off a speck of dust.

"Well, it's almost too wonderful to take in," Summer said.

"Precisely." Desmond grinned.

She seemed to study the engineering marvel of it for a moment, and then asked, "You mentioned your parents, Desmond. How are they doing? Do they still live in this—"

"They're abroad," Desmond said before Martin could reply. "In Europe."

"A long vacation then?" Summer asked. "How wonderful to—"

"Yes, you could safely say it's a very long vacation, but not so wonderful." Desmond blinked as he gazed down at the marble floor. "Since you'll know soon enough through Martin, I'll say this. Our parents left when Ivan turned eighteen, and they've never been back."

A puzzling concern consumed Summer's face. "Well then, you three must enjoy going to visit them."

"That's not really the way things work in our family. There aren't any visits." Desmond ran his finger along the edge of the railing. "And our mother and father divorced before they left for Europe."

"Oh, I didn't know." Summer clutched her purse more tightly. "I'm truly sorry."

"Yes, well." Desmond released his classic humorless chuckle. "It's a burden we've borne for a long time. But we won't endure it forever. There will come a day—" He stared up at the top of the staircase and then back at Summer with a glassy grin. "Dinner is ready if you are."

"I'm ready," she said quietly.

"Good." Martin offered his arm, since she looked a little uneasy. "I hope you're hungry."

"I am. I'm always hungry."

"I'll give you a tour of the house after supper if you'd like."

Summer looked up at him and gave his arm a squeeze. "I would like that."

Oh, how Martin had missed that sweet smile of hers—the one that told the whole world that there could still be a few gentle souls out there roaming the earth. So was that the reason why, even at a tender age, he'd fallen in love with her? Or was it because no one else had ever understood his eccentricities like she had, to the point of celebrating them? Or could it be because his memories of Summer had brightened some unhappy times?

If his love for Summer distilled down into no more than those simple reasons, then God help him, since it seemed superficial and selfish of him, and she deserved so much more. But that girl, now a woman, had touched a place in his heart that had never been stirred before. He'd never forgotten, could never forget, even if he tried. And now, Summer had returned. Martin mulled this over while escorting her through the entry hall and into the dining room.

Ivan joined them. "Hello, Summer. I didn't know you'd be here for our dinner."

Summer let go of Martin and circled her arms around her middle. "Well, Martin invited me. I hope it's okay."

"Of course it's all right," Desmond said, coming up behind them. "Our caterer has left us with a buffet this evening. We are to help ourselves. Summer, I hope you like veal."

"I'm sure I will. Everything looks so good," she said, picking up a plate from the stack. "At home I don't get much fancier than spaghetti, beans, or tuna out of a can."

"Really?" Desmond gave her a choking expression. "How can you stand it?"

"Well, I'm a terrible cook for one thing." Summer loaded up her plate with this and that from the buffet. "And to be honest, my income doesn't allow for a lot of extras."

"I'm sorry to hear that." Desmond lifted a large hunk of rare beef onto his dinner plate. "To me life is unbearable without a few of the niceties. Good food. Good clothes. Good—"

"Good company," Martin added, glancing at Summer.

"Are you sure this isn't horse meat?" Ivan glared at the platter of meat.

"Very funny." Desmond shot him a poisonous look. "Actually, they eat horse meat in France and many other countries, so it's not unheard of anyway."

After they'd each taken turns filling their plates, they settled in around the table—with Desmond at the head and Ivan at the other end. Their ornate mahogany table always seemed to swallow them up by its enormous size, especially when his brothers insisted on sitting at either end. The silly thing wasn't practical in any way. But Desmond insisted the table had panache. Maybe it did, but there was little practicality and homey warmth in mere style alone.

Oh, well, moving on. Martin said a brief word of grace—his voice echoing eerily around the room—and then they dug into their feast.

In silence.

Martin tried not to stare at his special guest, but he caught himself stealing glances when he could. Summer was in his midst again. What a miracle.

Flashes from the past flickered across the screen of his thoughts, and he paused on a random memory—a time when he and Summer were children. When they had first gotten to know each other in her grandmother's bookshop, one of the boys had brought a jar of ladybugs for show and tell. But while no one was paying attention, Summer released them outside. The boy became a little ball of fury. When Summer was asked why she did it, she simply replied without apology, "Because the ladybugs were hurting themselves trying to get out." He smiled at the remembrance.

Desmond ran his hand over the surface of the table and stared into the wood as if searching for something. "Summer, occasionally I buy and sell antique pieces at auctions. In case you're interested in older furnishings, this table is gothic, hand-carved mahogany. One-of-a-kind."

Summer, who sat across from Martin, paused with her fork poised in midair. She put her utensil down and gave him her full attention. "It's really . . . um . . . unique."

Martin grinned. She was trying hard to be honest without hurting Desmond's feelings. But in truth, it was a hideous beast of a table.

"In fact," she went on to say, "I've never seen a table quite like it. Except in storybooks like—"

"Except in storybooks like Grimm's fairy tales," Martin absently finished Summer's sentence as he cut through his beef and took a bite.

Desmond's cackle was mirthless. "Oh, is that right. Well, Martin you're also one-of-a-kind, but the difference is, we can't sell you at auction."

Ivan exploded with laughter as he slapped his napkin against the table.

Again silence.

When Martin realized he'd hurt his brother with his offhanded remark, he said, "I'm sorry, Desmond. I was just thinking out loud. I shouldn't have said that about this table."

"No problem." Desmond waved his fork. "We'll just put your comment into the attic, along with all the other things that don't fit in this house."

Summer's fork landed on her plate with a sharp clattering snap, which made one of her cherry tomatoes spin off her dinner plate and then roll down the table like a cue ball.

"I'm so sorry." Summer flushed red. "I get clumsy sometimes."

"Cherry tomatoes are like planets. It's in their nature to spin," Martin said, hoping to make her feel better.

She smiled at him. "Thanks." Summer scooted her chair back, walked over to her cherry tomato and then, after wrapping it in her napkin, returned to her seat.

Ivan took a sip of his water. "There're more vegetables on the buffet table, Summer, in case you want to entertain us some more with those Cirque du Soleil routines." He grinned.

"I'll keep that in mind." Summer slipped him a grin in return. "By the way, these garlic mashed potatoes are so good." She scooped up another big bite. "Do you eat this way all the time?"

"No." Ivan stirred his potatoes around on his plate like they were caught in an eddy. "This is a special night."

"What are you celebrating?" Summer asked.

Silence.

She swallowed. "If you don't mind my asking."

"Sure, why not?" Ivan said.

"Of course we don't mind you asking," Martin said. "It's sort of a tradition. We—"

"A couple of times a year," Ivan said, interrupting his brother, "we hold a dinner in sort of a remembrance of our parents." He pointed to the formal portraits on the wall, the one of their mother and father posing together. "We have this hope that they'll return. Sometimes during the meal we tell stories of our past. But in the last year or so, we've run out of stories."

Summer gazed at the paintings and then at the empty chairs, her face awash with what looked like bewilderment.

This year's dinner did seem more than a little uncomfortable, Martin realized. Was it because Summer was in their midst, and somehow her presence subtly let him know that this tradition might seem sort of sad and pitiful? Probably. And she was right. It was a peculiar ritual. He forever walked on eggshells when talking to his brothers, to the point of retreating to his cottage, and yet if there were ever a time to speak up, it was now. "I was just thinking, doesn't it feel like we're living too much in the past with these dinners? If we keep it up, we'll eventually run out of a future."

"That sounds clever, but I have no idea what you mean by that," Ivan said.

"He means give up the dinners," Desmond said. "You know, walk away from our family as well as our hope."

"No, that's not what I mean." Martin set his fork down. "I want to be clear here. We should never give up hope for a family reconciliation. And remembering them is good too. But maybe it's time to take another approach. These dinners have been going on for a long time, and as we can clearly see, it isn't going to bring them back. Only prayer can do that."

"Or a private investigator," Desmond said between bites. "We know that Mother started out in Provence and Father in Munich. Eons ago, we did talk to them as you surely remember, but it was only briefly. They both have moved so many times, and they are notorious for not returning calls so that connecting with them has become impossible."

"But really, what else did we expect?" Ivan said, with an edge to his voice. "They broke off all ties with us."

"Of course, but I didn't just hire the detective to find their current residences and phone numbers," Desmond said. "It was also to uncover the reason why they left the way they did. Most unhappy parents merely split up. But our parents not only divorced, they left us our inheritances as if they were dead and then cut off communication. They stood in that foyer over there and without so much as tears in their eyes, they said the words, 'from this day forward, think of us as dead.'"

Desmond gazed up at their parents' portrait with a desperate look in his eyes. "I mean, who does that? Who says that except in a gothic novel? There was something going on back then. Some secret that we don't know about. Since our parents have never told us and never will, I'm determined to find out what it is."

Martin took a sip of his water to wash down the meat. The veal was good, but the lumps kept lodging in his throat. "I've wondered about that myself many times. There does seem to be some mystery in it." He glanced at Summer. She'd disengaged from the conversation, but she didn't seem uninterested or overly unnerved by their interaction—that is, the Langtree version of what it meant to be family.

Martin had wanted the evening to be pleasant for Summer, but that was not how it was panning out. And yet what else could he have realistically expected when his brothers got involved? Perhaps this view into the Langtree household, though, could at least give Summer a necessary look at their history. He felt she deserved to know, especially if they were going to continue to be friends in the future. He just hoped that this brief insight into their dysfunctional lives wouldn't scare her off. "Desmond, did the detective find anything?" Martin finally asked, as he took another bite of his salad.

"He found nothing." Desmond pulled out his little gold pillbox from his pocket and set it on the table, lining it up perfectly in front of his plate. "But what I—"

At that moment the phone rang in the kitchen. Desmond rose. "Excuse me. It might be important." He left the room, and while he was gone, Martin asked Summer about simpler things to lighten the mood, such as the traffic to Bellaire and the warmer weather.

In the meantime, Ivan remained quiet as a sphinx, barely eating his food.

In a few minutes Desmond returned, but his eyes appeared haunted and his skin pale.

"Who was it?" Martin asked. "Are you all right?"

"There is something you should know." Desmond glanced over at their parents' portrait.

Ivan stared at Desmond. "Speak up. What is it?"

Every time Desmond spoke in that somber way with those particular words, some part of their lives seemed to collapse. Martin wiped his mouth with his napkin. "Desmond, really. What is it? Something we should know?"

"You two sound like a couple of parrots." Desmond popped a pill from the box and washed it down with water.

Summer twiddled with her spoon in her iced tea, trying to stir in some sugar, but when the tinkling clank echoed around the room, she cringed and set the utensil on the table.

Summer was fingering her earlobe as if in deep thought, but then suddenly she looked up and gave him a sunrise kind of smile. Martin knew it was to lift his spirits, and it did, but he felt sorry that he'd dragged her into such a mess.

"I've been waiting for this phone call. It was a friend of mine who also happens to be my accountant. I just wish it hadn't come during dinner. But the problem is . . ." Desmond daubed the napkin to his forehead. "With the detective's ongoing fees and the household bills, and no more money coming in, well, the inheritance money is dwindling."

"Really?" Martin asked. "Are you sure?"

"Yes." Desmond snapped his pillbox shut. "Private investigators are expensive, even the lousy ones. But it's much more than that.

Our inheritance hasn't been able to cover our bills as our parents had hoped. This house is very expensive to keep up."

"Do you mean you both have spent almost *all* your inheritance?" Martin asked.

"Wait a minute. You said *our* inheritance." Ivan spit the words at Desmond. "You surely didn't use *my* money for this detective of yours. Did you?"

"I pooled our monies together, because you said it was all right. Don't you remember?" Desmond twiddled with his shirt.

"Not that well, no."

"Yes, I did use *our* money for this detective because this was about *us* . . . and *our* parents' lives. And too, I had to use these general funds to support this house. There have been huge bills in keeping a place like this going. I don't think you have a clue—"

"What? You've used up my money. Is that what you're saying?"

Desmond's jaw quivered but he said nothing.

Ivan shot up out of his chair, knocking it over.

Desmond pointed to the chair with a jittery finger. "The chair, Ivan. You just knocked over a three-thousand-dollar chair."

Ivan leaned toward Desmond as he spread his palms on the table. "I don't care about the stupid chair. This is an outrage. I demand—"

"Let me finish. Please." Desmond played with the signet ring on his finger, turning it around and around. "There have been repairs, utilities, our housekeeper, a gardening staff, and—"

"No, there is no excuse for this." Ivan gestured wildly with his hands. "You should have kept me informed, since it was my money too." He shook his finger at Desmond. "Wait. Wait just a minute. You told me some months ago that an investment banker, a man named Xavier, was going to help us grow our portfolio. You know, make a plan for us, so that we could make more money for the future. What happened to that?"

Desmond opened and closed the little clasp on the pillbox. "Xavier did invest the rest of our inheritance—most of what was left anyway—into a financial scheme he said was foolproof. Xavier said he believed in the plan so much he invested his own money into it."

"And?"

"It failed. Utterly."

"Failed," Ivan said in a whisper. "Desmond, why didn't you tell me this?"

Desmond made a fist around his pillbox. "I'm telling you now."

"That's not good enough. It was *my* money you were playing with too."

"I know." Desmond sighed. "I know. I'm sorry, Ivan."

"I can't believe it. This sort of thing always happens to somebody else. We've lost everything then? Everything? I want to hear it again." Ivan's voice faltered. "Desmond. Answer me!"

"Okay! We didn't lose everything, but almost. Our parents have abandoned us yet again." Desmond pushed his plate away. "You and I are nearly destitute."

"I trusted you." Ivan shook his head, his expression dazed. "How could I have been so foolish to depend on you? No, our parents haven't abandoned us again. You have!"

"We need to remain calm." Martin's head filled with the sound of his pounding heart until he felt lightheaded. "Getting worked up isn't going to—"

"I don't want to remain calm." Ivan pounded his hand on the table. "The time for calm was months or years ago when we had a chance to turn this thing around."

Desmond took another pill out of his box and washed it down with a swig of water. "You're right, Ivan. It was foolish to trust me, wasn't it?" he said, sounding defeated.

Ivan righted his chair, sat back down, and glowered at Desmond. "But you're the oldest. You're supposed to watch out for me."

"I want to be clear here," Desmond said, mimicking Martin's earlier words. "I'm not my brother's keeper. And besides, I'm *not* the oldest brother in this family, Martin is."

"Martin is not the oldest brother in our family because he *isn't* our family," Ivan said. "He's adopted."

Martin lowered his gaze. "We all know I'm adopted, Ivan. I'm sorry you feel that I'm not part of this family." His brothers had on occasion looked at him as if he were a stranger among them, but neither one of them had actually said the words out loud—that he was not considered to be a real member of the family—until now. That lonely feeling he'd known ever since he'd come to be in the Langtree family was never closer to him as it was now.

It was a shame that Summer was there to hear it, see it all. Why had he asked her to come? What a fool he'd been to even consider it.

❧❦❧

Summer's heart skipped a few beats and then pounded hard enough to make her face feel hot. How dreadful to know that Martin had been trapped inside the confines of a family where he was not welcome, let alone cherished. She took a quick sip of iced tea to calm herself. "I'm so sorry," she spoke up, breaking the sudden silence of the room. "I shouldn't be here. This is a private family matter." She smiled at Martin, folded her napkin, and slid back her chair. "Thank you for dinner."

"I'm sorry that you were here during a family crisis," Martin said to Summer. "But I know you wanted to talk to me about something, and I sense that it was important. I won't let you keep going away without telling me. Please don't go. We can talk in private."

"I don't care if you go or stay, Summer Snow. So you might as well stay." Desmond's words slurred a bit as he placed the pillbox to his forehead. "But I'd better not hear this news on any social networking sites." He wagged his finger at her and broke out into a goofy grin. "It'll be pretty humiliating if any of my friends were to get wind of it."

"I can't believe this," Ivan said. "Is that all you can think about at a time like this? How embarrassed you'll be in front of your friends when they find out that you've lost almost everything? That *we've* lost everything?"

Summer rose and gave Martin a sincere look of apology.

"Stay Summer." Ivan impaled her with his abrupt stare. "Come to think of it, you might be the only voice of reason here right now. My brother seems to have lost his mind." He softened his expression, but only a little. "Please stay, Summer. Okay?"

She already felt herself regretting her decision as she relented and said, "All right. I will stay for now if you think I can help in some way." Summer sat back down. "But I do want to say this. I have no intention of speaking to anyone about this, so know that whatever is said at this table will go no further than this room. And I am very sorry about your troubles. I know this must be very hard." She gave Martin a reassuring smile, but braced herself for a bumpy ride.

"Well then." Suddenly Desmond's eyes flashed, his expression slightly maniacal. "In honor of our guest who will be staying." He lifted his steak knife, plunged it into his lump of rare beef, and raised it up like he was giving a toast. "Welcome, Summer Snow, to the Hotel California!" Then Desmond howled with laughter.

CHAPTER
ten

Martin knew the lyrics of the song—that Desmond's bizarre theatrics alluded to—and it made him shiver. His brother had officially lost control of himself. It was a dreadful sight for Summer to see, and what he knew he had to do next was going to be even more unpleasant. Martin rose.

"This is disgusting," Ivan said to Desmond. "You really have lost your mind, haven't you?"

Desmond cackled. "Yes, the lovely Langtree legacy is, let's see, is languishing ludicrously low." He chuckled deep in his throat, making a gurgling sound.

It was a noise that didn't sound quite human, but one Martin had heard more and more from his brother, especially when he'd taken one too many of those little round pills. Martin strode over to Desmond.

"I wish I were as good at making money as I am at alliteration." Desmond fumbled with his pillbox again, trying to open it. "Islands in a still blue sea."

"What do you mean, Desmond?"

He hesitated. "I have no idea, but it must have been deep." Desmond chortled again. "Get it? Deep blue sea?"

Martin lowered his hand in front of Desmond, making his gesture as clear as he could without humiliating him. "Please give me the pills."

Desmond shook his head like an angry toddler.

"You're popping those drugs like they're candy," Martin said. "What you're doing is very dangerous."

"Well, I've discovered something, and you'll appreciate this. It's a deep theological discovery on my part. Yes. Now if I can just remember what it was." Desmond rested his head on his arm and then shot up straight again as if suddenly awakened. "Oh, yes. That it doesn't matter how careful or good or tormented or freewheeling we are in this life. Trouble comes calling anyway."

"Some of that is true, but you're chasing trouble with the intent of catching it. And since we're bound to experience trouble in this life, why try to buy even more? Why work at making yourself miserable?"

"Because life is a farce." Desmond winced as if trying to wrap his mind around all the angles of what his brother had said. "You and I and all of us around this table, we're part of a game being played out. No, it's more of a theatrical experience, theatre of the absurd. Yes, that's it. And this is the moment when the camera pans back and the violin music begins to play something sweetly melancholy."

"Please," Martin said again. "The meds."

This time his brother gazed up at him with fire blazing in his eyes. "As you know, this medicine is for my restless leg syndrome, so I can't let you take it." He lifted his hand and then let it fall with a hard thud on the table.

"Is that malady even real?" Martin asked. "It sounds fictitious."

"Of course it's real. Look it up on WebMD." Desmond patted Martin's hand. "I know how you live for research." His voice dripped with sarcasm.

"You're addicted to these meds, thanks to your doctor who has been looking the other way while you got hooked." Martin put his hand on the back of Desmond's chair. "Your mind needs to be clear for the months ahead. We'll have to make some changes."

A menacing silence consumed the dining room.

Ivan said, "Give Martin the stupid pills. Now, okay?"

"Humph." Desmond shot his two brothers another black look. "Whatever." Then he slapped the pillbox into his Martin's hand. "If you're wanting those for yourself, I'll need cash. No checks."

Martin dropped the pillbox into his pocket and offered Summer another sad look of apology. "The last of the supper seems to have gone cold, so maybe coffee would be good at this stage. I think it might help us all."

"I'd rather have a good stiff drink about now," Desmond said.

"And wind up in the emergency room?" Martin said to his brother. "That doesn't sound wise, does it?" He went over to the buffet table, poured a large mug of black coffee, walked back over to Desmond, and placed it on the table in front of him.

Desmond thanked him with a grunt but began to take a cautious sip or two.

"Summer? Ivan? Would you like some coffee?" Martin asked.

"No, thanks. Coffee gives me restless stomach syndrome." Ivan smirked.

Desmond growled.

Summer raised a finger gingerly like a little flag. "I would like some coffee."

"Cream and sugar?" Martin asked.

"A bit of cream if you have it."

"We have plenty. You deserve much more than cream for putting up with us this evening." Martin smiled at her, feeling the pull and tug of two emotions again—wishing he could have spared her their troubles and yet grateful for her presence and support.

Martin handed Summer her mug of coffee and then sat down with his own.

They all sat there in an aching kind of quiet as they took sips of their coffee.

Ivan reached over to the middle of the table, scooted one of the candlesticks closer to him, and let his finger cross back and forth over the flame as he stared into the fire.

"You're going to burn yourself," Martin said.

"What's a little burn when your whole way of life is going up in smoke?" Ivan asked Martin and then turned to Desmond. "Listen, I vote we sell the house and all these expensive furnishings. I assume my money was also used to feed this addiction to antiques of yours. Right?"

"I love antiques, yes, but they are *our* antiques, brother," Desmond said. "Big difference. But we're not selling them. No way."

"I don't give a flying fig for antiques if we can't pay our bills. Listen, the house is nearly paid off. Isn't that what you said some months ago?" Ivan drummed his fingers on the table.

"Yes. But I don't want to sell this place." Desmond set his mug back down with a bang, making the liquid splash out and land on the table. "It's all we have left of them." He carefully wiped up the liquid with his napkin.

"I don't want to sell it either. But someday holding on to this place won't be an option. We may, however, have one more possibility." Slowly, Ivan turned to Martin. "You received an inheritance too. Just the same as we did, right?"

"Yes, I did." Martin straightened in his seat.

"And you have some of it left?" Ivan raised an inquisitive brow.

"Yes, I do."

"How much?" Ivan asked. "Exactly?"

"I have almost all of my inheritance left." Martin clasped his hands together on the table. "I've held on to it all these years . . . for my retirement."

"You have almost *all* of your inheritance left?" Ivan reared back in his chair. "You're kidding, right?"

"Why would I joke about a thing like that?" Martin asked.

"No, I guess you wouldn't. But how do you live?" Ivan asked. "Don't you eat? How do you pay your bills? Do you still work?"

"Yes. My part-time job pays well." Martin took a sip from his mug. "I live frugally. There aren't that many expenses, since my cottage is so small."

"So what is it you do again?" Ivan asked. "I always forget."

Martin looked at him, incredulous that his brothers knew so little about his life. "I work for a think tank called Sunrise Enterprises, and they pay me for my creative ideas and problem-solving skills. I've been working for them on and off for years."

"But you don't seem to drive into the office much. What's up with that?" Ivan leaned forward, looking almost interested now.

"I work mostly at home when they need me," Martin replied, "which isn't all the time."

"There's money in that sort of thing? That think tank business? Sounds sort of made-up, like Desmond's ailments." Ivan's smile was grim.

"Hey, watch it." Desmond pounded the table with his fist.

"There's money in all kinds of things." Martin took another sip of his brew. "But you have to work at it."

Ivan rolled his eyes. "Don't get all high and mighty with us, now that you hold our futures in the palm of your hand. And you do," he said, simmering down a bit. "You do hold our destinies in your hands." He rapped his knuckles on the table. "What do you intend to do to help us, Martin?"

"Well, since you just told me earlier that I wasn't a member of this family, I'm not sure I'm obligated to do anything," Martin pointed out calmly.

Ivan grunted. "How can you be so hard-hearted?"

"I'm not trying to be hard-hearted," Martin said. "I just think you both need to take this situation seriously."

"We do," Desmond finally spoke up, this time sounding more sober after drinking his coffee. "And I guess Ivan is right. Martin, you're the only one who can help us now."

"God can help you." Martin looked intently as his brothers. Lord, let them see the truth.

"I'm not sure He cares much for us anymore. If I were God, I'd be pretty sick of us by now," Ivan said. "But *you* have money. You can save us without bothering God. I'm sure He has a lot more on His mind than *Desmond's* folly."

"I saved my inheritance money for when I retire someday. Do you feel this is fair? What are you asking me to do—bail you out?" Martin asked.

Ivan waved his hand like he was swatting at a gnat. Then he reached over to the candle in front of him and pinched the flame out with his fingers. The fire sizzled to its end.

Martin recalled the story of the prodigal son, and it stirred his conscious into approaching his brothers in a different way. He took in a deep breath, and said, "But I am willing to give you both a small portion of my inheritance while you get on your feet and to save you both from selling your home—*our* home. I hate to see it sold too, even though it's far from practical to live here. A house like this should be used. Really used. It should be filled with children and laughter. Seems like we've turned it into a museum."

"Well, that's the spirit, eh?" Ivan slapped the table. "I knew you'd come through for us, Martin. I knew it."

"You couldn't possibly have known if I would do this," Martin said, "since *I* didn't even know for sure if I would do this for you."

"Why not?" Desmond leaned forward, sounding more lucid.

"Because you both have abused your inheritance. It wasn't meant to be your sole support all these years as well as your retirement money. But you've treated it that way." Martin scratched his head, wishing he didn't have to sound so harsh. "Neither one of you has ever worked a real job. But in spite of that fact, you both live so lavishly that I'm surprised this crisis didn't happen years ago."

"Yes, we get the gist of our failures, Martin. I think we've plumbed the depths of that subject. So let's cut to the chase. What do you intend to do for us—I mean in detail—to save us from Desmond's dastardly disaster?" Ivan twiddled his fingers while he scowled at Desmond. "How's that for alliteration, oh brother-of-mine?"

Desmond rolled his eyes.

Ivan released a low growl at his brother.

Miss Beetle, an older woman who'd been their faithful housekeeper since Martin had come to stay when he was a boy, sauntered over to the edge of the dining room, and let loose with, "Jumping Jehoshaphat. What's all the hullabaloo I hear?"

"Nothing to worry your pretty head with," Desmond said, his voice echoing around the room.

Martin introduced Miss Beetle to Summer, and after a brief and friendly exchange, Miss Beetle looked back and forth at Ivan and Desmond and then dropped her smile. "Well, I came back for my purse, and it's a good thing I did. What exactly are you boys up to? You playing nice?"

"No, we're not," Ivan said plainly. "And knowing us, I doubt we plan to."

"Well, I'm going home to pray for you then like I have ever since you were little 'uns. I keep hoping something will change round here." Miss Beetle positioned her hands on her ample hips like she did when she meant business.

"We're a lost cause," Desmond said. "Surely you know that by now. Not sure we're worth your prayers."

"God'll be the judge of that." Miss Beetle's eye twitched as it usually did when she was upset. She pressed her finger on her eyelid. "But here's what I think. Nobody is a lost cause. Not while Jesus is on the throne."

"Sure." Ivan waved to her. "Have a good one."

"You boys can wave me off all you want, but mark my words, one of these days this Langtree family is going to see a day of deliverance." Her dark eyes flashed redemption fire, and against her pale skin, it made for a sobering sight. On her way out, she gave the front door a hard slam—and to use Miss Beetle's lively language—a door slam hard enough to rattle the bones of King Hezekiah.

Ivan raised his hands. "Why do we let the help abuse us this way?"

"The *help*?" Martin said ominously, hoping they wouldn't miss the displeasure in his voice. "Excuse me? I can't believe you just said that."

Desmond looked up at the portrait of their parents. "Ivan, we let Miss Beetle treat us this way because if we died today, she is one of the few people who would truly mourn. I mean some of our friends might grieve . . . but . . ." his voice faded. Desmond motioned with his hands. "We're off the subject. Martin, what are you expecting us to do? I know your money isn't going to come without a few strings."

Perhaps he should escort Summer out of the dining room and forget the whole thing. But they were his brothers, after all, even if they didn't like to acknowledge it. "Here's what we're going to do." He cleared his throat. "First, it would be nice if you could both show me a little human courtesy, even if you don't consider me to be a member of this family."

CHAPTER
eleven

Ivan tugged on his sleeves, as if pondering whether or not he could pull off Martin's suggestion of treating him in a civilized way. Then he blurted out, "All right. Maybe I was a little out of bounds when I said you weren't really our brother. I was in a fit of rage, though. You could see that. At the moment, the last thing on my mind was how—"

"How it might be wounding?" Martin asked as he touched the rim of his mug.

Ivan seemed to dwell on those words for a moment and then said, "Maybe."

Martin went over to the buffet, picked up a platter of homemade pastries and, starting with Summer, went around the table offering each of them a treat. When everyone was savoring their desserts and in a slightly better mood, Martin went on to say, "And secondly, it would be nice if we could all try to get along better."

"But won't we just be pretending?" Ivan licked the cherry goo off his lips.

Martin sighed at his brother's comment as he swallowed his bite of cherry strudel. Would Ivan ever learn? He glanced at Summer, who sat picking at her dessert as if in deep thought. What must she be thinking of them? Why was it that families got into such deep ruts when it came to matters of the heart? It seemed that once they fell into those cavernous potholes, nothing could pull them back out, except for the stirring hand of providence. Maybe God would use this family crisis—this threat of near bankruptcy—to make them swerve out of the old ruts. "Ivan?"

"Yes, Martin?"

"It's just that I doubt it would please Father and Mother if they knew we'd fallen into such wrangling and quarrelling."

"I'm not sure they get much say in this because they fled the scene long ago." Ivan shrugged.

Good point. Martin washed down the strudel with the last of his coffee.

"And you have always been such an easy target." Ivan flickered with a look that almost bordered on contrition. "But I can see I have no excuse."

Martin lifted an eyebrow. "Yes, I'd say it might be best not to use me for target practice if you're hoping to use me as your loan officer."

Ivan bowed his head in acknowledgment of Martin's point. "Touché."

"We really can get through this crisis if we all stick together," Martin said. "Here is what you can expect from me. For now, I will cover all the expenses in running the big house, not just my part. However, you both will have to promise me in writing that you'll make all the changes I've asked for, including some *other* essential ones."

"Other essential ones? And what, pray tell, are those?" Desmond held up his hands. "Okay. All right. I'm sorry. I'll try harder to be Mr. Friendly. What do we have to do?"

"Well, you both need to put yourselves on a budget," Martin said. "Cook all your own meals, and stop spending so much money on clothes and furnishings and luxuries you don't need."

"And what about that membership at the country club?" Ivan added, glaring at Desmond. "That has cost you a fortune. And it's as necessary as that grandfather clock you bought."

"It's a Bulova, and it was meant to be an investment," Desmond said. "And what about those riding lessons of yours? You own a horse and you pay for boarding, Ivan, and yet you don't even ride."

"So?" Ivan got up and grabbed another piece of strudel from the platter. "That is a fraction of the cost of what you spend on that membership."

"I can't give up my membership at the country club," Desmond said. "That happens to be where I meet up with my friends on the weekends."

Laney crept into the dining room, head down, her nails tap-tap-tapping on the hardwood floors as she trotted up to Summer's chair.

"Laney," Summer said. "How nice to see you."

"Guess she wasn't all that happy with her food bowl in the kitchen, eh, Laney?" Martin said.

The dog jumped up, her spindly little legs resting on the side of Summer's chair. She whimpered, putting on a most pitiful performance—an act that Martin was very familiar with.

"She's trying to wangle her way onto somebody's lap." Summer picked up the little dog, and right away Laney snuggled down into her cradling arms.

Martin grinned.

Ivan pointed to the dog. "What is that *thing* doing here in the big house?"

"Oh, forget about the dog," Desmond said. "We have more important matters to deal with. As I was saying, I don't want to give up my membership at the country club. That's where I meet my friends on the weekends." He turned to Summer. "Well, don't you think that's unfair? I mean really? Surely I'm not expected to give up my friends as well as everything else."

Summer winced. "I don't think I have a say in this matter."

"But I'm asking you," Desmond said, "since Ivan calls you the voice of reason."

"You don't have to answer that if you don't feel comfortable," Martin said.

"It's okay." Summer stroked the dog's ears as she appeared to consider Desmond's question. "Well, it seems to me that if they are really your friends, Desmond, then they could meet with you anywhere. Not just at an expensive country club."

"A-*ha*." Ivan laughed. "Told you she was the voice of reason. I mean, Desmond, would those fancy country club friends of yours attend your funeral if you died?"

Desmond looked down at his half-eaten pastry. "I don't know. Maybe not if it was a good day to golf."

Ivan chuckled. "Well, at least that was an honest reply."

What a distressing commentary on the friendships his brothers had cultivated over the years.

Desmond turned his attention to Martin. "All right. My membership runs out in one month, so I will make a vow that I won't renew it; but just for now."

"Okay. Good. We're making some headway," Martin said. "But you'll also need to fire that detective. He's obviously soaking you for money without delivering any real information. And you'll need to find work. You're both smart and able-bodied. You'll be able to find something. You might even discover something you really enjoy."

Desmond slumped in his chair. "I can't work. I have too many health issues."

"Like what?" Ivan asked. "Please tell me, what is your disease du jour this time, Desmond?"

"Oh, you are just brimming with mirth today, aren't you?" Desmond said. "Lately, I've had even more bad news healthwise, but I've kept it to myself, since I didn't want to worry anyone. But I also have been diagnosed with stiff person's syndrome."

Ivan let out a thunderous cackle. "You just made that up on the fly, didn't you?"

"No, I did *not*."

"Well, I certainly can't see any of that stiff person's disease when Douglas asks you to play golf." Ivan waggled his head.

"That's *not* a disease," Desmond said. "It's an *affliction*, and it comes and goes."

"Excuse me, but I honestly can't see how you can have restless leg syndrome *and* stiff person's syndrome. There're sort of mutually exclusive, right? I think you're pulling my leg." Ivan spewed with a loud and obnoxious chortle. "Am I the only one who can see how crazy funny this is?"

Desmond fumed. "This is not funny. I want you—"

"Come on, Desmond, stop your mewling," Ivan said. "You're worse than a toddler sometimes."

Laney whimpered, and Summer cuddled her closer.

Martin looked beseechingly back and forth at Ivan and Desmond. "Come on, guys."

"Oh, right," Ivan said. "We're supposed to all be buddies. Desmond, look, I know if I can find something to do, you can too. It's not like you'll need to put on a hard hat and do manual labor. You can find a desk job. Or how about working in an antique shop? That's something you would do well at."

Martin smiled at his brother. One baby step forward.

Desmond made little circles on the table with his finger. "Maybe. I am good at it after all."

"Yes, you are," Martin said.

"Don't patronize me," Desmond ran his hand along his lapels, smoothing them. "Please."

"Hey," Ivan said, "if I have to play nice, so do you. And you know what else, Desmond? You don't have any right to be so self-righteous here. All of this hullabaloo is *your* fault." Ivan put up his hands. "All right. All right, Martin. I'm putting on my nice hat again. Okay?"

Martin scratched his head in exhaustion over his brothers' continued wrangling. "I've had about enough of both of you. But I do mean what I've said. I will help if you'll solemnly agree to what I've said. Are we all in agreement? And will you start looking for jobs this coming week?"

Both Desmond and Ivan stared at Martin as if they were in physical pain. In the end, both brothers nodded in agreement with Martin's plan.

Good, maybe they are finally taking their choices seriously. "That's great. You'll be happy about this decision in the months to come."

Ivan glared at the half-melted candle.

Desmond gaped into his coffee mug.

Martin smiled at Summer and rose. "Well, I have made Summer wait a long time to ask me something, so after I take her on a tour of this house, we're going to find a quiet spot so we can talk."

"That doesn't seem quite fair," Ivan said, "if you don't mind my saying so, Summer. We've opened our veins for you here at this table. You're now aware of some of our most private family matters. So whatever you have to say can easily be said in front of us. We can hold your secrets as well as you now hold ours." He raised his gaze a notch.

"I agree," Desmond said.

"Of course," Summer said. "I don't mind—"

"Summer, please excuse me for interrupting," Martin said, "But you don't need to do any such thing." He looked back and forth at his brothers. "Now how can this be fair to ask Summer to do that? We don't even know what she wants to ask me. Also, it's nothing short of rude to corner a dinner guest this way. Ivan, you asked Summer to stay for your own purposes, and she did so graciously, even though this family debacle of ours most certainly ruined her evening. And it grieves me that all of this came out just as she and I were finally reunited as friends after twenty years. This wasn't a good start for us, but I intend to make things right." Martin reached out his hand to Summer and helped her from her seat.

"Thank you." Martin led Summer out of the dining room, but just as they were about to turn the corner, he overheard Ivan say to Desmond in a low voice, "Martin never would have ordered us around if *she* hadn't been here. I will get a job to save this place, and you will too, but I loathe this new imperial Martin and his directives."

CHAPTER
twelve

Summer heard Ivan grumbling as she left the dining room with Martin, but she couldn't make out the words. Considering the foul temperaments of Martin's two younger brothers, she wasn't sure if she cared to hear any more of their rantings anyway. She'd never known anyone else like them—to carry on so ridiculously—except maybe the kids back in high school. No, wait, maybe grade school. It was more than evident that Martin's brothers were two thoroughly spoiled young men.

She circled her arm through Martin's as he led her toward a little sitting area just beneath the staircase. When they were seated, Martin went quiet for a moment. Perhaps he was trying to decompress after such a family ordeal. In all the Langtree tangles, it was Martin she grieved for the most in this family saga. He had obviously been mistreated with those verbal lashings from his sharp-tongued brothers, and it was also clear that he absorbed those little stinging agonies without retorting. He instead responded with patience and love. What a man. It had always been the way of Martin—it was one of the many things that made him the best friend she'd ever had.

After a moment or two, she said softly, "This has to have been an emotionally exhausting evening for you. Please don't feel like you need to show me the whole house unless you want to. But what I'm most interested in is your favorite room. I'll bet it's the library. Do you have one?"

"Good idea. We do have a library, and it *is* my favorite room in this house." He lit up some again. "Let's go there. It's a quiet place where we can talk."

Martin led her through a hallway full of alcoves, which were festooned with either a statue or a vase, each looking like heirloom pieces. He opened the door, and gestured for her to go ahead of him into the library.

The lights came on instantly as they entered. How cool was that? Summer looked around with appreciation—at the many shelves of books lining the walls, the tapestries, and the original oil and water color paintings. At the lush Persian rugs over polished wood. The subdued illuminations here and there, the stone fireplace, and the cozy look of the leather chairs. Wow, spare no expense. "What a wonderful place for reading and generally getting lost in a story."

"Yes, I did a lot of that here when I was younger. In this family, getting lost in a book was almost a necessity."

"I'm so sorry, Martin, that you had to live that way."

"Well, I did survive it, and I will continue to." He motioned for her to sit down. "Please, sit if you'd like."

When they were seated on a cozy leather couch, she said, "Before I ask you which one of these books was your favorite growing up, I'd like to say again how sorry I am that your family is going through this trial. For Desmond and Ivan to lose their inheritance, well . . . I barely know what to say, except that I'm sorry for them both—and for you."

"Thank you. And in answer to your question, it's *Dracula*."

"Really? Your favorite novel growing up? Why is that?"

"Because I enjoyed reading about people who were more messed up than my own family."

Summer laughed. "Sorry. Guess that's not so funny."

"I'm hoping someday it will be funnier than it is now." Martin grinned. "I'm glad you stayed this evening, but Ivan shouldn't have demanded it. That had to have been the most uncomfortable dinner conversation you've ever experienced. I hope it didn't give you indigestion."

Summer smiled. "No, it didn't. I'm fine. Although I admit it was pretty creepy when Desmond raised his knife and plunged it into his steak, welcoming me to the Hotel California."

Martin shook his head. "Desmond always did have a theatrical quality about him. I'm sorry he did that, though. It was inexcusable. Not to mention disturbing."

"And maybe a little funny too." Summer shrugged.

"Yeah, in a sickening sort of way."

After a short silence Summer said, "But what about you? They were brutal to you, Martin."

"Maybe." He loosened his tie. "I've gotten used to it, but I'm sorry you heard it."

"I think they are taking advantage of your goodness."

"My goodness? I've never thought of myself like that, but I guess sometimes they do take advantage of me. But tonight was different."

"Oh? How so, if it's okay to ask?"

"You being at the table made a difference. I've been thinking this crisis might happen at some point, and so this discussion should have happened a long time ago. I am the oldest, and I do feel a duty to watch out for them. But it was easier to stay in the guest cottage and ignore the symptoms. But tonight . . . well, with the combination of their predicament and you being there, it seemed like an open window. Your presence gave them pause while it gave me courage." Martin reached out to her. "I want to thank you in some way."

Summer took hold of his hand, and Martin shook it. But that gesture seemed too impersonal, so she leaned over and gave him a hug. They lingered in that embrace for a while, and it felt like the dearest affection of friendship.

And maybe something more.

They seemed to be breathing as one, just as they used to say the same thing at the same time when they were kids. When she reluctantly eased away, they looked into each other's eyes. Summer studied this friend of hers who'd now become a man. What were they searching for? Hard to tell, but maybe a different kind of life would be a good place to start.

The mantel clock chimed the hour.

"Summer?"

Oh, dear. He'd caught her drifting on *other* matters. "Yes?"

"What have you been wanting to ask me? I don't want anything else to interfere with your question."

"Yes. Yes, of course. I do have something important I wanted to ask you." Summer crossed her legs, and then she uncrossed them. "As you know, Granny is quite ill, and I will not deny her anything. I never could say no to her even when she was well. But now, more than ever, I want to do whatever I can to make her last months happy ones." She looked away toward one of the bookcases, trying to steady her emotions. "And she has asked me to doing something for her. Something wonderful, but sort of out of the ordinary."

"Your grandmother was always wonderfully different."

"Yes, she is. And she's made a list of adventures. It's sort of like a life-list of things she thinks are important for me to do."

"That sounds like fun." Martin's arm rested near her on the back of the couch, and for a second he lightly touched one of her curls, which lay next to his fingers. Suddenly he pulled his hand away as if he too had been caught drifting on *other* matters.

"I'm glad you feel that way," Summer said, "since she wanted you to do the list with me."

"Really? Me? She remembered me that well?"

"Of course she did. She's never forgotten you." *Nor did I.* "And she feels that you were meant to do this list with me."

"I would be honored, but why me? I'm sure there were dozens of people she could have chosen for this task."

"Granny was very fond of you, as I was. And she must feel I need a friend, a good one to help me as I fulfill this list."

"You don't have a close girlfriend then?" Martin asked.

"I've had lots of friends come and go over the years, but no, they weren't like you. None so . . . special." She hoped that was the right word—honest without being too forward.

"I would be honored to do the list with you."

Summer gave him a quick hug. "But wait." She pulled back. "You haven't even asked what's on the list yet. That's kind of dangerous, isn't it?"

"Not really, since I trust you and your grandmother. But okay, tell me, what's on this list?"

"Well, all sorts of things, like take a hot air balloon ride. Build a tree house. Go find a treasure. Solve a mystery. Watch a sunrise. Befriend a dog. That sort of thing."

"Well, I think you've already accomplished one of them with Laney."

Summer smiled. "Good."

Martin rested his elbows on his knees and then looked back at Summer, beaming with joy. "This list does sound like your grandmother. She always seemed to have an adventuresome spirit about her. Sure, I'll do it."

"Are you sure? But what about your work? You just gave your brothers this amazing lecture on how important work is, and then I take you away from yours. That can't be wise." She hated to talk him out of it, but Summer wanted to make sure she wasn't interfering too much with his life. The last thing she wanted to do was to make Martin's life harder in any way.

"It's all right since my work comes in spurts, and this is a downtime for me. As far as I can see now, there shouldn't be anything to keep me from your grandmother's request."

"Wonderful. I'll email you the whole list."

Martin went over to an oak desk, jotted something down, and then handed her the slip of paper. "It's my email address. I'll look forward to seeing the list. It will—"

The door to the library made the tiniest creaking sound, and Martin abruptly stopped talking. He tiptoed to the door and jerked it open. He leaned out beyond the door for a look up and down the hallway, and then he came back in the room.

"Was someone there?"

"I don't know," Martin said as he touched a rotating globe that set on a brass stand. "That door has always been unsteady." He gave the globe a gentle spin.

"I guess you thought it might be Ivan or Desmond?"

"They're not in the best mood right now, and I've learned from experience that, well . . ."

"What are they capable of? Not anything drastic, I'm sure," she said in a lighthearted tone. But then when Martin didn't answer she added. "Maybe I don't know what I mean."

"I just know that when people get desperate they don't always think rationally." Martin rubbed his forehead.

Oh dear. "Maybe this isn't a good time after all, you know, for the list. You do have a lot of family issues on your plate right now." When Martin stepped over to her, she gave his sleeve a gentle tug. "Please don't feel obligated. Granny wouldn't want it."

"I want to do this. I *will* do this list with you." He slipped off his sports jacket and tossed it onto an ottoman. "The things that have to happen in this house need to come from my brothers. I can't make these changes for them. I can't work my job and their jobs too. But in between our outings, I will make sure they're following through with their promises." He raised an eyebrow.

"All right. Good. Glad it's settled then if you're sure. Thank you again, Martin. This might be Granny's last request, so I'm happy you can do this with me. Maybe we should try to do them as quickly as possible, so in case you get busy or in case Granny takes a turn for the worse and . . ." Tears formed in her eyes. "Sorry. I'm just not ready to say goodbye." She steadied her voice. "I guess I won't ever be, though."

Martin sat down next to her, closer than he was before. "None of us want to say goodbye to someone we love."

There seemed to be more in Martin's words—in his expression—than just a solemn and soothing comment, and that "more" warmed her heart. "Yes, well, that's the truth." When tears threatened again, she hopped up and began to peruse the library, scanning titles, and hoping to learn more about Martin's favorite room.

"What is your—"

They both spoke at once, which made them laugh.

"You go first, Martin."

"All right. I'm wondering, what is the first thing on your list?"

Summer replied happily, "*You* were the first thing on that list. Number One. It read, 'Find your childhood friend Martin Langtree and convince him to fulfill the life-list with you.'"

"I'm happy to say that Summer Snow has definitely found Martin Langtree." He smiled. "So what does your list say to do next?"

"It says I'm supposed to learn to whistle."

Martin looked surprised. "Come on now. You don't know how to whistle?"

"I put my lips together and I blow, but nothing comes out. I'm whistle challenged, I guess." Summer puckered her lips and blew to show him how pathetic she was at whistling.

"You're right. That is sad." He grinned. "But what makes you think I can teach you?"

"I have no idea." Summer filtered through some childhood memories. "You know what? I do know. I remember you whistling in the bookshop sometimes when you read. You'd sit in one of the beanbag chairs in the backroom and whistle like a songbird. It was so unusual to hear someone do that, especially someone so young."

Martin came over to her by the bookshelf. "My father taught me how to whistle."

"He did?" Summer reached out her hand briefly but didn't touch Martin. "By the way, I didn't want to bring it up before, thinking it might upset you. But I'm so sorry your parents left you the way they did. It must have been hard on all of you."

"It was." He fingered a book or two on the shelf. "I don't think any of us ever recovered. It's one of the reasons that Ivan and Desmond struggle to find their way. Even though we were legally adults when our parents left for Europe, we weren't ready to take over the responsibilities of this huge house without some direction. We weren't mature enough to cope with why they left so suddenly. They not only divorced each other, but they divorced us with no reason or hope for future contact. I guess maybe that's another reason I give my brothers so much leniency. But in the end, I guess those indulgences became more debilitating than redeeming." He made a little wave with his hand. "I'm sorry. I didn't mean to get off on all that."

"I asked you, and I wanted to know. Do you want to talk about it some more?"

"Maybe someday. But right now, I'd rather teach you to whistle. That seems pretty important."

Summer grinned. "Okay." She raised her chin. "So what's the secret to this whistling thing?"

"It's very simple. Make your lips look like this." Martin made his into an *O*.

"I do that very thing every time, but it never works. But for you I'll try it." Summer made her lips into the proper shape.

"Now place your tongue up against your bottom teeth."

"But that's where my tongue is parked most of the time anyway."

"Let me see," Martin instructed.

Summer opened her mouth to let Martin check her tongue and then she laughed. "Do I have it right?"

"You do. Now blow."

Summer blew. "Nothing." She tried again. "Nothing." She tried again. "Nothing."

Martin laughed.

"Hey, stop your guffawing."

"Is that what I was doing?" He grinned. "Guffawing?"

"Maybe it was more of a titter, but your eyes said guffaw."

"Come on now, nice and easy as you go. Play and experiment with that shape of your mouth until you hear something musical come out."

Summer slowed the air coming out of her mouth and kept moving and reshaping her lips until the tiniest sound came out.

"That's it. I think you're getting it. Sort of."

She grinned and tried it again. This time a bit of actual melody could be heard. "That's it. I did it."

"Yes." Martin slapped his hands together. "You did it."

"Thanks." Summer whistled a bit more and smiled proudly.

"You've got it. Now all you need to do is practice a bit. You're a born nightingale."

"Maybe I am." Summer was suddenly in such a good mood—a giddy and frisky mood—that she lifted a throw pillow off one of the chairs with the intent on giving him a smack with it.

He held up his finger. "About the nightingale, you might find it interesting to know that—"

Summer gave Martin a billowy thump across the face, which muffled his words.

When the pillow thumping was complete, Martin pulled back and took on the look of a disapproving butler as he flared his nostrils in mock horror at what she'd done. "How could you do such a thing? Thwack me like that?"

"Thwack?" Summer laughed.

"Yes, thwack. What a senseless act of brutality. It was—"

Summer gave him another hit with the pillow, which once again stopped him cold.

While Summer prepared for yet another strike, Martin must have been planning his own assault—with the clandestine maneuvering of a snake, she thought afterward—since he suddenly brought a pillow out from behind him and gave Summer a good wallop on the arm.

After that, it was all-out war as they found pillows here and there, using them for ammo and hiding behind couches to plan a fresh attack. They continued with their good-natured skirmish— whamming each other and laughing until they finally collapsed on the couch in happy exhaustion.

As they were still chuckling, the blare of an alarm interrupted their joy.

"What?"

Martin frowned. "Oh, great. Sounds like one of the smoke alarms."

"Really?"

"I don't smell any smoke, but we'd better go." Martin opened the library door the rest of the way and quickly escorted Summer down the hallway.

But as they hurried toward the entry, she couldn't help but wonder if the shrieking alarm wasn't a false one and somehow connected to Martin's brothers. In the past, since Desmond and Ivan hadn't supported their friendship, perhaps they still didn't approve. What those bullying and childish and peevish brothers were capable of now was difficult to know. If they became desperate in some way, as Martin had suggested, would their artless scheming become more creative and perhaps even threatening? Time would tell.

PART TWO

snags

CHAPTER
thirteen

Two days later, Summer got on the freeway and sped back toward Martin's house. She had to keep letting off the gas, since she caught herself going faster and faster to get there. She and Martin had barely reunited, and yet they were already celebrating their third date? No, not quite. A friendly get-together? Sounded so 1950s. Did she want it to be a date? Possibly. It was certainly something lovely to think about later.

Summer grinned. She'd done a lot of that grinning thing since she'd found Martin. They had reconnected in spite of the trickery of his brothers. As was her guess, Desmond and Ivan really had set off the smoke alarm, but from what the two of them claimed, it was purely an accident. Right. She tapped her finger against the steering wheel. She believed that nugget of falsehood as much as she believed that Houston could have snow in summer.

She tightened her grip until her knuckles went white. Actually, it grieved her deeply to think so poorly of Martin's brothers—she had always taken the view that a person was a decent sort until proven otherwise—but the younger Langtree brothers seemed to be riddled with an inordinate amount of "otherwise." And the thing that really got her goat was the way the two could abuse Martin's generosity. That she couldn't bear, even if they *had* wasted their inheritance. *Lord, please don't let me hate them. I fear I'm getting close.*

A few minutes later, when Summer arrived at the Langtree house, Martin was already there waiting for her at the back gate.

"Aiya," he said.

It was the way he used to greet her when they were teens—"hello" in one of the Elvish languages from *The Lord of the Rings.* She repeated it back to him and added, "I hope you haven't been waiting long."

"Well, I've been waiting about twenty years for you, but who's counting?" Martin grinned.

Summer smiled back. "Traffic was heavier than expected on 610. Two fender benders."

"All too common. I'm glad you're here. Come follow me."

"You said that you have everything set up to do the next thing on our list. Really? You mean, today we're going to build a tree house?" Summer had to take two steps to keep up with Martin's long, lanky-legged strides.

"Yes, sort of." He stopped suddenly and gave her his full attention. "Would your grandmother mind if we remodel an old tree house rather than build a new one? I have one behind the cottage that's in disrepair. It needs a few new boards and a lot of love."

"I know Granny wouldn't mind. Last night when I called her to give my report, she said we could improvise. She's so happy we've become friends again that she'll be thrilled that I even spent some time in a tree house, let alone remodeled one."

"Your report, huh? I guess she heard about our family dinner. You know, what a disaster it was."

"I did tell her some of it, yes," Summer said. "I'm sorry, maybe I shouldn't have."

"No, it's okay. It's just that . . . oh, boy, what she must think of us." He raised his hands in a flustered gesture. "I'll bet she thinks we're this living proof of the chaos theory."

"Martin, Granny loves you. And she hopes and prays for the best always. That's all."

"Yes, I could have expected that from her. Of course." Martin stuffed his hands in the backs of his pockets, which gave him a boyish look. "By the way, I really would like to see your grandmother again sometime. When she feels up to it."

"And she wants to see you too. But she's waiting until we get a few things checked off this list. I'm telling you, Martin, she is intent about this, almost obsessed."

"But why?" he asked. "What does this list really mean to her? You never did tell me exactly why these particular things are so important."

"I will tell you. I promise. But let's repair your tree house first," Summer said. "Then we'll have a quiet place to talk." *A private place.*

"Good idea."

Martin led her around the cottage to a small backyard. A smattering of pines grew up tall here and there as well as some red cedar. But in the middle of the yard was a giant live oak, and its mighty arms seemed to embrace the whole of the backyard. He pointed to the tree dwelling up in that oak. The tiny abode could boast of windows and shutters and a nifty rooster weathervane on top, but the bragging rights ended there. Martin was right. The tree house was indeed a shambles. "It does look like it needs some loving attention. When did you build it?"

He placed his hand on the trunk of the mighty oak. "Not long after we moved to this house. It was Ivan's idea. We all decided to do it together, which was a first for us. I thought it would be a great way to have a little camaraderie with my brothers. So I read some how-to books from the library and we got started. But Desmond got tired of the work and Ivan whined and argued so much, that in the end, well, I finished it for them."

What a surprise.

Martin looked up at the tree house and sighed.

"Did you boys at least spend some time in the tree house? You know, pretending to be pirates and all that?"

"No, we never did, which makes me believe that if you don't put the work into something, it doesn't mean as much. They didn't hit their finger with the hammer like I did, multiple times. They didn't experience the satisfaction of figuring out how to get the window shutters to open and close properly. They didn't hang up the welcome sign. Since they didn't go through the pain and the joy of building it, they never got that sense of ownership."

She patted the tree. "Sounds like wisdom."

"Well, I certainly wasn't very wise back then, since I was foolish enough to do all the work myself," Martin added dryly.

"You were faithful to the project no matter the weather. Can't fault that," Summer said.

"Maybe. But when the tree house was all done, my only wish as a kid was that I could share it with a friend."

What Martin didn't say fully, well, it was there in his eyes—that he'd wished he could have shared the tree house with her.

Nice. "You have a friend to share it with you now." Summer felt flushed, and so to cool off, she walked over to Martin's neat stack of supplies—fresh boards, two saws, two hammers, a box of nails, and some bottles of water. She picked up a hammer and waved it in the air. "Let's do this thing. I'm stoked."

"All right." He headed upwards on the makeshift ladder. "When I get up part way, hand me the tools and boards, and then you can come on up. Got it?"

"Sir, yes, sir." Summer saluted him.

Martin laughed.

When all the supplies and tools had been hauled up to the tree house and they had worked steadily for several hours—except for snack times and laughter breaks—and they'd replaced all the rotten boards with new ones, Martin said, "I think we're there. What do you think?"

Summer wiped the sweat off her face with her T-shirt. "Well, it might not stand up to a Houston hurricane, but it's perfect for two friends to enjoy springtime."

"Hear, hear!" Martin sat down on the floor, leaned against the wall of the tree house, and took a swig from his water bottle. "Now you can officially say that you've renovated an old tree house."

"Granny will be thrilled."

He made a checking sign with his finger. "Check."

"Yea."

"We need to make this official." He raised his water bottle. "I hereby christen this abode the Summer Langtree Castle, but we can call it The Nest for short." He smashed the bottle against the open window frame, but the plastic container bounced and flew out of his hand onto the ground below.

They both laughed.

"Not exactly a resplendent ceremonial," Martin said.

"But it's ours, and it's more than enough." Summer sat down on the floor of the tree house, opposite from Martin.

Martin wiped his face with his flannel shirt. "What a perfect April day."

"Indeed."

They went quiet for a bit, but Summer felt anything but uncomfortable. With her former fiancé, things had to always keep moving, even if it was only for movement's sake. Martin, though, even though he obviously loved being immersed in projects, he knew how to merely "be." He knew the value of quiet, and the priceless serenity of an unhurried moment.

After a little while, Martin said, "Do you hear it?"

"What's that?"

"The sounds of creation without that pesky traffic noise that you hear in front of the big house. Out here you can hear more of what God made rather than what people have made."

Their natural surroundings did indeed come to life, rewarding them for the listening. Birds serenaded one another on nearby branches. Bees droned, going about the business of making the world bloom from their allogamy. And the wind teased the edges of their tiny castle, whispering secrets in some mystical language. "What a sanctuary."

"But it's more than the peace of this place. It's the comfort of *us*," Martin said, not looking at her. He added, "If you're ready, please tell me some more about this list. Was there some special reason your grandmother asked you to do it? Seems to me there's more going on here."

"That's very intuitive of you. You're right. There is." Summer crossed her legs at the ankles, trying to get comfy on the hard wood. Not an easy task. "First, let me preface my story with something you probably don't know. During the years we were apart . . . well, my parents passed away."

"I had no idea." He looked at her intently. "I'm so sorry."

"I think of them every day and still miss them. It seems you never really get over the death of a parent. That I know now. You just learn to live with the grief. But it changes you. You can't ever be the same again no matter how hard you try. Grief sort of becomes a part of you like a broken limb that never heals quite right. You can move again, eventually, but not as smoothly as before." Of course, she knew what her granny would say—that if life didn't have those kinds of losses then no one would long for heaven—their real home.

"Life is far from easy."

"True."

"I'm sorry I hadn't taken the time to ask about them before."

"That's okay," Summer said. "You didn't really know my parents all that well. They rarely visited the shop, so you didn't get a chance to get to know them very well."

"What happened to your parents? Are you okay talking about it?"

"I don't mind. At least, I don't mind talking to *you* about it." Summer gathered her thoughts. "Just before I was supposed to leave for college, my parents got in a car accident. It was serious, and they sustained some internal injuries. You know, damaged organs that they couldn't seem to heal from. They did get treatments, which were paid for by the settlement from the accident, but mostly Granny and I took care of them during those years. They had good days and bad days, but then the bad days became more frequent for both of them. And then they both died. Well, my mom died and then my dad not long after. He just sort of gave up. He so desperately wanted to follow her to heaven. I had a lot of time to prepare, but it still wasn't easy. Not at all."

"I'm sure it wasn't." They were once again engulfed by the sounds of nature when suddenly he asked, "You didn't get a chance to go to college then?"

"Oh, I could have gone. My parents left me a bit of money, and it was enough to go to a small community college, but not long after their passing, Granny retired from the bookshop. She asked if I'd like to run it. I had so many happy memories from that place that it seemed natural for me to take over the business. Once again, it felt like the right thing to do. But yes, there have been times that I get those *what if* moments." Summer noticed a fallen paper wasp nest—which no longer had any inhabitants in it—so being curious, she picked it up.

Martin seemed to study her as he said, "Did you know that paper wasps are social insects?"

"No, I didn't. That's interesting." She turned the wispy shell around in the light.

"Social. Unlike me." He chuckled. "I did attend college and then got a master's degree in physics, but it was hard because of my lack of social skills. I was just always better with concepts than anything communal. Except with you, of course. I always felt at ease with you."

Summer smiled.

"Sometimes, do you wish you'd gone to college?" he asked.

"Maybe. Yes. But I was also glad to take care of my parents. They certainly took care of me growing up, in good times and bad. I knew taking care of them was the right thing to do, and so there was great comfort in that on those days when I pined for a different kind of life. So that is one of several reasons why my granny insisted I do these adventures. That I turn over the shop to my assistant and take a short leave of absence. Anyway, I guess you could say that Granny thinks I didn't get enough youth in my youth. You know, that I was forced into a caregiving role before I'd had a chance to explore life. And also, she feels guilty that she asked me to take over the store. She believes it was selfish on her part. I don't agree, of course. I had what many kids never got growing up—lots and lots of love." She shrugged. "What more can a girl ask for, really?"

Martin reached up and adjusted a wooden shutter so that it would let in more sunlight. "Most people would think that's a sad story, but you made it beautiful with your outlook. You always did that when we were kids too."

"That's a sweet thing to say about me, but be careful putting me on a pedestal. I'll fall off and hit my head before I've even made it to the top."

Martin grinned. "But there's another reason. You said there were several reasons for the adventure list, and if I'm not mistaken you've only mentioned two."

"Yes, well." How could she bring up the last point without making Granny sound like she was heavily suggesting that Martin might be the one? Impossible. "Um . . . I don't know how to say it, except that I've been a little lost in love."

CHAPTER
fourteen

"Lost in love?" Martin repeated. "I'm not sure I understand. How does that happen?"

Summer laughed. "It's pretty easy. For me anyway. You get lost in love by not dating the right men. By lacking discernment. By agreeing to marry men who seem to say all the right things, but who are not what . . ." Her words drifted away.

"You've been engaged?"

She took one more look at the wasp nest and set it down on a plank. "Yes. I've been engaged twice. Nine years ago. That time, my fiancé, Patrick, broke it off, and this second time, recently, *I* broke it off."

"How recent?"

"Last week." Summer cringed, thinking how pathetic she sounded. Not to mention fickle. But she was determined to follow her granny's instructions, and considering her condition, moving with haste was paramount. She sensed an urgency in her spirit. Was it from God?

"Really?"

"Yeah. I know, hard to believe."

"No. But you must still feel the sting of that."

"It feels more like a lonesome kind of ache. I hate unhappy endings, even in the stories that I read. Sounds silly, since I was the one who caused the unhappy ending. I'm the one who called things off. But more than any pain, I feel much more relief now that it's over.

And in time, he'll come to feel that way too. Maybe he already does. At least I hope so. But I know Granny wonders if I'll ever know my own heart well enough to find the right man."

"Maybe that isn't the problem. You're so kind and giving that you have trouble saying no to a proposal—to a man who you might be fond of, but you don't necessarily love—at least not for a lifetime." Martin looked away briefly and then shook his head. "Sorry. That wasn't my business to say that."

"We're old friends. You may say whatever you'd like. And as far as the way you summarized my love life, well, there may be some truth in it. I'm not saying I'm all that kindhearted, but I do say yes too soon, before I know what I'm really getting myself into."

Martin gave her a special *knowing* look she remembered from her youth—a look that told her he knew she was hiding something, and that he would get to the bottom of it eventually.

What Summer didn't expect were the nuances of that look in those deep brown eyes of his and how it might make her feel. His expression was no longer kidlike, but mannish with a bit of spice that made her skin go as hot as cayenne pepper. It was too soon for a new relationship, and yet this wasn't just any man. It was Martin. "I wanted to say that I'm sorry your teen years were made so unhappy by your brothers. Did they badger you a lot? Especially about being adopted?"

Martin rearranged his long legs until he appeared to get comfortable again. "I was an easy target, I guess. Unfortunately my father made comments that were sort of one-sided. He would brag on me about my grades and accomplishments, but he didn't carry on about my brothers. I suffered some embarrassment every time he did it, because it made Desmond and Ivan angry. Which was understandable. And it also caused my mother some distress. I can't imagine why, but my father seemed to get a perverse pleasure in upsetting her in that way."

"Your adoptive father must have loved you," Summer said. "You know, to brag on you like that."

"I would like to think so. He did come around when I was little, but it was sporadic. I never knew who he was, except I guess I thought he was a friend of my mother's. Once I became a part of the family, he did spend some time with me but he was always so wrapped up in his oil business dealings that it was hard to get close to him." Martin's expression seemed to be overcome with troubling memories.

"That's hard for me to imagine, since I really was close to my dad . . . and my mom." She let out a tiny chortle. "Goodness. Listen to me. I'm making us sound so *Leave It to Beaver*-ish. I can assure you that our family wasn't perfect, but we did love each other a lot." Now it was her turn to be overpowered by memories, and yet, so many of them were good ones. So many that her eyes misted over with the wonder of it. If only Martin could have known such joy in his youth.

"I wish I'd been able to get to know your parents more," he said.

"I do too. The little bit that my parents knew of you, they liked." Summer took another drink from her water bottle. "What you said about your adoptive mother made me curious about her. Did you have a good relationship?"

"I'm sure she loved me in her own way, but some parents understand kids better than others. I don't think my mother understood me. I seemed to always be a stranger in her house. So much so, that I often wondered why she adopted me."

"Do you ever wonder about your natural father . . . if he's still alive?" Summer asked.

"It's easy to be curious, but I don't have any information. I was glad to have had fourteen years with my birth mother before she passed away. When she died I thought I'd die too. It was a dark time for me. I knew she loved me, and that has kept me going through the years. But she refused to talk about my father. I guess it was too painful for her to talk about him, so I let it go. For her sake." Martin wiped some dust off his pants. "But now, sometimes I wish I'd asked more questions. Maybe she would have finally felt comfortable enough to talk about him. But those days are gone. You can see why now that your grandmother meant so much to me. How she changed my life for the better."

Summer smiled. "I know Granny would love to hear that from you."

"I hope I can tell her someday."

"You will, soon, I'm sure. You know, one of the things on Granny's list is to solve a mystery. I have no idea what she meant by that and I forgot to ask. But there are pieces of your life that appear to be shrouded in mystery, especially the way your parents divorced and left you the way they did."

"Their timing wasn't so much a mystery," Martin said, "since I think they were waiting for Ivan to turn eighteen, but the actual reasons why they left are, as you said, a mystery."

Summer wished so hard to help Martin that her thoughts turned into a prayer. *What can I do for him, Lord?* "Did your parents leave anything behind that might give you any clues?"

"Not really. As you know, they left us the house and all its furnishings, but they took their personal belongings," Martin said. "Except for furniture, my parents' bedrooms are empty."

"Did you say *bedrooms*?" Summer couldn't hide the surprise in her voice. "Sorry, I'm getting too nosy."

"No, it's okay. I don't mind you knowing. My parents each had their own bedroom in the last two years before they divorced and moved away. It was sad, but true."

When quiet settled between them, the sounds of nature once again engulfed them. Summer picked up the wasp nest and looked inside again. The tubelike nursery chambers, so skillfully and delicately made, had once upon a time sheltered their babies. Sometimes maybe insects did a better job of caring for their families than people did.

"I know what you're thinking; that the Langtree family is beyond dysfunctional."

"No, I don't think that."

Martin reached into the pocket of his flannel shirt, pulled out a packet of gum, and offered her a stick just like he used to do when they were kids.

She looked at the packet. "Black licorice? It's my favorite."

"I know."

"Where did you find it? I didn't even know they made it anymore."

"I keep it on hand because I've always liked it too."

"You're kidding." Summer shook her head at him and grinned. She took a stick of the gum, unwrapped it, and took a deep whiff. "Mmm, that's so good. I'd forgotten. Thanks." Then she folded up the chalky gray piece of sweetness into her mouth and let the unique flavor bring a wiggle to her toes.

When they were contentedly chewing, Martin said in a more serious tone, "Now to fully answer your question, I've checked the attic. It's quite large, but there doesn't seem to be much up there except for leftover junk. Really, sometime I need to clean it out and give most of it away to a local charity. But that takes time."

Summer perked up. "I know what we can do."

"No. I already know what you're going to ask. I don't want you spending your valuable adventure time on cleaning out the Langtree attic." Martin rose from the floor and dusted himself off.

"But Martin, it might be fun. And what if we were to find something that answered this huge question in your life? It would give you as well as your brothers some closure. Maybe it would help them to move on with their lives. They seem to be in a holding pattern or something."

He wagged his finger at her. "You're just as persuasive as you were when you were a kid."

"I know. Well, when I want to be. Please say yes. If you think I can help you with this, I really do want to." Summer gave him a pout that was aimed at his heart.

"Come on." Martin reached down his hand to her, and with one easy movement he lifted her up off the floor. "It always was impossible to say no to you. And I see that has never changed. All right. I'll say yes, since doing this happens to be on your list to solve a mystery. But you may do it under one condition. Otherwise the answer is no."

"Name it," Summer said. "I'll agree to it."

"You're not going to *clean* the attic. You may help me look for clues about my parents and why they left home. That's it. I mean, you've already rebuilt my house here." He gestured with his hands as if they were inside a grand manor instead of a tree house.

Summer waved her arm around as those showcasing a mansion. "Your palatial shanty, my lord?"

"Well, it's more than good enough for me, because you're here." Martin gave her another one of his "looks" again. But this time something lingered on his face. Was it more than friendship in his eyes? Perhaps when the right time came she would give him that "look" right back. But not so soon.

"Before we go, I have something I want to show you." Martin pulled back an ancient piece of tree house curtain that had managed to survive the weather, but barely. Underneath the tattered fabric was a carving in the wood.

She moved in closer to read the word that someone had neatly scored into the wall.

The word etched there was "Summer."

"Oh." She pressed her hand over her mouth. "I'm touched. Really."

"I'm glad. I can tell you that I wouldn't have marred my castle with anything unless it was for a good purpose."

Without thinking, Summer reached up and touched his cheek. "You always were the best friend any girl could have ever hoped for. Thank you for that."

"You're welcome."

To ease the tension of what seemed to be transpiring into something dreamy and something she wasn't quite ready for, Summer tilted her chin upward and added, "By the way, before we start on the attic, you need to buy me some pizza. I need sustenance."

He looked at his watch. "I can't believe it's almost noon. I'm a lousy host, aren't I?"

"Indeed, you are." She grinned.

"I'll have some pizza delivered. Anchovy, right?"

"Ah. You remembered my favorite." Summer gave him a friendly slap on the back. "I'll try not to breathe on you later. I know the—" She stopped talking to listen to the sudden pitter-patter on the roof. "It's sprinkling."

"Good. We'll see if our cabin has been made ready." Within seconds raindrops began a slow drip through the cracks. "Guess not."

They laughed.

Thunder rumbled and grumbled its way around the tree house.

Martin opened the shutters all the way, and they leaned on the wide window frame.

Together, they gazed down onto the garden, which was decorated with a cobblestone walkway that meandered by a koi pond. Lovely.

The billowy clouds just ahead of them looked frothy and foamy like the whipped cream dolloped on a hot fudge sundae. "Remember the stormy days in Granny's bookshop? You know, when it was too wet to play outside at home, but just right for reading and imagining the hours away. Do you remember the stories you made up?"

"You mean the legends of old, m'lady," Martin said with a Scottish accent. "Aye, there still may be a tale or two left to be told."

"Please do, m'lord."

He lifted her water bottle to his lips and blew until he'd created the deep sound of a foghorn. Then he donned a forsaken expression. "Ahh, yes. Captain Pattack and his crew had been lost at sea for some days, and their rations had worn thin. Darkness shrouded them like the black veil of a widow, and the waves surged higher and higher as if the water had been transformed into a sea monster ready to devour their ship."

"How truly dreadful." She pretended to fan herself.

"Ah, yes, m'lady. The storm raged on until the captain's men became exhausted and so disheartened they wanted to throw themselves into the sea. When all appeared hopeless there came a distant glow on the horizon. The closer the light came the more the men shouted in victory. 'It's a miracle,' Captain Pattack said to his men." Martin paused as if mesmerized by his own story. "Because with the light came a—"

"What was it?" she asked.

"It was the light of the pizza delivery boat with an extra-large anchovy pizza."

Summer laughed and gave him a playful punch. Oh, how she missed his stories and his—what could they be called—Martin-isms?

"Come on. I'm starving too."

"Maybe we—"

The high-pitched bark of a dog interrupted her. *Laney?* She looked out one of the windows.

Martin leaned out the door and looked down the ladder. "Laney, you little rascal."

"Is she upset, barking like that?" Summer asked.

"She must have seen a squirrel." Martin shook his head. "How did you get out of your crate? I'm going to have to start calling you Houdini."

Summer thought she might know how Laney got out and the explanation contained the names of the two brothers Grimm. Perhaps Ivan and Desmond knew about Granny's list, and they wanted to interfere in some way.

CHAPTER
fifteen

"Do you have a leash for Laney?" Summer asked.

Remembering the dog's antics, he replied with a grin. "No, every time I show Laney a leash, she runs away."

"You're a savvy little lady, Laney," Summer called down to her.

The dog lowered her head and wagged her tail.

Summer said, "Guess she wants to play."

"That's because she already loves you." Martin looked at Summer and then shook off the new direction of his thoughts by concentrating on the ladder. "Now, be careful; this wood is slippery because of the rain, so let me go down first." He lowered himself, and when he was on the ground, he held up his hands for Summer.

When she got close to the ground, Summer turned around and playfully leaped the rest of the short distance into his arms.

Such a simple act, and yet it thrilled him that she would trust him to catch her. When he held her for that brief moment after setting her down on the ground, she felt so soft and irresistible—like that favorite old couch of his. She smelled like the licorice gum she'd been chewing, and she also carried an earthy fragrance like the broadleaf weeds that grew by his front door. But he knew enough to leave those thoughts right where they belonged—in his head.

Summer scooped Laney up in her arms, and the little dog licked her cheek. "Martin, would it be okay for Laney to go with us to the attic to explore?"

"Sure. Let's get out of this rain, though. I think it's about to turn into a deluge."

They headed to the big house, Laney still in Summer's arms, and Martin jogging alongside Summer. Just as they reached the awning over the porch, the rain turned into a tropical drenching torrent.

"Glad we missed that," Summer said, holding Laney close. "I think it's bringing in a cold front too." She shivered.

"Houston weather." He slipped off his flannel shirt and placed it around her shoulders.

"Thanks for the shirt," Summer said, "but how are you going to stay warm in that thin T-shirt?"

A kiss would warm me up just fine. Martin made himself back away from that intriguing thought and said, "It's always warm in the attic. Come on. Let's go up the back stairs. It's easier." Martin opened the door for her, and they headed up two flights of narrow steps to the attic. He opened the door, and in they went, taking in the dust and the musty smell of all things old. Boxes and crates and dilapidated furniture were scattered everywhere with no labeling or logical order. "What a shambles. I don't remember it being this bad."

Thunder boomed, making the window glass rattle like it might shatter.

Summer held Laney close as she looked around. "It's like most people's attics. Messy. Granny would call this higgledy-piggledy." She winced and turned away from him.

She was surely thinking of her grandmother at that moment and how she would miss her. Martin wasn't certain how to comfort her. Perhaps talking about it would bring her even more sadness. So he simply gestured around the room and said, "Feel free to snoop around as much as you like. I'll order us some pizza."

Laney wriggled in Summer's arms, so she gave her a hug and then let her down. "You're right. It is warm up here." She took Martin's flannel shirt off her shoulders and draped it across a chair. "I think I'll start in the back. Maybe it's a place that hasn't been looked at in a while."

"Good thinking." Martin flipped on the rest of the light switches, which lit up some of the nooks and crannies.

Then Summer took off with Laney in tow toward the back of the attic.

Martin pulled out his cellphone and ordered pizza while also being careful to tell the delivery folks to phone him when it arrived, so his brothers might not be tempted to confiscate it at the door. When his ordering was accomplished, he joined Summer.

She had been rummaging around in the back, opening a few boxes, but they appeared to be full of nothing more than old clothes and junk. What she now held in her hands, though, surprised him. A vase—a beautiful one. Summer was busy examining the bottom of it. "Looks like you found something interesting."

"Not what we were looking for, but yeah, this is fascinating." Summer carefully turned the vase upright again. "It might be valuable."

"You know something about antiques like Desmond does?"

"I know a little. Enough, as they say, to be dangerous." She grinned as she ran her finger along the delicate designs.

"Where did you find it?" Martin walked over to her for a closer look at the vase.

Summer pointed to a dilapidated cabinet. "I found it underneath that escritoire. It was covered over by a pile of old rags."

"Looks like it's from China. May I see it?" Martin spit his gum out into the wrapper, stuffed it into his pocket, and then with careful movements allowed Summer to hand him the vase. He examined the intricate blue, hand-painted designs.

"This is an amazing find. If I'm not mistaken, this antique could be rare and very valuable."

Martin looked up at her. "How did you learn about antiques?"

"What little I know, Granny taught me. And Grandpa too, in the early years before he died. Granny and I used to hunt around junk shops and estate sales, looking for treasures. And we did find a few. Then she'd sell them. In fact, that was one of the ways Granny supplemented her income, since the bookshop never did make much money for her to live on. But Granny and I never did find anything like this vase."

"So you think it really is valuable?"

"It might be worth a lot, but I hate to get your hopes up."

"How about a ballpark figure? I won't hold you to it. I'm just curious."

"I saw a vase like this in one of Granny's antique books, and if I'm correct, it could be as valuable as a hundred thousand dollars."

"Really? That much. I wonder why my parents left something so valuable behind. I know they left in a hurry. Perhaps they found this at an estate sale and didn't know it was worth anything." Martin tightened his grip on the vase as he thought through the ramifications of telling his brothers about the find. "If it is *that* valuable, I'm not sure I should tell Desmond and Ivan. They would immediately halt their search for jobs, sell the vase, and live off that income. That would not be good. They will never know what they could have been."

"Of course, it's up to you whether you tell them or not," Summer said, "but if I were you, I'd have this vase appraised by someone who is an expert."

Laney trotted up to her, and jumped up against her leg. Summer picked her up and right away the little dog took up residence in the crook of her arm.

"I will have the vase appraised. Good idea. And in the meantime I think I'll set this potential treasure down in a safer place than on the floor under some old rags." Martin turned to do that very thing when someone said his name from the dimly lit recesses of the attic. Impossible not to know who that voice was attached to.

Martin looked toward the stacks of boxes as Desmond stepped out from a dark corner.

"Well, aren't you two a quaint duo here?" Desmond said. "Thank you, Summer, for that valuable assessment concerning the vase."

Summer remained silent.

Desmond lighted his finger along an end table. "You never learn, do you, Martin? About the vulnerabilities when a door is left ajar."

"And you never did learn the meaning of the word privacy." Martin sighed. His brother was about to disappoint him. Again. He thought he even heard a tiny sigh from Summer. "But I'd rather be vulnerable than impermeable."

"The way I see it, impermeable means resilient and hardy. Vulnerable means susceptible and weak." Desmond's smirk was locked into place. "You know what? I think I'll take that vase off your hands, Martin. Since you say that I have some expertise in the area of antiques, then I should be the one to do the research on this fine piece. And I should be the one who sells it, if I choose to do so."

"Maybe we should talk about it."

Desmond frowned. "Oh, *now* you want to talk. How ironic. Just a moment ago you hadn't planned on doing one bit of that, not to me anyway. You planned to withhold this find from Ivan and me in an effort to control us. In an effort to cheat us out of what is rightfully ours." He strolled over to Martin with a cocky swagger as fire danced in his gray eyes. "Tell me this; who gave you permission to be our parent?"

Was now the time to say it? "In answer to your question, it was our father who gave me permission before he left. Actually, he begged me."

"What are you talking about? That can't be true." Desmond spit out the words.

"It is. As I'm sure you remember, before our parents walked out the door Father called us each into the library to talk to us separately.

He pleaded with me to do my best to watch over you like a father would. He said that it would give him peace in the years to come."

Desmond gathered his fingers into fists. "How can that be?" His body shook as if from a sudden chill. "You were only his *adopted* son. Why would he leave that legacy with you and not me?"

"I'm not sure why he asked—"

Desmond hit one of the boxes with his fist, knocking it onto the floor and dumping its contents. "I don't want to hear any more. Do you hear me? It will only be a sermon, and I'm sick to death of them."

"I'm sorry if you feel—"

Desmond came toward him and reached out his hands. "Give me that vase—now."

Martin hesitated letting go, knowing that giving in to to Desmond's demands might be the worst possible move.

"Let go of it," he growled.

Laney whimpered in Summer's arms.

His brother's eyes glazed a bit as they did the night of the dinner. *Not again.* Had his brother found another stash of pills somewhere? "Okay. Desmond, listen to me. Since we're going to end up breaking this vase, I'm going to let go. Slowly, okay? But first tell me if you have a good hold on it—"

Desmond yanked the vase out of Martin's hand, and the next sound was his brother's gasp.

CHAPTER
sixteen

"Martin, what have you done?" Desmond's voice rose while he clutched the vase in a rigor mortis--like grip.

"What do you mean?" Martin asked. "You're holding the vase. All is well." Could his brother be so out of his senses that he didn't even realize he held the vase safely in his hands?

"No. Don't you see?" Desmond turned the vase to give him a view of the other side. "Your hands had been covering a crack. A big one. Which one of you broke it?"

"Of course neither of us did," Martin said. "Summer held it with great care, and so did I. We just didn't notice the crack on the other side."

Desmond held the vase under the illumination of a nearby lightbulb and examined it more closely. "The fissure is toward the base, but there are these tiny fractures rising up, like veins." He seemed to be talking more to himself as his eyes misted over. "These flaws are serious, and they ruin the value of this great piece of art." His shoulders drooped. "It is beyond hope." He released a dreary sigh. "Just like our family."

"We aren't beyond hope," Martin said, "not at all."

Desmond set the vase down on a wooden crate. "Well, I guess you can gloat. I'll have to get a job after all."

"I'm not gloating, but I am concerned that you find your place in the world. I keep thinking that you'd be—"

Desmond waved him off. "I don't want to hear any more. I'm done." He dusted his hands off in his classic theatrical fashion, exited the attic, and slammed the door behind him.

Summer exhaled as if she'd been holding her breath.

In some ways it felt as though Martin had been holding his breath ever since he'd come to live in this house and in this family.

"Oww-wee." She blew on her bangs.

Laney wriggled as if she wanted down, and Summer set her on the floor.

After the dog scampered off to explore the attic, Summer stood apart, distractedly rubbing her earlobe. Something was always on her mind when she did that.

"What is it?"

"Oh, Martin, I wish I'd never found that vase. This is all my fault."

"No, it isn't."

"It sure feels that way."

"It's always been like this with my brothers. To be honest, I'm nearly at my wit's end with them."

"I have no right to say this, but why do you let them treat you that way? I don't think calling it abuse is overstating it. You're too kind and good, and they know it. They're taking full advantage of your virtues, and it breaks my heart to see it."

"I'm sorry you've had to witness these outbursts of theirs." Martin sat down on a crate. "It's like this. Finding a balance between tough love and turning the other cheek is a balancing act like trying to cross a high-wire across Niagara Falls. Pretty well impossible." He fingered one of the buttons on his shirt. When it fell off into his hand, he dropped it into his pocket. He couldn't even keep his shirts together.

Summer huffed. "Yeah, well, you have more patience than I do, because I'd like to give both of them a good thrashing."

"I think it's time to tell you something that might help you to understand what makes the situation with my brothers more complicated." Martin pulled out a handkerchief from his pocket, laid it out over the crate across from him, and gestured for her to sit down.

"Thanks."

When Summer made herself comfortable, he began his story, "When I was in college I heard about an older student who beat up one of the younger ones. The incident happened on the lawn of the campus while some of the student body watched. The younger one, John, took the punches one after the other, without even trying to defend himself."

Martin paused and then went on to say, "I was so confused by the news that later I went to talk to my professor about it. He said he thought it was because John had heard that the older student's parents had just been killed during a mission trip to Sudan. My professor also went on to say that when it comes to a spirit of compassion, sometimes the strongest man may not be the one left standing. It didn't make a lot of sense at the time, but it does now."

"That is a good story." Summer reached out to him and gave his arm a gentle squeeze. "And you're right. It does help me to understand why you deal with your brothers the way you do. But . . ."

"Yes?"

She shook her head. "I'm meddling where I shouldn't be."

"If you are meddling—and I don't see it that way," Martin said, "—then there is no one else on earth I'd rather have meddling in my life than you."

"Okay." Summer grinned. "Then I'll say this. In light of your story, how are Desmond and Ivan weaker than you?"

"Well, one reason is because their parents abandoned them. Yes, technically they were old enough to be on their own, but only legally. They were still pretty young to try to grasp the situation. They were both hurt deeply by what happened. It was a little like you mentioned about grief not really going away, but just changing you."

"I'm sure it was real sorrow," Summer said. "No doubt. I don't want to make light of it. But I'm saying, what about you? You were left behind just like they were, and you were almost as young as they were. When do *you* get a break? Like in that story you told, when does anyone take the punch for you, Martin?"

Summer stood then, her expression so earnest he thought it might be time to tell her a bit more of his story.

"There is more to Desmond and Ivan's history."

"Oh?" She eased back down on the crate.

"You heard me remind Desmond of the time Father called us each into the library just before they left."

"Yes."

"Earlier, I did tell Desmond the truth, but not all of the details. I'm glad he didn't ask why Father wanted me to be like a parent to them, since to answer him would have been pretty painful for both of us."

Summer waited for him to go on.

"That day in the library, my father brought up the fact that both Ivan and Desmond have slight learning disabilities. I already knew this, and of course, Ivan and Desmond knew about it, because they struggled in school. But it was something that was taboo to discuss." Martin halted briefly, remembering. "You see, that was the reason my father wanted me to watch over my brothers in this special way. He felt because of their disadvantages, they would need extra help."

Summer pressed her hands along her jeans. "It must have been hard on them. Were your brothers born with these issues?"

"No. That's why our family didn't like talking about it. You see, according to my father, Mother insisted the boys have a nanny when they were babies. I guess the nanny wasn't a very attentive or patient woman, and apparently she shook both Ivan and Desmond when they fussed to get them to stop crying."

"Oh, no." Summer's palm splayed across her heart. "How could she?"

"I know. Brutal. And criminal." Martin sighed. "And it may have caused some slight brain damage. By the time my mother saw what the nanny was up to, it was too late."

CHAPTER
seventeen

"How horrible." Summer looked at him, her eyes filled with sadness. "Did your parents turn the nanny in to the police?"

"No, but they fired her immediately with no references."

"But why didn't they do more? I would think they'd want her brought up on charges."

"I'm not sure why they didn't pursue it any further. There could have been a number of reasons. Maybe they couldn't prove for certain about any injuries until sometime later when the boys were older. Or maybe my parents didn't report it because it was too painful. You see, I think my mother blamed herself since she'd been the one who insisted on hiring the woman and because she hadn't been paying close attention to the nanny. Mother spent a great deal of time at her charities and club meetings. At least this is what my father claimed. I think he may have told Mother that she was partially responsible for the nanny's abuse. And I thought I heard Ivan say once that she had a nervous breakdown when they were little. But some of this information is sketchy. I've been putting bits and pieces of information together over the years."

"Do you think that's one of the reasons for your parents' divorce? That your father blamed her, and she couldn't handle it?"

"It might have been. It certainly couldn't have helped their marriage. People have broken up for lesser reasons than that. But even if it does explain the divorce, it doesn't tell us why they left the way they did."

Summer picked at one of the frayed holes in her jeans. "I'm curious about something, but you don't have to answer it."

"Yes?"

"Well, does the rest of your family blame your mother for what happened?"

"I certainly don't blame her. Of course, I hadn't been adopted until many years later, so it wasn't anything that I had to deal with. In my opinion, it was the nanny who failed my brothers. But I'm not sure how they feel about it."

"Do both of your brothers know what the nanny did to them when they were infants?"

"Yes, they know, but we've never had any real solid discussions about it. Actually, there's a lot we haven't talked about over the years. Sometimes I think our family has been living in an hourglass. Not really existing on the outside of life, but on the inside, doing nothing more than counting those passing grains of sand." Martin wiped the perspiration off his forehead with his T-shirt. "Makes me think of the words 'the truth will set you free.'"

Summer looked at her hands, which were now gathered on her lap. "I can see that you took the vow you made to your father very seriously."

"I was so young and I was desperately wanting to be a real part of the family and, well, for him to be proud of me. It was a pretty heady thing, you see, having a father for the first time. So I told him that I wouldn't fail him. At the time I thought our parents would come back. And when they did, I wanted my father to find me standing on the wall so to speak, keeping watch. I guess I'm still keeping watch, but I've done a terrible job at it. I can see that now."

"You've given it your whole heart, and it's admirable." Summer's eyes pooled with tears. "In spite of what I said earlier, I love it that you care so much about your brothers to get it right. Besides my father, you are the most loyal and compassionate man I've ever known."

"Please don't put me on a pedestal too high," Martin said, "or I'll fall off and crack my poor head open."

"Mmm. Where have I heard that?" She grinned at him. "I just wish there was something I could do for you."

"You already have. I've begun to talk about the past, and you've listened. With too little discussion comes a shallow kind of anger, and that's also what's wrong with our family. For too long, our family had the philosophy that if you kept quiet about something it might go away. But that isn't true. It's an easy way out, but in the end, it's the hardest way and the most painful. Like a wound that never heals because no one has taken the time to remove the pieces of broken glass. And maybe I'm guilty too, since I didn't tell Desmond the whole story just now. But I didn't want to cause him any more grief about his disability." Martin reached over and fingered an old lantern that was sitting by his hand.

"You meant well, and that counts for a lot."

"Yes, but even well-intended deeds can do irreparable harm. Desmond went away still not knowing everything. I guess I didn't trust him with the information. That he could handle it, and yet I know he can. He's not a boy. Maybe Desmond and Ivan don't need a father anymore. They need a brother." Martin swiped away the cobwebs that laced their way from the lantern over to the crate.

"That sounds like a revelation." Summer smiled, but traces of concern still furrowed her brow.

Oh, how he'd like to dispel the anxieties that had creased her lovely face—that ones he was responsible for putting there. If it would help, he would like to hold her, perhaps even give her a friendly kiss. Well, to be true to himself, he wanted the kiss to be more than just a friendly one—lately he was thinking along the lines of heartfelt and fervent. Dare he say impassioned? But since the moment was riddled with talk of family strife, a kiss seemed manipulative. Someday he'd broach the subject—that is, of any new feelings they might have since their reunion—but he'd need to approach with caution, since social discernment wasn't his best asset.

Someone knocked on the door.

"Must be Miss Beetle. She's the only one around here who knocks." He grinned. "Come in." He went over to the door and opened it.

Sure enough, it was Miss Beetle, and she was holding a large plastic bag. "Look what came for you. Desmond said you were up here."

"That pizza place was supposed to call me. I'm sorry you had to fool with it."

"Guess they got their wires crossed. No biggie."

"Come on in and have a slice."

"Don't mind if I do." Miss Beetle pulled out everything from the paper bag—the box of pizza, napkins, and sodas—and Martin and Summer helped her set up their little feast on a wooden crate.

"What kind of pizza you got here?" Miss Beetle said. "Smells almost good enough to eat."

"It's anchovy," Martin said.

"What?" Miss Beetle let loose with a blustery whoop. "Well, that's worse than eating worms right off the front lawn."

"I'm the guilty one," Summer said. "It's my favorite." She lifted the lid on the pizza box, breathed in the aroma, and said to Miss Beetle, "Are you sure you wouldn't like to try a piece? That salty taste is deviously addicting once you've had it."

"Hmm." Miss Beetle peered over at the pizza as if it might bite her. "Maybe just one itty-bitty piece. That way nobody can say I don't know how to live on the edge." Miss Beetle fluttered her fingers, touching several pieces, and then she finally lifted out a large slice and set it on a napkin.

Martin took out a slice and ate off the very tip. He hated to tell Summer that anchovy pizza was the only kind he didn't like, but he would do nothing to spoil the moment. "Don't you need to spit out your gum?"

"No, I accidentally swallowed my gum when Desmond appeared out of the blue."

"It *was* a little unnerving," Martin said wryly.

"That don't surprise me," Miss Beetle said between bites. "That boy used to sneak around all the time when he was growing up. He used to get some kind of wicked pleasure in scaring the heebie-jeebies out of me. I'd scream, and he'd just laugh. And then later in the day he'd do it all over again. He enjoyed my scream so much that sometimes I just pretended to be scared."

Maybe some of their times growing up were only riddled with mild dysfunction. Memories had a way of morphing over the years, Martin reflected. Maybe people altered them to suit their convictions.

When they were all three munching merrily, Summer asked, "What do you think? Too fishy?"

Miss Beetle rocked her head back and forth. "Not bad. This pizza is like my friend Jossie. She's off-putting when you first meet her, but once you get a taste or two, she has enough intrigue about her that you're willing to come back for more."

"Ahh, so you want another piece?" Martin slid the box a little closer to her.

Miss Beetle eyeballed the pizza again. "I might need just one more slice just to make sure I don't hate it."

Summer grinned.

Martin lifted an anchovy up off his pizza and shook it, causing the skinny little fish to wiggle over his open mouth like a worm. "I think Miss Beetle is right." He lowered the anchovy into his upturned mouth and then began to slowly chew.

Miss Beetle gave Martin a good-humored slap on the arm. "That is disgusting. Come to think of it, you used to torture me too. Just in different ways than the other boys. Summer, he used to make me part of his science experiments. He was a real Dr. Frankenstein, I'm telling ya."

Summer and Martin laughed.

"By the way, did you pay for this pizza out of your own money?" Martin reached into his back pocket for his wallet.

"No, now don't be getting out your wallet. I didn't pay for the pizza."

"Who did?"

"Well, Ivan started to, but his wallet was empty. So Desmond paid the man."

"Really?" Martin had to process that information for a moment. "Desmond paid for our pizza?"

"I know. It's as believable as a flying moose." Miss Beetle put up her hand. "Now I'm not saying any more. But Mr. Martin, I will add this. Your brothers aren't one hundred percent bad. God can surely work with that other thirty percent."

CHAPTER
eighteen

"I'm sure He can too." Martin said, still thinking about Desmond paying for the pizza. "But I do wish you'd just call me Martin. You don't put the word *mister* in front of my brothers' names."

"I know. But I have my own reasons for calling you that. And besides, you call me Miss Beetle." She wiped her mouth with a napkin.

"That's because I was taught to respect my elders and because you're rather special in this house." Martin lifted a slice of pizza from the box.

"Well now," Miss Beetle said, "as long as I'm your housekeeper, I intend to keep calling you Mr. Martin."

He grinned. "Have you been watching reruns of *Downton Abbey* again?"

Miss Beetle laughed. "Maybe." She pointed across the attic. "What is that I spy over there. A vase?"

"Yes, Summer found it on the floor covered in rags."

While sipping on a soda, Miss Beetle went over to the vase and examined it. "Pretty thing." She held it up. "Ohhh, and it reminds me of the one my mother had when I was but a little bud of a girl. My momma would have given me that vase as a legacy, but she had to sell it to feed me." Her black marble eyes took on a beseeching look.

Martin smiled. "You may have the vase if you want, but I must warn you, it has a big crack in it."

Miss Beetle shrugged. "Yeah, well, this family has a big crack in it too, but that's never stopped me from loving it."

Martin laughed.

"Thanks for the vase." Miss Beetle set her soda can down and cradled the vase like it was a baby.

"You're more than welcome." Yes, good old Miss Beetle. Since she'd faithfully served the Langtree family through the good times and bad, she deserved a priceless vase, not just one with a big crack in it. But it brought him joy to see her so happy about the treasure.

Laney trotted over to the pizza box and whimpered, looking hungry.

"Why don't I take Laney off your hands," Miss Beetle said. "She's due for some lunch and a nap about now."

"Thanks. But don't be sneaking her any table food."

"Never." Miss Beetle looked aghast. "Would I do that?"

"Uh, yeah."

Miss Beetle cocked her head at him then looked down at the dog. "Come along then, Laney girl." She looked in the pizza box again, fingered a few smaller slices, took the largest, and set it on a napkin.

The dog danced in circles. "That is the cutest little trick, Miss Laney, but you still can't have any pizza. I have something better for you." When Laney whimpered, Miss Beetle looked like she was about to give in—but not quite. She instead headed to the attic door, and Laney trotted alongside her. "It's time for me to stop jawing anyway and get back to work." She opened the door. "I've been cleaning floors and commodes all day, and I'm nearly to the finish line."

Martin and Summer said goodbye, but as soon as Miss Beetle left with Laney, they stared into the box at the last of the pizza.

"Commodes? I'm sure she washed her hands." Summer laughed.

"I'm sure she did too."

Summer took a sip of her soda. "So you didn't mind giving away that vase? What if it was worth something even with the crack?"

"If the vase is still valuable, I'm sure Miss Beetle has earned it a thousand times over for taking care of my brothers."

"Does Miss Beetle clean your cottage too?"

"Does my cottage *look* like it's ever been cleaned?" Martin retorted good-naturedly.

"Good point."

"I'm afraid Miss Beetle would want to tidy my papers and projects, and I'd never find anything again. There is an order to my chaos." A dripping, sound caught Martin's attention. *No, not a leak.* Sure enough, he saw a dribble from the upper rafters. "Guess the attic leaks." He saw a bucket—which must have been put up there for that very reason by Miss Beetle—and placed it under the leak. "I'll need to get that fixed."

Now the drip made a loud pinging echo in the metal bucket.

"Maybe this will help." Summer picked up an old rag and dropped it into the bucket. Now the noise turned into a *splat.* "Maybe we should get back to work." She placed her cold soda next to her face.

"Sorry it's so stuffy up here. I think the thermostat is haywire, and the windows are all sealed shut. I have no idea why." *More mystery.*

"I don't mind. A little sweat never hurt anybody." Summer opened an old cupboard.

Martin busied himself looking through a box of clothes. Suspenders. Shoes. Old suits and heavy coats. Not much illumination there.

"By the way, I was wondering about something."

"Yes?" Martin closed the lid and set the box aside to take to the local thrift store.

"I told you about my breakups with men." Summer shut the door on the cupboard and looked over at him. "Did you . . . just wondering, did you date a lot of women during those twenty years? I was just curious. You never said, and I was . . ." Her speech grew fainter as her face took on a pouty little expression that seemed adorable to Martin.

Wonder what brought on that topic. "Yes, I did. But nothing ever seemed to work, so I eventually gave up. The women I went out with all seemed to be like that globe you saw in the big house. Impressively made, showy, but in the end, sort of hollow."

"Oh." Summer seemed to chew on that reply.

Martin hoped she'd be happy with his response and that she'd no longer desire to be merely old friends reunited. Perhaps Summer's grandmother had intended more to come from the list than what was said—maybe she hoped they would fall in love. What a grand thought. Perhaps too grand, considering what a rare find Summer was. There would hardly be a man living who wouldn't be instantly smitten with the wonder of her.

Summer peeked inside a toy box, pulled out an umbrella, and waved it around. "Look at this—a Japanese parasol." She opened it up, rested it against her shoulder, and gave it a few twirls. Then she dug out an old baseball cap, came over to him, and set it on his head.

Martin pulled the cap snug on his head. "I remember this old hat."

"You used to play?"

"Only a little. I tried baseball, but I'm afraid I was the kid who always sat on the sidelines, watching. Just couldn't get the hang of it like the other boys. But that's okay. I was meant for other things." Of course, what he hated to tell Summer were the malicious words that had been shouted from his teammates, because he didn't fit in. He pulled the cap off, willing himself to forget.

"You were meant for many great things, Martin. Besides, all I ever liked about baseball was the excuse to eat hot dogs and ice cream."

He grinned and tossed the cap onto a table.

She gave the parasol one more twirl, set it on the box, and sighed. "I see that I'm being too random with my search. I think I'll start at the back again."

"I'll join you."

They headed to the dark reaches of the attic and for the next hour or so, they worked their way toward the front, looking for any hints that might solve some of the mysteries of the Langtree past. After much searching through boxes and crates and cabinets full of old junk, they came to a disappointing end. Nothing of any significance was found in their search.

With a sigh of resignation, Martin closed the lid on the last box.

"I'm sorry we didn't find anything." Summer fanned herself with a piece of cardboard.

"That's okay. I'm grateful for your help. More than you know." He looked at her, hoping she could understand how much he meant those words.

"Looking through all these boxes of old things made me think how funny it is that people find a hiding place for things that are defective or old. It might be something that had once meant a great deal to us, but the moment it's flawed, the thing, no longer a treasure, gets put away in a dusty attic." Summer's expression, which had been previously sunny, darkened with anxiety.

"I hadn't thought of it that way, but it's true."

"Too true."

"Hey." Martin touched her arm. "You okay? I hope this didn't wear you out. I know it's hot up here."

"No, no, I'm fine that way."

"Please tell me what's wrong."

"I'm not sure. I don't believe in premonitions, but I just got an odd sensation of uneasiness concerning Granny. I think maybe she's holding back on me. Not telling me everything about her illness. She's trying to shelter me, of course. But I'm concerned that while

I'm busy doing everything on this list she'll be busy letting go of the last of her life. It's like she's trying to pass some sort of mantle onto me with this list. Some maturity and purpose, but I'd rather have my granny for as long as I can be with her." Summer lowered herself onto a crate and ran her palms along the edges. "Listen to me. I sound so selfish. Like it's all about me when Granny is the one who's suffering. She's the one who's—" She winced. "How can you even stand to be my friend?"

"What do you mean?" Martin sat down on a crate across from her. "You're only saying these things because you love your grandmother so deeply." Oh, to be loved like that. Now it was envy that niggled at him. Absently he'd traced his finger in the thick dust of a table, but when he realized he'd drawn the first letters of her name, he swiped away the evidence. "You're blessed to have a grandmother like you do, but she's fortunate as well to have a granddaughter who loves her so much."

Summer stared at him, mist in her eyes again. "Oh Martin, when it comes to the way you see me, you seem to be wearing rose-colored glasses."

"Not so." He leaned forward and gave her an earnest look. "I have perfect vision."

Summer smiled.

"Do you want to stop working on the list for a while? Maybe you could move in with your grandmother. Would that help?"

"That's what I told her I wanted to do," Summer said. "But she won't let me. She is determined to do this her way." Summer's shoulders wilted.

"Do you think you should go see her right now? That might make you feel better."

"Maybe. Yes, I think that is a good idea. You don't mind?"

"Not at all. And I'm glad we got some things checked off your list. I hope that brings your grandmother some joy."

"It will. I need to focus on bringing Granny joy in any way I can rather than constantly thinking about my pain in losing her. So I'll tell her that we checked some items off the list today. She'll like that. The tree house and the treasure. Well, sort of. A damaged treasure anyway."

"Still counts." Martin rose when Summer did. He would like to have said that he'd found a treasure in her, but he thought that compliment was a little too unoriginal and inappropriate—even if it was true. Instead he said, "Since you want to spend time with your grandmother, we could have her come along. Would that work?"

"What a great idea," Summer said. "Now why didn't I think of that?"

"Remind me what was on that list again."

"A hot air balloon ride is one of them, but that might be too much for her with her heart. But she could go with me when I sing in public."

"Where are you planning on doing that?"

"I have been putting some thought into that one." She pressed her finger on the dimple on her chin. "Actually, I do know of a place in the Heights that is sort of a beatnik coffee joint. When they have open mic times, some people play a guitar or sing or read a poem they've written. Granny would call it bohemian, and she'd love it."

"Have you ever sung in public before?"

"In church, but there are lots of other people around to drown me out. Which might be best."

"That can't be true." Thunder rumbled around them, but its angry growl had diminished some. "Why did your grandmother put singing in public on the list?"

"I think because when I was growing up I always said I wanted to be a singer. I'm sure she put it on the list as a nudge to get me to try what I thought might only be a dream."

"Your Grandmother Snow is one-of-a-kind."

"Yes, she is. They'll be no one born on this earth who'll ever be able to replace her." Summer rose. "I'd better go. We can talk about the list tomorrow. That is, if you still have time to do this."

"Of course I do." Martin wanted to say he had all the time in the world for her, but he feared going too far with admitting his feelings too soon, especially since she'd just broken off an engagement. He knew well that once a series of notes was played, they could never be unplayed. "Let me walk you to your car."

"No, it's not necessary."

"I don't mind. You sure?"

"Yes, thanks. I'll let myself out the back door."

Her smile lit up the attic in spite of the stormy day.

Martin opened the door for her, but he didn't want to let her go. Didn't want the day to end.

She touched his shoulder briefly. "Thanks again for doing this list with me. I don't know of another man who would have done it."

"Not even your fiancé?" Maybe he'd pushed the envelope too far with that question.

Summer rested her hand on the doorframe. "Former fiancé," she corrected. "No, not even him. But then I guess he wasn't my best friend."

Taking a chance, Martin reached up to the doorframe and placed his hand over hers. "Just a reminder, Miss Snow."

"A reminder?"

Martin gazed at their hands, which were not quite intertwined, and then looked back down at her. "Don't forget that your coach turns back into a pumpkin at midnight."

"I won't. And don't forget to bring my glass slipper," she said lightly.

"How could I ever forget?" he said, leaning toward her. Then in a moment of courage or audacity—he didn't know which—Martin lifted Summer's hand from the doorframe and over to his lips.

Briefly, he kissed her hand and then released her. It all happened so quickly, they both stared at each other.

Ahh, the fragrant and lovely ways of Summer. He would never change a thing about her. One could not alter what was already perfect. The last thing Martin wanted to do was pull his gaze from those lovely blue eyes. "Bluebonnets," he finally said in such a small whisper that it seemed to be more in his thoughts than on his lips.

"Yes?" Summer asked.

"Your eyes. When we were kids I always knew your eyes were pretty. But now, well, they're like a field of bluebonnets. They're so saturated with color and light . . . so mesmeric, they could stop a heart."

Summer snickered. "I hope I don't slay anyone!"

I think you've already slain me.

CHAPTER
nineteen

"Sorry. I shouldn't laugh." She lighted her finger over her mouth, which drew even more attention to her lips. "What I should have said is, thank you for the compliment, Martin."

"You're welcome. I hope it was a good compliment. Not too syrupy or too businesslike. I've never been very astute at that sort of thing. Compliments are an unknown quantity. Actually, there're a little scary."

"How so?"

"Too many variables. Not like a formula I can control. You never know if you're saying the compliment right. Or how it will be received. Or if it comes off like cheap flattery."

She grinned.

"I've always been better at math and science," he reminded her.

"I know. But remember, I like whatever you say, Martin, because I know your words come from your heart." She patted his arm. "I'd better go. I'll see you soon."

"Please let me know how your grandmother is."

"I will."

"Bye for now."

"Bye."

Martin stayed there, watching her walk down the hallway, turn the corner to the backstairs, and disappear from his sight. Then he listened to her footsteps until the sound was gone.

Loneliness replaced the sound and sight of Summer.

He drank in the previous moments, hoping to feel a bit more of her warmth. He'd always immersed himself into so many projects that it had been easier to keep his lonesomeness at a distance. But not now. No longer could he do that. Suddenly, he saw all that he'd been missing through the years—his dear, sweet Summer—and the knowledge of it tore at him, body and soul.

Martin walked over to one of the small alcoves in the attic and sat in the window seat. From that high vantage point, which over-looked the small cottage and beyond, one could see the live oak and the tree house. The rain had ceased now, and the sun was breaking through the storm clouds in streams of pure white light. He placed his palm on the windowpane, wishing he could paint the scene, keep it always, since that sunburst reminded him of Summer's smile.

Martin rose and walked back to the attic door. He switched off the lights, one by one, and took one last look into the darkened room. His day with Summer was now only a memory—but it was a memory that would stay with him for a lifetime.

As he walked down the hallway, he met with Miss Beetle as well as Laney, who was trotting alongside her. Miss Beetle's eyes ap-peared red-rimmed as if she'd been crying. "Is something wrong?" he asked a little distractedly since he was still thinking of Summer.

The woman held out the paper bag she was carrying, and then lowered it. "I am so upset I don't know what to say."

"Please tell me what's wrong."

"I would tell you, Mr. Martin, but it's such a beastly thing." Miss Beetle picked up Laney and set her into Martin's arms. "You'd best take care of her for a while."

"Your hands are shaking. What's going on? Are you ill?"

"I wish I were ill. Oh, dear me, I wish it were only that." She raised her hands as if in a blustery exasperation. "It was my fault really. I wasn't watching Laney like I should. You see, Laney jumped up at the legs of the little table, the one at the top of the main stair-case. It has such frail legs as you know. Spindly little things that are just like the legs of a spider. That's why I always called it the spider table."

Miss Beetle hung her head low and wagged it back and forth for so long, Martin thought she might have forgotten what she intended to tell him.

She finally said, "Laney jumped at the legs of the table and—"

"Yes?"

"Oh, tell me, tell me that you'll forgive me," Miss Beetle exploded with emotion, her eyes big and her smile turned upside down.

"Of course I'll forgive you, but I'll need to know what I'm forgiving." Martin smiled, hoping to calm her down and put her mind as ease. He'd never seen her in such a state. "If the table broke, it's okay. I've always hated that thing anyway."

Miss Beetle sighed a deep sigh. "The thing is, I'd just put your gift, that pretty vase, on that table, away from Laney to keep it extra safe. But Laney must have thought it was a game or a treat or something she could have. Anyway, she jumped up at the legs of that spider table, and the vase tittered. Well, to make a long story short, the vase fell off the table, hit the marble floor, and shattered into pieces before I could reach out and catch it." Miss Beetle's voice quavered as she covered her face with a hanky. "I'm so sorry to be the one to give you such painful news."

Martin touched her shoulder and said, "I really don't mind. It's okay. It had a crack in it anyway. I'm just sorry that your gift is broken and it's caused you so much grief."

"Was it really valuable?"

"Maybe. It might have been, but most likely the initial crack would have reduced the value quite a bit anyway."

"Okay." Miss Beetle wiped off her face. "I guess I feel a little better."

"Good. Don't worry about it anymore."

"I saved every piece in case it can be mended." She handed him the paper bag, and the contents rattled.

"Thanks." Martin smiled. "But I will take Laney back to the cottage now so she can't get into any more mischief."

"Right. Good idea." Miss Beetle patted her apron. "Oh, I almost forgot." She pulled something out from one of the pockets. "This was stuck down inside the vase. Looks like a bunch of letters."

Martin set the bag down and accepted the wad of letters, which were tied up with ribbons. "Letters? Thank you." He stared at the little bundle. Then he looked up and down the hallway, grateful Desmond and Ivan weren't around.

"Maybe there is something there. Something important," Miss Beetle said. "You seemed to be up in the attic looking for something. I know it grieves you boys that your parents left the way they did. Maybe there's something in those letters."

"Could be. It's certainly worth reading them all."

Miss Beetle hesitated and then said, "You know, I was here that day when your parents left."

"You were? I'd forgotten."

She fiddled with her hands inside her pockets like they were trying to escape. "I'm not sure anybody noticed me, since I was in the background, trying not to get in the way. But I knew what was going on. I saw the agony you boys felt during that horrible farewell. And that misery was in the eyes of your parents as well. I don't think they ever wanted to leave any of you."

"Really?" Her words went straight to the heart, making him ache to know more. "You don't think they wanted to go?"

"As I've mulled it over through the years, I think they felt bound to leave. Like there was something dark chasing them. What that thing was, I don't know. But I did feel the pain with all of you, and I have felt it ever since. Now I'm not saying any more." Miss Beetle put up a hand. "But I will add this. I think if walls could soak up the grief of its owners, then this house has taken it on all the way to its timbers." She nodded as if in agreement with herself.

"Maybe one of the reasons I retreated to the cottage wasn't just that I wanted to be able to make a mess with my projects, but to escape from the memories that haunt these rooms."

"I thought maybe that was your thinking."

Martin glanced down at Laney and gave her a scratch behind the ears. "Is that why you stayed all these years? Because you felt bad about what happened?"

Miss Beetle gave him a slow nod. "I couldn't leave you boys. Not ever after what happened. Not unless you wanted me to go."

"For that I am truly grateful," Martin said. "I'm sure Desmond and Ivan are too."

"They have trouble trusting folks and showing their emotions. I mean, they can get mighty riled up, and showed lots of angst, but it's not what's real. There's more to those boys than what we've seen. I know it. Mark my word. If I didn't believe that, I might have headed on out of here long ago. But I know if I died, they'd grieve. Maybe behind closed doors, but God would see their grief."

"I hope you're not planning on putting that to the test anytime soon, are you?" Martin eyeballed her in a scrutinizing manner, trying to lighten the mood.

Miss Beetle smiled at him. "No, I don't intend to die for a long time, Lord willing."

"Good."

"By the way, after I picked up the pieces from that vase, I saw Ivan down the hall coming out of his room. I quickly hid the letters in my pocket. I knew he'd snatch them away if he saw them, and I wasn't sure what he'd do with them. So I thought you'd better see them first."

"I appreciate that. And I promise you that after I read these I will share them with my brothers."

"That's what I thought. I knew you'd do right." Miss Beetle looked up and down the hallway and lowered her voice. "I'm not sure your brothers would do the same for you. But it pains me to say it." She briefly mashed her finger on her eyelid to stop the sudden twitch.

"Well, it pains me to agree with you." Martin held up the letters. "I just hope there's more to these letters than someone sharing a recipe with my mother."

"You'll know soon enough. I'd better leave you to it." Miss Beetle turned to go.

"Thanks."

While Martin held Laney in his arms, he hurried down the back stairs. He really didn't want to get his hopes up, but it was too late. Once in his hobbit hole and Laney was busy having her snack, he cleared a place to sit down, plopped onto his favorite couch, and then carefully opened the first letter in the stack. It was from his grandmother who'd passed away. The envelope was addressed to Mrs. Edward Langtree, his adoptive mother. He scanned and then reread. There wasn't anything significant to the letter, mostly everyday things. He quickly went on to the next letter and then the next, but nothing seemed to be enlightening concerning their past. As he perused the last letter in the stack it appeared to deal with much more of what he'd hoped for. The letter read:

> *My dear Margaret,*
>
> *You have asked for advice, and I will give it to you, although I doubt my suggestions are what you're wanting to hear. I know your husband's unfaithfulness has been a brutal disappointment to you, especially since it came so soon after your wedding, but you must find a way to rise above it. Forgiveness is the answer, and it will give you your sanity back, even if Edward isn't willing to ask for forgiveness. If you find you can never see beyond his betrayal, then rise above it by pouring yourself into your boys. And please, my dear one, don't withhold your affection to Martin out of resentment.*
>
> *Martin can't help it that he was born out of sin from Edward's act of adultery with that Odell woman.*

In a rush of emotion, Martin lowered the letter, nearly tearing it. Before he went on reading he had to stop and digest the information. "That Odell woman" his grandmother spoke of was his biological mother. So there had been a hidden affair. He had never known. But why hadn't he figured it out? He did look a little bit like his father, but he'd always thought it was wishful imaginings. And this, of course, explained those awkward visits from the man when he was young. The times he tried to help him with his homework, or play a game, or drop by on his birthdays. But Martin had written all of that off too, thinking Mr. Langtree was merely a friend of his mother's. Friend indeed.

All this time, he'd not only known his biological father, he'd lived under the same roof with him. That part seemed joyful, but that happiness was short-lived when he thought of the rest of the circumstances. To think that his father had been unfaithful in his marriage was painful enough but to also discover that his betrayal included his biological mother, Odell, was even harder to take. In spite of the pain, Martin read on.

> *Also, you should not continue to tell your family and friends that Martin was adopted when that is a lie. You must convince Edward to makes things right and to choose the truth. It is the way you were raised, and you know it is the only way to live right before God. I know these are hard things to hear, but they are also hard for me to write.*
>
> *Your loving mother*

Martin slipped the letter back into the envelope. Now he knew why he'd never seen any adoption papers, or why his parents had avoided the topic.

How would he ever tell Desmond and Ivan the truth? For them to find out that his biological mother had participated in an affair and had helped to cause the ruin of their family would not go down well. And they would surely single out his mother as the chief offender—the guilty party who had seduced their father—and not the other way around. Then any possible headway he'd made over the years in building a relationship with his brothers would vanish in an instant.

He was glad to know the truth after two decades that were shrouded in mystery, but the knowledge didn't come without some stinging realities. No wonder his new mother hadn't fully embraced him as part of the family. He was a product of one of the worst possible marital betrayals—an affair. Martin would have been a daily reminder to his new mother of her husband's betrayal.

In addition, all of this history might explain why his father bragged on him above his other brothers. It certainly accounted for his new mother's distress when he did it. All those years ago, when Martin had been brought into their home, he'd hoped those harsh looks from his new mother had only been her general aggravation with life, but it had indeed been his presence. And how could he blame her? It was only natural to feel that way about an intruder. That is, a child who didn't bring love into the house, but disharmony, distrust, and ultimately divorce.

Martin folded the letter and then folded it again and again. Maybe he wished to make it so small that it would diminish its implications. Along with the distressing answers came more questions for him. Perhaps Edward Langtree and his mother, Odell, had loved each other. Of course, that didn't excuse their affair in any way, but it might explain why his biological mother seemed sad at times when she thought he wasn't watching her. The doctors said his mother died of heart failure, but maybe her unhappiness hastened her death.

And what about his father's desire that he be taken into their family after his real mom died? Was it because he didn't want him to be raised by strangers in foster care? That too he would never know. More mystery.

Laney must have eaten her snack, because she was nuzzling him on the leg with a look that said it was time for her to curl up on his lap for a snooze. But when Martin picked up the dog, she whimpered as if she couldn't find a way to settle down. He knew why. Laney was such a smart and intuitive dog, she knew his every mood. Whether he was in the throes and excitement of a new experiment or a project for work. If he was tired and sleepy and maybe a little grumpy. Or if he was pondering the past and feeling a little disheartened as he was now. Laney knew.

Martin scratched the little dog behind the ears. "I'm all right. I will survive. I always have. It'll be all right, girl."

Laney stirred one more time and nestled down on his lap. With her head down, she gazed up at him with the saddest eyes. That look was meant to comfort him, which it did. Too bad people weren't always as loving as dogs.

Martin had promised Miss Beetle that he would tell his brothers about the letters, and he meant to keep his word. But for a moment, he stayed still. He let Laney fall asleep, and he let himself mourn a bit. Tears stung his eyes. He grieved for the past, the consequences of sin, and all the sorrow it brought down on people. For the loss of trust and goodness and love for so many, including himself.

After a while, Martin cleaned himself up, placed Laney in her kennel, and then left the cottage in search of his brothers.

CHAPTER
twenty

The closer Summer got to Granny's house, the faster she drove. The splinter in her palm, which she'd gotten from swiping her hands along the wooden crates, was now embedded in her hand and turning an angry red. But what was that pain compared to what her grandmother was facing? It was nothing. She turned into Granny's driveway with such speed that her tires squealed as she almost hit the trash bin. She parked and strode up the sidewalk to the front porch.

When her grandmother didn't answer the door after repeated knocks, Summer headed around the side, hoping she was in her backyard, enjoying the cool April afternoon. *Please, Lord, let it be nothing more than that.*

She speed-walked and then ran toward the backyard. Then she caught sight of her granny, looking well and relaxed. Summer stayed back just behind the crepe myrtle and watched for a moment. Her grandmother was having some fun on one of the rope swings that was attached to a huge live oak tree in her backyard. Ah, yes, those old oaks were good for so many things—tree houses and rope swings. Usually her granny merely swayed gently on the swing, but this time she was pumping herself higher and higher and throwing her head back in laughter.

What a wonderful sight. Even though it was probably too far away to take a photo, she took out her phone from her pocket and snapped a picture. So good to see her granny laughing in pure delight. Simply beautiful.

As she stood there, watching and relishing the sight, somewhere in her spirit she sensed how it would be in heaven—such freedom, such joy. *But I can't let her go, Lord. Not yet.* "Granny!" Summer yelled as she plucked a blossom and emerged from the bushes.

Granny slowed herself to a stop on the swing and looked toward the shout. She grinned when she saw Summer emerging from the shrubbery. "Hello dearie," she yoo-hooed back as she started to get up.

"Stay put, and I'll come to you." Summer rushed over to her grandmother and, leaning down, gave her a long, bear hug. Her granny's breathing was still a bit too fast as well as rattley, but the deep strain she sometimes had to catch her breath didn't seem as severe as it was before.

When Summer eased back, Granny said, "You okay?"

"Sure." Summer gave her a decisive nod to put her worries away.

Granny studied her. "There are tears in your eyes and you seem as shivery as a leaf in a windstorm."

"I'm fine."

"You don't look so fine. Are you and Martin doing okay?"

"Yes. More than okay," Summer said, glad to hide behind a new topic. "I think your plan for us is unfolding as you'd hoped. At least it is for me. I think I really can see him as more than a friend." Summer handed her grandmother the flower and sat down on the swing next to her.

"And I'll bet Martin is starting to feel the same way. That is what I pray for anyway."

"Maybe he is, but I don't know for sure. It might be that he's glad to have a friend."

"I'm sorry to hear that, but it will work out." Granny planted her shoes in a muddy spot, and she seemed amused at the sound of the funny smacking sound that they made on the mud.

"How can you know that, Granny?" Summer asked softly. "That it will work out?"

"I don't know it for certain, but it's just an inkling in my spirit. I've been getting more of those lately."

Summer paused before she asked the question, "Is it because of your illness? Those inklings?"

"I think it is." Granny stuck the crepe myrtle blossom in her hair. "But I've been spending a lot more time in prayer lately, especially for you."

"I'm glad. I love your prayers, and I'm sure I need them. But I wish you'd pray for your health to return. That is what I really want more than anything."

"I pray for that too. But I realize that even Jesus prayed, 'Father, Your will be done.' That is what I've come to now. Whatever *His* will is, because I know He has my best interest at heart. And I think I know the real reason why you're shivering. You haven't prayed that last part of the prayer concerning my illness, have you?" Granny looked at her then—one of her serious looks.

Summer didn't need to think about it. She knew her innermost thoughts and so she answered simply, "No, Granny. I'm not ready to pray that last part yet."

"I know, little love. I know. One more thought. When Jesus was here, people were always desperate for Him to care about power. About politics. And all the various problems of the day. That desperation came from their humanness, so it was understandable, but it was shortsighted. The Lord cared more about matters of the heart. Because we are eternal creatures, you and I. We were made for eternity, not this broken life. It's unfortunate that death became this porthole to the other life, but that came from man's choice to sin, not God's will for us." Granny gazed across the yard and then back at her. "And I have enough peace now that I no longer feel the need to toss my dishes over the railing anymore. I'm making progress, don't you think?"

Summer glanced over to the concrete patio, and there were no longer piles of broken dishes sitting there. "That is good, Granny."

"I would have run out of dishes eventually anyway."

Summer's laugh was tinged with sadness—her pathetic attempt to lighten her spirit.

Granny slapped her hands on her knees and said, "Well, you know what? I'm not dead yet, so I want some updates. How's it going with Martin and the list? I want *real* details."

Summer gave her all the latest news she could think of—including refurbishing Martin's tree house, making friends with Laney, finding the heirloom vase, and the attic search for clues to Martin's past.

"You are making fine headway with that list, which was bathed in prayer as I told you."

Summer reached up, plucked a leaf off the tree, and twirled it around by its stem. "But I wish we could have found something in Martin's attic. It would help him have closure with their family situation, you know, with what we talked about yesterday."

"You both working together . . . well, you'll find something eventually." Granny rocked herself on the swing. "But right now, I have a story to tell you about Martin."

Summer brushed the leaf across her cheek, but it felt scratchy against her skin instead of velvety as she'd expected. She looked at her granny, waiting for her story about Martin.

"When I was running the bookshop, you may remember that I had a dream box. Well, that's what I always called it anyway. I let the kids decorate it with glitter and whatnot, and I kept it on the counter for them. When they thought of something they hoped for, big or small, I let them write it out on a piece of paper and slip it into the box. At the end of the month, when I was by myself, I would take out the papers, read each of them, and pray over them. In all those years, Martin only put in one slip of paper. I guess he had one big dream. Do you know what that was?"

"I'd love to know."

"Martin wrote something like, *I wish I knew who my father was. I wish I knew if he had ever loved me. Why are there so many secrets?*"

"Oh, wow. That is so sad." Summer's spirit ached for Martin. "After all this time, you remembered that." She let go of the leaf and watched as it drifted to the ground.

"I remembered. And just as I've always prayed for you, I've prayed for Martin too, even though we never knew what happened to him back then after the family moved him away." Granny paused. "When you told me yesterday about the tragic way Martin's family broke up, it was a terrible thing to hear. I do hope you can help Martin understand his past and some of those secrets."

"Me too."

"I will say this too. You might even be surprised to hear it, but I felt prompted to add 'find a mystery and solve it' to your life-list. It seemed like the right thing to do, but at the time, I didn't know why I wrote it down. Only that I felt God wanted me to."

Summer mused. "God is a mystery, isn't He?"

"And mercy." Granny gazed at the sky. "Maybe you can also help Martin solve the mystery of what made his parents leave so suddenly to Europe. It might bring him some closure. And it could be the vehicle that could someday reunite the whole family. I'm not sure how that can be done at this point, but God knows. Now what's next on that list I gave you?"

"I think it's to enjoy the beauty of a sunrise and take a hot air balloon ride."

"Those are good ones. Right?"

"Yes. And they bring me to another topic. Martin thought it would be fun to have you join us for a couple of the adventures. I agree with him, but I think a hot air balloon ride might be too taxing for you. It might even be dangerous in your condition. I doubt your heart doctor would ever agree to it." Summer hated those words, since it sounded overly motherly. And her granny had always had a spirit of adventure. She hated to see her lose more and more of her independence.

"That is the Martin I remember, to ask me to tag along on your adventures. I say yes. I would love it, flying up high in the sky like that, almost touching the heavens."

"You didn't hear a word I said about the potential risks to your health."

"Nope."

"But are you sure you're up for it? Granny, if anything happened to you it would be my fault. I would never forgive myself. But I have an idea." Summer raised her finger to make a point, but her grandmother latched onto it and dropped a kiss on the tip of her finger.

Summer chuckled. "I really do have an alternative idea."

"All right. I'm all ears. But it better be good." Granny smiled.

"I read somewhere that we could take a hot air balloon ride with ropes tethering us to the ground. What do you think of that? Safety and fun all in one. Win-win, right?"

Granny nearly came out of her seat. "Oh little love, that's not really an adventure if it doesn't go anywhere. That experience wouldn't be all that different from sitting on this swing. If the good Lord is going to release me from the ties of this earth soon, then I would love to know now what it might feel like to fly free." Granny reached over and took Summer's hand in hers. "Look, I know why you're hesitating, and I love you for it. I really do. But please don't deny me this."

"Are you absolutely sure?"

"I am."

Summer slapped her shoes in the mud like her grandmother had done, but she felt no enjoyment in it.

"The doctors have been fretting, yes, but what is the point?" Granny said. "When a doctor tells you that you're dying and that there's nothing else they can do for you, then I don't see the need to take it easy. Don't you see?"

"I see, but I don't want to." Summer tried to hold up her head, but she knew it was sagging a bit.

"There's a quote I like even though I can't remember who said it. 'The value of life lies not in the length of days, but in the use we make of them; a man may live long yet live very little.' That is a good philosophy. I'd rather live my last days full than stay in bed, clinging to each breath as if those last breaths were all there was to living and dying."

"I admit it's a good quote, but—"

"Let's go on the balloon ride this week. Can you arrange it for the three of us?"

Summer sighed. There was no talking Granny out of it. Occasionally she had a stubborn streak as tough as shingles. "I'm not sure, but I will do my best. I know they go early in the morning at sunrise. Something about the air currents being more stable at that time of day or something like that. So we could see the sunrise as well as go on the ride."

"Two birds with one stone, eh?" Granny laughed and then went into a coughing jag. She held up her hand. "I'm good."

She gently rubbed her granny's shoulder. Summer still thought the balloon ride was a risky idea in Granny's condition, but what could she do? How could she tell Granny that she couldn't enjoy the last of her life? What an impossible situation.

Granny cleared her throat. "I wanted to ask you something about Elliot. Your breakup with him is still pretty fresh. How are you feeling?"

That was so Granny, always thinking about everyone but herself. "I'm okay with it. Really. I still feel some sadness that I hurt him. That I had to say goodbye. But in general, I'm relieved. I've been so busy with Martin and the list that I haven't had much time to think about him. Should I feel guilty?"

"No."

"Now that Elliot's had more time to think about the breakup, maybe he sees things more clearly. Surely now, he agrees that it wouldn't have worked between us. Not the way he wanted it to work anyway."

Granny asked, "Have you thought about that item close to the bottom of the list—about making amends with someone you might have wronged?"

"To be honest, I'm not sure what to do with that one. Was there a special reason you put that one on the list? Usually when I've hurt someone, I know it immediately, so I apologize right then or soon after. That way it's not hanging over my head."

"Yes. You do have the kindest heart, dearie. But have you thought of the past?"

"No, not much. Did you think I hurt Martin when we were kids?"

"No."

A sudden breeze ruffled their clothes and hair, and her grandmother buttoned up her sweater.

"Maybe you need a coat instead of that thin sweater. It's starting to get a little chilly out here," Summer suggested.

"Yes, Mother, I guess I do."

Summer grinned. "Maybe we should go inside to talk."

"No, I like the cool air, and I'd like to stay out here with the sky and the clouds. But I will take you up on the idea of a jacket. Why don't you go inside and get my coat out of the front closet. Then stop by my reading room and bring me the book from that little coffee table."

Summer zipped up her jacket, went into the house, and followed through with Granny's request. She found the coat in the front closet and then headed back to the little den. On the way she stopped for a moment in the dining room to look at the current jigsaw puzzle Granny was putting together. It was a picture of a garden lit by a brilliant sun, and it was finished—almost. One piece was missing, and it was a vital one, since it was that final piece that would have completed the face of a child who'd been strolling through the garden. When Summer gazed into the box, it was empty. That always irked Granny when she got to the end of the puzzle and a piece was missing. *Ah, well, such is life.*

She took one more look at the puzzle picture, then went to the den and found a single book on her coffee table. It was a copy of one of the Hardy Boys. Always a good read for kids, but she wondered why Granny wanted to see it.

As Summer walked through the maze of cozy rooms and hallways that made up Granny's house, pleasant memories trickled through her mind, as well as some recollections that weren't so pleasant. The book that she held did indeed have a history behind it. Not the Hardy mystery itself, but the setting in which it was read long ago and an unhappy incident that rose from a thoughtless gesture on her part. How could she have misplaced that scene from her youth? How could she have forgotten how she jeered at Ivan and Desmond?

Summer took a breather in the hallway as the full brunt of what she'd done came to her. During story time at the bookshop—while Granny had stepped into the backroom for some snacks and juice to pass around—Ivan had volunteered to read out loud. But right away he stumbled on his words, and when Desmond tried to help his brother, he stuttered. Summer had laughed at them and had gotten some of the other kids to laugh right along with her. Ivan and Desmond's expressions had turned to embarrassment and then misery. She couldn't possibly have known at the time that Ivan and Desmond would someday become Martin's brothers—that their lives would all intersect in such a way—and yet it really didn't matter who they were. What she'd done had been shameful, plain and simple, especially considering the news Martin had told her about their learning disabilities. But something else niggled at her memory. After she'd laughed at their poor reading, she'd made a joke about their haircuts, saying they looked sillier than gooney birds. All the other kids laughed again. Oh dear.

Summer's hope was that Ivan and Desmond had forgotten that brief episode, and yet the reality was that childhood incidents like that had the potential to leave permanent damage. *Oh, Lord, what have I done?*

CHAPTER
twenty-one

Summer strode over to Granny, helped her on with her coat, and then handed her the book. "I see now why you wanted me to retrieve this book. I remember what I did to Martin's brothers." Her chin quivered. "I was one of the mean girls, wasn't I?"

"No. You weren't a mean girl. Maybe you were just having an off day. The good Lord knows I do. Come here." Granny rose from the swing and wrapped her in a comforting embrace.

Summer clung to her, the same way she always did when life got too tangled or too painful. She took in the warmth of her hug and the ever-present and soothing scent of lilac powder. "How could I have done such a thing?"

"Desmond and Ivan, well, I could tell the minute they came traipsing into my bookshop that they had plenty of attitude. Those boys were impossible to forget."

"But it doesn't excuse me." Summer motioned to the swings. "I think we'd better sit down. There's more to their story than you know." When they were seated on the swings again, Summer told Granny about Desmond and Ivan's nanny, about her heartless behavior when they were infants, and the years of struggle with their learning disabilities.

When Summer had given her all the story that Martin had relayed, Granny said, "Oh my. I guess it is a reminder to us all that we don't know all the details of why a person becomes who they are. We don't know their background, and that history makes such a difference. That is why God is the judge and not us, which I am grateful for."

"True." Summer sighed. "But come to think of it, that was the first time Desmond and Ivan ever came to the bookshop. And because of me, Granny, it was the last time they ever came. I drove them away. Even though I was just a kid at the time, it still makes me shudder to think of my insensitivity. I can't imagine doing anything like that with the children in my bookshop now." But the more she examined those childhood days more closely, the more other incidents of haughtiness came to mind—ones she'd conveniently erased from her memory. The way she always liked to dress up in white, pretending she was a princess—that her grandmother's bookstore was her kingdom and all the customers her loyal subjects. "Oh, dear. What a perfect little snot of a kid I was," she muttered.

"Now don't be too hard on yourself. Not everyone would bother grieving about something like this. They would simply dismiss it as childishness. But you, I can tell you want to make this right. But it still needs to be your choice, my dear."

"Of course I'm willing to make it right. I have to. But what if they've forgotten all about it? Won't I just be stirring up trouble and pain all over again, reminding them of their errors?"

"That's a reasonable question." Granny gazed up to the sky again, which had now taken on a deep golden hue. She closed her eyes for a moment and then looked at Summer. "But it seems to me," she went on to say, "that it is better to err on the side of humility and be chastised for it than to be stingy with one's confessions and risk wounding someone."

"I do see the wisdom in that. But those two brothers seem so hard-hearted now. They have more than a mere 'tude, I can tell you."

"I imagine you're right," Granny said. "And yet the smallest crack can cause the hardest dam to break." She shook her head. "I was amazed way back then as I still am that Martin was adopted so suddenly and that two members of his new family would be Ivan and Desmond. God does have a plan in all of this. I can feel it. We just can't always see the whole picture."

"Yes, I know." Summer thought about Granny's words. "I will go over there tomorrow. I know I hurt them, and I do want to make things right."

"I see your sadness, and maybe I shouldn't have brought it up. I should—"

"No. I know what you're going to say, and it's not true. You did the right thing by bringing it up."

Granny reached over and patted her arm. "I too have had to ask folks for forgiveness as I put my affairs in order."

"You? I can't imagine, Granny. And who is that if you don't mind me asking."

"Well, one was an old friend, Shirley. You may remember her. Anyway, some months ago, Shirley said I wasn't healed of my on-going heart condition because I didn't have enough faith." Granny picked at the printed flowers on her sweatpants. "Shirley was quite dogmatic about it."

"I know that's not true. I'm sorry to say that Shirley is out to lunch. You have more faith than anyone I've ever known."

"Yes, and I told her something to that effect, and needless to say it didn't go over well. There is no one so hard to convince as someone who's all fired up with someone else's sin—or what they think might be sin. I don't really regret what I said, but I was sorry for the way I said it. I got pretty sharp, and for a while it caused a falling-out between us. I knew I needed to make it right. And I did."

Summer tried to ignore her hand, which still throbbed with pain from the splinter. "And are you friends again?"

"No, but we're working on it." She smiled. "So your old granny doesn't get it right all the time either. I think some of the misery of this world isn't just the mean things other people do to us, but it's the closed-heartedness in our own actions." Granny paused. "And soon, those kinds of earthy struggles will be gone. Aren't you, in some way, envious of my journey to heaven?"

"Of course, except that your journey takes you away from me."

"We won't be separated forever. Only a time. But you know that."

"Yes, I know, but the thought of it still tears me to pieces."

"You are my treasure, so it pains me too," Granny said softly, almost like a prayer. "But God will have His way."

Summer picked up a pinecone that had fallen to the ground and studied it. "Yes. I just wish this life weren't so fragile. Too much pain. Too many goodbyes."

"Well, heaven will be a land of greetings. We'll never have to say farewell again, at least not in the sorrowful way we do here."

No matter how hard Summer tried to be strong for Granny, tears still came. She shook her head. "I'm sorry."

"Nothing to be sorry about, little love. Listen, I have a story. I know how you love them. I'm sure you remember when you were little and I took you to the Cypress Acres Amusement Park. Well, when you first got there, you were ecstatic. You couldn't decide which ride to go on first. You wanted to do them all. And I think you almost did. You had such a good day, and your joy was mine too."

"I do remember that. It was fun."

"Well, after all the rides, you wanted to try all the amusement park foods—the cotton candy, the corndogs, and the ice cream. I was silly enough back then to let you have whatever you wanted. You were such a darling girl."

"And sometimes I was a little twit." Tired of the prickles, Summer threw the pinecone across the yard.

Granny protested. "You were a darling girl to me, and you still are. Anyway, this is my story to tell, so I'll tell it like I see it." She grinned. "Eventually, our fun came to a close that day, and we headed toward the parking lot. I know your eyes were sparkling with all the memories of the day; the rides, some were good and made you giggle but some of them scared you. And as we walked, you told me you had this ache in your tummy from all the food, which was understandable, of course, since I let you eat everything in sight." She shook her head. "Then as we got closer and closer to my car, well, all you wanted to do was hold my hand tightly and talk about home."

"Okay, I see where you're going with this now." Summer's stomach tightened.

"Yes, I'm sure you do. Well, more and more, that is the way I feel now, little love, as I know my time is coming to a close here. I've have a good life full of rides, some wonderful, some that made me giggle, and even some that were scary. I had a bookshop that brought children great pleasure over the years. I've known the love of family and friends and *you*, who have brought me tremendous joy. And I've known my Lord. In other words, I've been to the park and I've ridden all the rides and I've eaten all the foods. But now, well, I've got this gnawing sensation in my gut, and all I can think about is holding the hand of my Lord tightly and heading on home."

CHAPTER
twenty-two

This round, Summer held back the tears even though they were fighting to be released. She would be brave for Granny. "That was a good story. I understand better. A little, anyway."

"Good." Granny said the word with excitement, but there was an unmistakable wheezing in her breath.

Should she bring it up? "I'm willing to spend the night here if you think you might need me. You know, it could be like old—"

"Like old times? That's sweet. But, no. You go on home and get a good night's rest. You'll sleep better at your apartment."

Summer doubted it but agreed. "All right. Are you going in now? It's getting even chillier out here."

"No, I want to keep company with the clouds a bit longer. It makes me feel closer to heaven out here."

"Well, don't get too close to heaven while I'm gone, okay?"

Granny grinned. "Okay."

Summer gazed upward from the swing. "I just noticed. One of the ropes on this swing is unraveling. We'd better not use this one again until it can be fixed."

"Good eye. Thanks for catching that." Granny looked up. "I doubt I'll have it fixed, though. I'll just have my next-door neighbor take it down the next time he drops by. He helps me with heavy things from time to time."

"Okay. Whatever you say." Summer wasn't going to say another word on the topic, since her granny's answer made her sad. The reason she was no longer repairing things was because she really didn't expect to live much longer. *Oh, Lord, what can I do?* Summer rose and kissed her grandmother on the forehead. "I love you big and high—"

"As the Texas sky," Granny finished and then shook her finger at her. "Remember, that no grandmother could be prouder of her grandchild. You're a remarkable young woman, Summer. Never forget that."

"And you're the best granny any girl could ever have."

"Thanks, little love."

Summer walked away, but then turned back to wave. When her grandmother thought she'd gone on her way, Summer stayed behind again to watch her. Her grandmother swung gently as she sang a familiar old hymn.

Summer sighed—that deep kind of sigh that only God could hear. Then she headed toward her car, her spirit unsettled, her mind filled again with uneasiness. Had there been a hint of a fever when she kissed her granny on the forehead? Was she declining faster than the doctors had predicted? It surely couldn't be helping her to stay out in the chilly air.

Summer climbed into her car, turned on the engine, and drove home to her apartment—a place that now seemed more than a little bit lonesome. She flipped on some lights and gazed around her cozy abode. How had her furniture gotten so drab, the small rooms even smaller, and the walls so dingy? Everything was exactly the same, of course, but it was obviously her outlook that had deteriorated.

She felt another bout of downheartedness coming on concerning her granny, so she stopped in front of the hall mirror to look at herself. She forced a smile, but the expression looked more frightening than friendly. Guess her heart wasn't in it.

Summer snatched an apple from the fruit bowl in the kitchen. *Okay, Granny. I'll try to lighten up. I will.* She plopped on her bed— which made a creaking sound as if the springs were about sprung—

and took a bite of the fruit, kicking off her shoes. She fingered her cellphone. On a whim, she called Martin. Maybe she shouldn't call him so soon. Maybe it still wasn't kosher for the woman to call the man in such instances. But they weren't dating—they were merely friends.

No one answered, so maybe she should give up. Summer set her apple down on the night table. No, that would be the spineless thing to do. *I am woman. I am fearless.*

Yeah, right.

Just as she was about to end the call, Martin answered the phone.

"Hi, Summer."

"Caller ID, huh?"

"No, it was just a hunch."

"Really?" Summer smiled. "I hope I'm not intruding." She wiggled her toes. Boy, did she need a pedicure. Too bad she couldn't afford it.

"Intruding? That's not possible," Martin said. "At least it could never be true of you."

She liked the sound of that. He was smiling through the phone with his tone, which was a good sign. She missed the olden days when she could curl her finger around the phone cord, so she curled her hair instead.

"Anything particular on your mind?" he asked. "How's Granny?"

"She's about the same. Thanks for asking."

"Sorry that I slipped into calling her Granny. I confess when I was a kid in her bookshop, I used to pretend she was my grandmother."

Summer rested back against the headboard. "Granny would love to hear you say that. It was the feel she tried to give the store. That everyone was welcome like family. That every child who entered her shop would be loved and accepted."

"Well, it worked."

"By the way, Granny wants to take you up on going with us for the hot air balloon ride. She claims she's up for it. Do you mind going if I can set it up day after tomorrow?"

"I'd love to. I've always been curious about those rides," Martin said. "But are you sure she should?"

"She won't be talked out of it. I tried. She thinks it would be quite the adventure, which it will be." Summer wrapped her arms around her legs in a hug.

"All right. It's a plan then."

"I also had something I needed to say to your brothers. Would it be okay to come over tomorrow?" Summer asked. "Will they be home?"

"Well, they sleep in some, but they never miss their breakfast. Why don't you come at nine? You've got me curious. What's this all about?"

Summer chewed on her lower lip. "I'll leave it for tomorrow, if that's okay. Is that okay?" She was sliding into a preteen mode the longer they spoke. Good grief.

"Sure. In fact, I have something I need to tell you as well, and it's important enough that I don't want to say it over the phone."

"Oh, wow. Now that's the perfect way to keep a girl from getting any sleep at all."

Martin chuckled.

They went on chatting some more, and it brought Summer so much joy that she almost forgot about the heartbeat pounding in her palm from the splinter.

By the time they said goodbye—two hours later—Martin hadn't given away even a hint of the news he wanted to announce in the morning.

But then neither had she.

The next morning, on her way to Martin's house in Bellaire, she decided to make a quick stop by Once Upon a Time. Wouldn't hurt, right? She wouldn't break her promise to Granny by going back to work, but she had to have a peek before working hours.

Once parked, she walked up to the front of the shop—admiring as always, the frontage of her quaint bookstore with its hunter green wood and swinging antique sign. She gazed at the new window display, enjoying its simple enchantments. Amelia had made a sleepy-time theme. The display featured some of the newer picture book releases, which were read-alouds for bedtime, and she'd added fluffy clouds and chubby sheep to the scene to make it cozy and welcoming. What a charming vignette. The kids would love it. The moms would too.

Ahh, the shop. It was so much more of a home to her than her apartment. What was not to love about it? Shelves and shelves of books full of stories that brought delight to all the children that passed through her doors.

Summer gave Elliot a place in her thoughts—not that she pined away for him, but she would no doubt miss what would have come with marriage—a home and a family. But then Elliot hadn't really liked children. The most he'd agreed to was one child. He'd always said, "When it comes to having kids, I just don't understand what all the fuss is about. The more kids, the more work. The more money depleted and resources consumed. And they can be such ungrateful little buggers." Oh, how his arguments when on and on. Elliot seemed to have forgotten that he'd been a child once upon a time. Or maybe Elliot really hadn't gone through childhood. He was the type who had gone straight from infancy to adulthood.

She smiled to herself as she cupped her hands over her eyes to gaze more deeply into the shop. Funny that all the things she thought Elliot was lacking, well, Martin had in abundance. She imagined how Martin would thrive with children all around him. Their dolls would probably be dressed like hobbits, their games would be filled with imagination, and their shelves would be stacked with books. Their little lives would never lack for a sense of joy and wonder. And love. Already she could see their shining faces, glowing with admiration as they gazed up at their dad.

Summer placed her hand on the warm glass of the window, wishing it was Martin's face. He had such a friendly face with a gentle way about his features. No hard lines—like Elliot, who seemed to have a lot of angles—and angles tended to have gloomy corners for things to hide. But Martin, on the other hand . . . well . . .

Come back down from the clouds, Summer. Your thoughts have drifted too far off course.

Then suddenly she heard, "Summer," so she turned from her daydream to the person calling her name.

Amelia came up to her with a grin firmly planted on her face. The jig was up. Her friend and beloved assistant knew the truth— that she just couldn't stay away from the shop.

They gave each other a warm hug.

"Hey, girl," she said.

Summer pulled back and said, "You've changed your hair color. It's a good look on you."

"Thanks." She bounced the bottom of her curls with her palm.

"You do look terrific."

"Oh, I love it when you lie."

Summer chuckled.

"By the way, what are you doing here? Never mind. I don't know why I asked that, since I know why. But I thought you were on strict orders from your granny to play hooky for a while." Amelia pulled a set of keys out of her purse.

"I stopped by for a look. That's all. I knew you'd have everything under control, but I already miss the place. And you and the kids too, of course."

"I know. I would miss it too, so I understand."

Summer pointed to the window. "I love your bedtime display. Very whimsical."

"Thanks. I like sheep. What can I say? I see plenty of them when I try to count them at night."

"What's keeping you awake?"

"Oh, I don't know. Well, one thing is, I'm always dreaming up ways to build up revenue and enhance the shop."

Summer studied Amelia. They were cut from the same cloth, in that they were both plugged into the shop with the determination to keep it charged up and running. "I'm the same way, but I'm sorry it keeps you awake."

"I don't mind. I really don't." Amelia sighed. "After Charlie died I needed to pour myself into something. I expected to have a hard time adjusting when I lost my husband, but it was even worse than I imagined." She lifted the shop key into the air with a triumphant gesture. "But it was this place that gave me something to do. It was just the hope I needed to get me up in the morning, to keep breathing, to keep going, instead of letting myself be completely taken over by grief." Mist filled her eyes. "I know this shop is like home to you. Well, that's the way I feel too. A home and a way out of my sorrow."

Summer gave Amelia another hug. "I'm so glad. Truly." *Oh, Lord, please let this shop stay open, even if only for Amelia.* "You've been the best all-around assistant any shop owner could ever have. There doesn't seem to be anything you can't do. I don't know what I'd do without you."

"I want to make this place work, more than anything." Was there something more in what Amelia was trying to say?

"I hate to ask this, but I know you've been doing the books. So what is the latest? Are we doing that poorly financially?"

"Well, I hated to tell you, since you've had enough to worry about with your granny been so ill and all. So I'm not sure this is the best time to tell you—"

Summer touched her arm. "Please. I need to know."

"Well, we're doing okay, but revenues are still going down slightly."

"It's the increase in online buying. I'm sure." Summer shook her head. Oh, how she'd hoped that her grandmother would see the shop flourish, even just once, but that hope seemed to be dwindling.

"You're right. I'm sure all the convenience of online buying is affecting our profits. But I'm still convinced there are folks who like to have a special place like this where their kids can gather. You know, where they can get excited about stories."

"I just hope this brick and mortar concept doesn't become a dinosaur. I fear it might already be."

"Never." Amelia raised her shop key in the air. "Yes, it might seem old-fashioned in a way, but that might also work in our favor, since online shopping can be impersonal and well, faceless and cold."

"You're so right," Summer said. It was the same pep talk she told herself, but it did feel good to hear it from Amelia. "So why are you here so early?"

"Restocking the shelves. Nothing major."

Someone yoo-hooed from the pastry shop nearby—one of their regular customers and her two preschoolers—and Summer and Amelia waved back.

Amelia turned to Summer. "Hey, how's it going for you and your grandmother's list? You and Martin staying busy?"

"Well, that's what I'm headed to do just now, and apparently Martin has something important to tell me."

"Oh, really? I wonder what that is."

"Don't get any ideas. We're just friends. But with the hope that it could become more." *Much more.*

"Well, keep me posted. I want details."

Summer grinned. "Will do."

They fist-bumped, and Summer headed on her way.

✌✌

At a few minutes to nine Summer arrived at the big house, but Martin noticed right away that she looked distracted. Something was on her mind. Something of a serious nature. After a few greetings and a few prickly questions from Desmond and Ivan as to why they'd been summoned to the dining room, they all four sat down at the table with a round of iced tea and an assortment of *looks*.

"What's this all about?" Ivan asked, fingering something in his shirt pocket. "You two are so cryptic."

Martin ignored Ivan and turned to Summer. "Would you like me to go first? Or do you want to?"

"I'll go." She gazed back and forth at Martin's two brothers.

Ivan's thick black hair hadn't been combed yet, and with the way it jutted up on both sides, the impression was that he was growing horns. *Curious look*. In the meantime, Desmond rubbed his eyes as if they were sleepy—or spaced-out. Wonder if he was craving his meds again. *This is not an encouraging way to start.*

Summer placed her hands on the table and laced her fingers together. "I asked to see you, Desmond and Ivan, because I had something to say to both of you."

"What is it?" Desmond a tapped a finger on the table.

"Well, the reason I came today was to, well, I'll just say it straight out. I came to apologize."

"What for?" Ivan slunk down in his chair, already looking bored. He once again played with the item in his pocket, which looked like a charcoal pencil. His fingers came away smudged with black, and he absently wiped them on his shirt.

"I'll explain." Summer adjusted a little cameo that rested at the top of her blouse. "A long time ago, when we were all kids, before Martin came into your family, you and Desmond visited my grandmother's bookshop one day after school. During story time, Ivan, well, you volunteered to read, but you stumbled on your words, and then when Desmond tried to help you he stuttered a bit. Instead of being kind or helpful, I laughed, and I encouraged the other kids to laugh. Then I made fun of your haircuts, which made the kids laugh all over again."

Summer took a sip of her tea. "I'm not sure why I did it, but it can't be for any good reason. I don't know if either of you remember that incident. Actually, I hope you've forgotten. It's just that I wanted to make it right, even if it was long forgotten." Her words spilled out faster and faster as if she were afraid she might not get the words out. "I am sorry for that unkindness. Truly."

Desmond leaned forward on the table and said in a gravelly voice, "As it turns out, I do remember that dastardly depressing day."

Martin groaned inside, hoping his brother wasn't about to launch an angry missile to destroy Summer's sweet-tempered apology.

"Yeah, I remember it too." Ivan scrunched up his paper napkin into a tight wad and gave it a plunk with his fingers, making it sail across the table, almost hitting Summer. "It messed me up for a while I admit, but come to think of it, most of my friends have done far worse to me over the years."

"Well, I am sorry for what I did. It was cruel. I hope you will forgive me." Summer lined up the wad of paper and gave it a flick right back to Ivan. "Friends?" She offered him a smile.

"Sure, why not?" Ivan shrugged.

"Summer, that's all you came here for?" Desmond asked.

"Yep." Summer massaged her palm as if she were in pain. "That's it."

"And why did you feel the need to bring it up now? Seems like a random kind of thing," Desmond said.

Summer straightened. "My granny, who owned that bookshop, well, she remembered what I did, and she thought it might be a good time to make things right."

"And why would your grandmother care about that?" Ivan said. "It was so long ago."

"Well, she's a little more sensitive about that sort of thing lately. I guess when you're . . . ill, you think more about forgiveness and reconciliation."

Desmond cocked his head at her. "Did you say ill?"

Summer seemed to hesitate, and Martin knew why. To tell Desmond and Ivan what was happening with her dear grandmother would be like throwing pearls before swine. *God, forgive me.*

"To be clear," Summer said, "my granny is not well at all. She is . . . not going to get better, and she asked me to do this today. It was a good idea, and so that's why I'm here."

"Oh? Your grandmother is dying," Desmond said, sounding mildly interested. "And what is she dying of?"

"Congestive heart failure."

Martin searched his brother's eyes for a softening in their expressions, but none came. "Let's not torture Summer," he said. "She's made a lovely apology, and you both should accept it. I don't even remember the incident she's talking about."

"Of course *you* don't." The pitch of Ivan's voice went up a notch. "You never made a mistake in your life."

"That's not true," Martin said.

"It may not be true to you, but it feels true to us," Ivan flicked the wad of paper again so that it hit Martin in the face.

Martin closed his eyes for a second. *Lord, give me patience with my brothers.* He slipped the wad of paper into his pocket. "Look, it was never my intention to lift myself up as someone who was perfect. I'm far from it."

"That part is right." Desmond's jaw muscles twitched as he spoke. "It was our father who lifted you up. The teachers who lifted you up. It was every living breathing soul around us, Martin. Ever since you came to live with us."

Maybe that's all true, but I worked hard. Doesn't that deserve some reward? Or had pride seeped in along with the striving? He'd have to ponder that one a bit more. "Then it's a good time to talk about it, don't you think? We've been dancing around the past for years. Maybe this is the right time to talk things through so we can move on. So we can have some kind of closure." Martin took several sips of his iced tea to cool off.

"Closure? Why do you say it in that particular way?" Desmond asked. "Do you know something? Did you find something while you were in the attic?"

Martin hesitated. He glanced up at the family portraits, especially the one of his father and stepmother. Their expressions now seemed to be tinged with displeasure—something he hadn't noticed before. Unnerving. He dismissed that irregular thought and said, "I did find something. Or I should say that Summer found something. That vase. The one you saw had something hidden inside. I should first say that Miss Beetle came into the attic and seemed to be pretty taken with the vase, so I gave it to her. I didn't see any harm in it. Well, later Miss Beetle set the vase on a small table, and Laney jumped up and knocked the table, which jarred it enough to make the vase fall onto the floor and break into pieces."

"Are you kidding me?" Desmond asked. "That heirloom vase broke? How come you didn't tell me? And how could you give it away without even asking us?"

Martin rested his head on his hands and rubbed his forehead, wondering why—when it came to his brothers—everything had to be an argument. "I can't imagine that it had any real value since the crack was so severe. If I had thought it really meant something to you, well, of course, I wouldn't have given it to Miss Beetle. But once you saw that it probably had no monetary value after all, you walked away from it as if it meant nothing to—"

"Maybe so, but you had no—"

"Desmond, please hear me out," Martin said. "What I'm trying to say here is that when the vase broke, it revealed some letters that had been stuck down inside. These letters had been written to Mother from *her* mother. I've read all the letters, and they're interesting, but one of the letters is truly significant." He paused and considered his next words carefully. "It says that I wasn't adopted after all, which would explain why no adoption papers have ever been found. I am not adopted. I am our father's biological son." He cleared his throat. "Ivan and Desmond, I am your half brother."

"Half brother?" Ivan said. "Half brother," he repeated again, his frown deepening.

Desmond rose, went over to the window, and fingered the tassels on the draperies. "What are you saying here? Does that mean my father and your biological mother had an affair at some point?"

"Yes," Martin said. "That's correct."

Desmond stared out the window. "That is not good news at all. Actually, it's despicable. I'll want to read these letters."

"I'd like to see them too," Ivan said.

"Of course you may have the letters. I want you to read them all," Martin said. "Even though I wasn't sure how you would feel about this new information, I wanted to tell you both. I really don't want to withhold information from you, even if the news might not be—"

Desmond whirled around to face him again. "Then why didn't you tell me about the letters yesterday?"

"I went searching for both of you," Martin said, "but I couldn't find you."

"Probably because we've been busy making a list of places to go job hunting." Ivan gave Martin a dark look.

"Job hunting is good." Martin moved his tea glass around in the crystal coaster. "You won't regret it. Anyway, as I said, I want to speak the truth. But even though what my mother and our father did was sinful, and even though it caused our family grief, I am at least relieved to know who my biological father is. And this must solve some, if not all of the mystery surrounding our family."

"And so the letters state that their affair happened while our mother and father were married?" Desmond sat back down in his chair.

"Yes, unfortunately, that is correct," Martin said. "And considering their wedding date and my age, that all lines up correctly too. Please let me add, though, that in spite of this, I'm pleased to be a part of the Langtree family, to be your half brother. I am hoping you both can come to feel the same way." Martin sighed. "I always felt like an outsider, so this does make—"

"You felt like an outsider, Martin, because you *were* an outsider," Ivan exploded. "You still are. Can't you feel it? Most people, that is, when they aren't so severely inept socially, can figure out when they aren't wanted. When they've *never* been wanted."

Summer stiffened in her chair as if she were about to say something fiery. She then took in a deep breath and pressed her palms around her iced tea glass.

His dear Summer had gotten tangled in the Langtree web again. Martin wished it weren't so, but it was too late to turn back now. He said to Ivan, "Why would you say such a thing? I have loved you as my brother all these years. I have loved you both."

Desmond yanked on his vest. "I know why Ivan says it. Because as kids, our lives were going along pretty well, not great, of course, but they were at least good enough, until you showed up at the door with your sad brown eyes . . . the lost puppy of dubious origins. Now we know why you showed up. Your mother, Odell, no doubt seduced our father, and you are this illegitimate mongrel of a child that our mother was forced to take in, to deal with, feed and clothe, and treat like her own. It's obvious now why everything was kept hush-hush. They were ashamed of the past. Ashamed of you, and they wanted to keep it quiet. So they made up a big lie, and they got away with it for a very long time."

No one in the room seemed to breathe for a moment.

Meanwhile Martin died a little more on the inside.

Ivan set his iced tea glass back down with a heavy hand, which made an unhappy clink in the coaster. "This is one of the reasons that Desmond paid that detective such a big chunk of our inheritance. To get answers. And here they are. The ugly truth of it."

Ivan shook his head. "I wondered if something like this might have happened, but I always dismissed it. Now we know the whys of our parents and their miseries. And I guess this also explains why they divorced and fled. I guess they could no longer endure the truth of the past. Mother was tortured by *your* mother's sin, and the sin she brought on our family. And maybe Father was full of guilt over what happened. Your presence would have been a constant reminder of the past, the disgrace. And you are the product of that sin, a misbegotten child." He pounded his fist on the table.

Summer squirmed in her chair, looking like it was taking every bit of wit and will to keep from exploding with her own blistering words against his brothers.

Martin gave her a smile and a tiny shake of his head, hoping she would get his silent message.

Summer seemed to understand and sat back in her chair.

Martin then placed his hands under the table and clasped them together so tightly his fingers ached. "I'm so sorry that you feel this way. I think once you've had time to think about this some more, you both might feel differently. I know I am a product of their sin, but I didn't participate. Maybe I shouldn't be condemned for what others did. Then when my mother died, I had no place else to go."

"You could have been placed in a foster home. That would have solved all the problems. Out-of-sight, out-of-mind for our mother, who might have been able to forgive our father's transgression had you not been that never-ending reminder of the past."

"Yes." Martin lowered his gaze. "When you word it that way, maybe it would have been a better way to handle the situation. Foster care might have . . ." The sense of hope Martin had felt earlier—

the hope he'd so fervently prayed for—seemed to teeter on the edge now, ready to break into pieces, just like the heirloom vase.

Summer rose from her chair, her face flushed. She looked at Ivan and then at Desmond. "If you guys aren't actually monsters, you sure are doing one convincing impersonation."

"Ahh, silent Summer rises." Desmond rose, his expression steeped in venom. "Now listen to me. You both need to leave this house immediately. Martin, if you were ever a part of this family, you certainly aren't now." He glared at Summer and then at Martin as he pointed toward the entry. "Now both of you . . . get out."

PART THREE

texas sky

CHAPTER
twenty-three

Floating along at a great height, over a lush mélange of fields and houses, Summer watched the sun come up in all its glory—first spreading itself across the horizon like great golden wings and then rising to cover their world with splendor. What a once-in-a-lifetime moment. And that moment was being shared with two of the finest people she had ever known.

Granny looked down over the land, her hands gripping the ropes of the balloon's basket. "Look at all this. Bewildering in the most miraculous way." She pointed toward the ground and smiled. "Look at the cars and the people way down there. I guess they see us way up here just below the clouds. I wonder what they're thinking. 'Oh, look, there goes a troupe of adventurers, a merry band of buccaneers.'"

Summer grinned. She'd never seen her granny so elated. Guess it had been okay after all not to talk Granny out of such a risky trip. "I'm glad you're having fun."

"The best, my dear. The very best. I hope *you're* having fun," Granny said. "I want this to be wonderful for you and Martin too."

"Oh, don't worry about Martin. I can tell he's relishing the idea of asking the pilot every technical question imaginable." Summer caught Martin's eye, and he smiled at her.

"But what about you, little love?" Granny asked. "Aren't you having a good time too?"

"Yes. Well, I did lose my stomach a few times as we were lifting off, but now that we're gliding along, it's wonderful. Unexpectedly so. Thanks, Granny. It was one of your classic ideas." What Summer left out of her little spiel was that she would enjoy the experience much more if she weren't so riddled with worry about her granny's health.

The pilot—a young man named Karl Truman—opened a valve of some kind, and the burner flared up again with a fiery whooshing sound.

They drifted higher, which made Granny sigh with pleasure. "Ohh, what are we doing now, Mr. Truman?"

"I'm having us ascend in altitude a bit to catch a different current of air. All is well," Karl said. "Mrs. Snow, what has been the biggest surprise to you so far on this trip?"

Granny turned to Karl and said, "Almost all of it is a surprise. But I was shocked at all the work you had to go through to meticulously lay out the balloon; oh, I think you called that part of it, the envelope. Anyway, it was amazing to see how you laid it all it out, got it heated up, and it sort of awakened like a giant creature rising out of the sea."

Karl grinned.

"But now that we're up here," Granny said. "I guess I expected us to be whirling in the sky like you would speed along in a car. Except for when you turn on that flame, there is such a peaceful quiet up here. A feeling of aloneness but not loneliness. I guess a better word is tranquility."

"Yes, I agree." Karl gave the wicker basket an affectionate pat. "It was that word that made me become a pilot. I love it up here. That tranquility you talked about. You can't get that feeling with any other kind of flying."

Summer studied Granny while she was busy talking to Karl. She had noticed some occasional wheezing, but it appeared to be noticeable only to her, since her ears were tuned to that sound. But since Granny was smiling and laughing and didn't seem to be having any problem catching her breath, Summer tried to stop herself from constantly fretting. She just wished her grandmother hadn't upped her meds for the trip. How much had she taken? And was she supposed to be increasing her dosage without the doctor's permission? *Lord, please help Granny to be okay on this trip, and please help me to stop worrying for one minute.*

A light breeze kicked up then, tickling Summer's cheeks. They had all expected the air temperature to be cold, and they'd even brought jackets preparing to be shivering, but amazingly—perhaps miraculously—the breeze was pleasantly cool rather than chilly. She breathed deeply, hoping to embrace the moment. The feel of sailing along with such a lofty view was indeed a heady rush. And too, when she calmed herself and let some of her inner turmoil go to God where it belonged, there was also a potent sense of serenity that came with it.

Granny pointed toward the south. "You don't realize what a patchwork world we live in until you see it from up here. The separate fields in so many varied shades; it reminds me of the quilts my mother used to make and just as pretty. We trudge on day in and day out with such a finite point of view, don't we? There's so much more to the world when you see it from up here."

"True," Karl said. "I mean, practically speaking, this is a silly way to get from place to place, but when you think of the inspirational factor, it's the best way to fly."

"I like that." Granny lighted her fingertips along the top of the basket as if they were dancing. "Do you believe in God, Mr. Truman?" she suddenly asked him.

"Funny you should ask me that," Karl said. "I didn't believe in God until I became a pilot."

Granny said, "Interesting."

Karl gazed out over to the horizon with the most pleasant expression. "I always asked my guests to describe this whole experience in two words. Who wants to go first?"

Granny pointed upward. "Heaven's porthole."

"I like that." Summer smiled. Granny's reply didn't surprise her, but it did make her heart sink a bit. She looked at the pilot and said her two-word description, "Being untethered."

"Excellent one too." Martin grinned. "I'll say *deep space*, even though I've never been there."

Karl chuckled. "Very good. You've come up with some of the best I've heard."

They all grew quiet. Summer guessed that they all wanted to make the most of the moment—a moment that might not ever come again.

Granny sighed with contentment. "Ahh. That silky-smooth wind. Perhaps it isn't the airstreams at all but the brush of angel wings against our basket." She said this in a whisper that didn't seem to be directed at anyone in particular.

Summer closed her eyes, trying to let her other senses take over. She let the balloon have its way, and a few more cares of the days got swept away. She glanced over at Martin, and she caught him staring at her. It was a look she'd seen on him before, one that had depth to it, and perhaps a world of "other" meaning, but just what that meaning was, she couldn't tell for sure. Were their thoughts in sync?

Martin had his hand resting on the side of the gondola, and without thinking, Summer reached over and touched the button on his flannel shirt, the one that seemed to be hanging on by a loose string. It would be a pleasure to sew that back on for him.

Her smile melted into a beseeching look, since there was so much she wanted to say, not just about their evolving relationship, but concerning the way in which his brothers had treated him a couple of days before. *Atrocious* would describe it well. They had talked about what had happened, of course, but mostly their discussion had consisted of Martin apologizing to her for his brothers' spiteful words. Martin had said little about his own hurt. Perhaps the incident was still too fresh, but oh, how she wanted to console him.

He gave her the slightest nod and wink as if he knew her thoughts and wanted to put her mind at ease.

Summer mouthed "Thanks" to him.

For now, she would say no more on the matter. Martin had said he wanted her grandmother's balloon ride to be perfect, which meant it was not a good time to talk about his brothers' foul behavior. After all, Summer had already discussed the unhappy incident with Granny. She agreed that some of the news did appear unsettling, but she was pleased that Martin now had the opportunity to know the truth about his father and the rest of his family. And Granny was encouraged that the strange deadlock—which had paralyzed the Langtree family for so long—had been broken, and there was at least a chance for movement. A possibility for healing. Granny had the assurance that God would take care of the rest in His good time. *Remember the old quote, she had said: "It's always darkest just before the dawn."*

Summer hoped and prayed Granny was right.

In a sudden gust, Summer gripped the edge of the basket to steady herself, and then winced in pain.

"You okay?" Martin asked.

"I'm fine." She looked at her palm. "I had this silly splinter in my hand, but with some coaxing it finally came out this morning. Apparently there's pain in the healing process." *Wish it weren't so.*

Martin took her hand in his and gingerly opened her fingers. He examined the slightly red and swollen spot on her skin. "I'll bet this is a souvenir from the Langtree tree house."

"Actually, I got it on a crate in the attic. But it's okay. It was worth it. I promise."

He leaned toward her cheek and said softly, "That's the very word I hear in my head when I look at you. Promise."

The air could have been frigid, but it wouldn't have mattered—since the warmth that traveled through her veins and spirit was more than enough to keep her toasty. Ahh, Martin. *You make me feel such joy.* Martin's ongoing gift for empathy and always putting the needs of others ahead of his own, was also pure Martin. And it was one of the many things about him that set him apart from other men. From so many other men—especially Elliot.

Just as Summer's shoulders relaxed, Granny turned to her with a flicker of fear.

"Summer?"

"Granny?" Summer disengaged herself from Martin and moved to the other side of the basket.

Her grandmother grasped her arm tightly and whispered in her ear, "I know who you are. You're my Summer. But who are these two men? And why am I up here in this thing? This balloon? How did I get here, Summer?"

CHAPTER
twenty-four

Dear Lord, please no. Summer fought to keep her emotions in check. She had read online that forgetfulness was symptomatic of the final stages of congestive heart failure. Her mind raced through various ways to handle the situation. Should she tell Martin or the pilot what was happening? Should they land immediately? But the last thing she wanted to do was to embarrass her grandmother or upset her perfect day unless it was a true emergency.

Finally Summer leaned her head over to Granny's and said quietly, "This is quite a day, isn't it? I'm so glad you came up with this idea for Martin and me to go on this balloon ride."

A look of confusion riddled Granny's face and then the puzzlement slowly faded. A few seconds later, she was nodding with obvious understanding. "Oh, I see what I've done now. Guess I was a bit bumfuzzled." She reached out and squeezed Summer's hand. "I'm okay now, little love. I'm myself again. Thank you."

Summer wanted to burst into tears, but now wasn't the time. She instead concentrated on the view as she tried to convince herself that Granny's absentminded slip was no more than the general forgetfulness that sometimes came with old age. But she was far from convinced. "Are you ready to go back down?"

"Yes, I think I am—if it's okay." Granny clung to the railing until her knuckles went pale.

Summer turned to the pilot. "We've had the best time, Karl, but I think we're ready to call it a day."

"No problem." Karl radioed to the ground crew and discussed a good landing site. Then he pulled on a cord, which opened a valve at the top of the balloon, which in turn let out enough air to start their descent.

An hour later and back at Granny's house, the three of them were still smiling over their grand Jules Verne–style adventure. Martin and Summer made sure Granny was in comfortable clothes, made her favorite beverage—a pot of white tea with pear flavorings—and then fluffed her pillows and tucked her into bed.

Unfortunately, though, Granny's breathing had gradually become more belabored since they'd gotten home. Even the additional medicine didn't seem to help. Every breath seemed to be a struggle—a searching for air that never seemed to be found.

Granny took a little slurp of her tea, but the tremor in her fingers rattled the teacup enough to spill some of the liquid into the saucer.

"Do you need some help drinking it?" Summer asked.

"No, but thanks. Now I've had the best time ever," Granny said, "so you're both welcome to go on home. I just need some good deep sleep."

"You seem to be struggling to breathe. Maybe I should take you to one of the local emergency centers."

"And what will they do, little love? They will ask me if I'm taking my meds. And I'll tell them that I am. End of story."

Her granny was sweet, but she did have a stubborn streak. Summer stroked Granny's hair. "But maybe they'll make an adjustment of some kind. Or maybe they've found a better drug by now. One that's more effective."

"I've just been to the doctor, and he's giving me the best there is."

"But they could watch over you, and they—"

"Little love." Her grandmother raised a finger, which silenced her pleading.

Summer sighed. "Okay."

"God is watching over me just fine." Granny looked up at Martin. "I'm so happy I got to see you again, Martin. You have been on my mind countless times over the years, and when you came to mind, I always prayed for you."

Martin stepped closer to the bed and gave her hand a pat. "I appreciate that very much, more than you know. I've always wanted to tell you how much you and your bookshop meant to me growing up. I wouldn't trade those years for all the money in the world. It changed my life. *You* changed my life."

"Thank you, dear boy."

"I hope we get to spend more time together in the future."

"Yes, Lord willing, we will." Granny smiled. "I think the medicine is making me drowsy. I don't think I'll be good company now."

"Okay." Summer rose from the bed, kissed her grandmother on the cheek, and she and Martin backed away from the bed. "See you later. Okay?"

"Goodbye," Granny whispered.

Summer waited there until her grandmother had fallen asleep. Her breathing sounded raspy and shallow, but what could she do? She'd been forbidden to take her to the hospital. Should she override Granny's wishes? *Lord, tell me what to do.*

After a few more moments of standing there watching her grandmother's breathing, she nodded to Martin, and they left her room. Summer pulled the house key out of her purse, and after they went out the front door and locked it, she froze on the porch. It had been such an otherworldly way in which her grandmother had said goodbye. Then a voice inside her seemed to speak softly with the words *It's time.* Was that her own inner voice, or was it God giving her a few last moments with her granny? She didn't know for sure, but she wasn't about to walk away now. "Martin. I can't leave. I need to go back inside."

"Your grandmother did look awfully pale." He came back up to the front step.

"Yes, she did. Oh, Martin, we've got to go back in. Quickly." Hands quaking, trying to fit the key back into the lock, finally she gave up, handed Martin the key, and he opened the door. They both rushed through the house to Granny's bedside.

Her grandmother was drawing breath in great heaving gulps. And there was a gurgling sound, almost as if she were drowning. How could she have declined so quickly?

Summer knelt beside the bed. "Granny," Summer said. "I'm going to call 911." She picked up the phone to do that very thing when her grandmother opened her eyes.

"No." Granny took in several more shallow breaths. "Please."

Summer slowly returned the phone to its holder, thinking she was making a terrible mistake. *What am I doing?* Perhaps her grandmother wasn't thinking clearly, and she was having another episode of forgetfulness. She glanced up at Martin, hoping for answers, but none came. He instead rested his hand on her shoulder, which steadied her and helped her to think. Yes, she knew her granny well, and how she'd wanted things to be—how she wanted to pass into heaven from her own home with the people she loved by her side, not surrounded by strangers rushing about with needles and sedatives and hospital tubes and—worst of all—a spirit of anxiousness. *Lord, tell me what to do.*

"It's okay." Granny took another swallow of air. "I'm going home now."

"Oh Lord, please not yet." Summer clutched the bed sheets, twisting them in her hand.

"Why do you pray that way?" Granny murmured between breaths. "I am at peace." She covered her hand over Summer's. "I am about to say hello to Jesus. Only this time not in prayer. This time . . . face to face."

"Yes, I see." Summer gazed down at her grandmother's frail hands. They were hands that had held her, loved her all her life. Over time, wrinkles and veins had tried to age and mar her skin, but to Summer, the veins were marks of wisdom and her hands, instruments of love. To her, they were beautiful. She took hold of Granny's hand and held it to her lips. "Can I do something to make you more comfortable? Anything at all?"

"Don't—forget."

"Forget?" Summer said, trying to force back the tears.

"The list." Granny tried to laugh, but she coughed instead. "It was a gift . . . from God."

"I won't forget. I promise." She kissed Granny's hand, but it was impossible to keep her hand from shaking.

"Don't be—afraid. I'm not."

"Okay."

"God is good. He . . . won't leave you."

"I know. I believe, Granny." She rested her palm against Granny's cheek. Her grandmother's skin had gone cold. "And you always remember that I love you as big and high—"

"As the Texas sky." Granny said in the barest whisper, "But now it will be as big and high as heaven. Even better. Yes?"

"Yes, Granny. It will be." A fresh batch of tears stung Summer's eyes.

Her grandmother stirred slightly and opened her eyes. She struggled for air and then said softly, "Oh, I can hear the words of the hymn . . . my mother used to sing. It . . . must be from the angels. I hear it so . . . clearly, 'Come home, come home. Ye who . . . ' her voiced failed.

"I'll sing it for you. Ye who are weary, come home; Earnestly, tenderly, Jesus is calling . . . " Summer continued to sing the hymn, the one her granny had taught her as a little girl. But she only got a few words of the lyric out when her voice broke with emotion.

"I see Him now." Granny's expression took on a distant gaze. "He's come for me." Granny lifted her finger, pointing toward the foot of the bed. "My Jesus. Oh, His smile, little love. So . . . beautiful."

Summer glanced toward the foot of the bed, desperate to see the Lord, but saw no one standing there. Oh, how she wished she could see Granny's vision, but she supposed the glorious sight of Christ was for her alone.

Granny stared toward the foot of the bed. "I'm ready." Her grandmother closed her eyes, and then her breathing became shallower until there was no breath at all.

"Oh, dear Granny . . ." After a long moment of silence, Summer felt her grandmother's wrist for a pulse. Nothing. She gave her grandmother's hand a squeeze, but she wouldn't feel it—she was busy now, running into the arms of Jesus.

Summer's heart skipped a beat or two and then pounded too hard, making her flush. She looked up at Martin. "She's gone." She smoothed out an imaginary wrinkle on her grandmother's shirt and then gave her a kiss on the forehead. "What will I do without you?"

Oh dear Lord, the pain is so great.

Martin knelt down beside her. He took hold of her hand. "It'll be hard, but your granny was right. The Lord won't leave you."

She stared at her granny's face. Her eyes were closed, but she had the faintest hint of a smile on her lips. *Oh, Granny.* No more of our chats. No more laughter. No more wisdom. The earth, along with her, would surely grieve. Summer buried her head into the soft bedding and wept. When she lifted her head, Martin was there handing her some tissues. The man was a godsend.

"Would you like to pray?" he asked.

Pain clouded her spirit, but she nodded. Together they bowed their heads and Summer began, "Our Father which art in heaven, Hallowed be thy name . . ."

CHAPTER
twenty-five

After the funeral—or the homecoming celebration as Granny wanted it called—Summer spent her days and nights at her grandmother's home. The house had been willed to her, and she was glad to stay there, since it made her feel closer to her granny. The rooms were still full of her personal effects, which brought along with them many comforting remembrances. There were her boxes of letters and family photos. Her window seat full of fluffy pillows for reading and dreaming. Her stacks and stacks of books and her spectacles, as she still liked to call them.

And then there was that ever-present scent of lilac.

She wondered how long it would be before that last trace of lilac would be gone—when the last of Granny would go missing from this world. Would it be then that the memories of her would begin to fade as well? But her grandmother's goodness would linger on the earth until the Lord returned. That was certain.

"And that is the truth," she whispered to herself.

Summer turned over in the twin bed and let out a groan. Her muscles had begun to get stiff from not getting up very often. She also felt weak from hunger, living on an occasional pot pie from the freezer and jars of juice from the pantry. It had been a week or so since the funeral. *Or had it been more?* Hard to know since she didn't care about the passing of time. Everything hurt—mind, body, and spirit. Losing the last of her relatives, and one so beloved, wasn't going to feel all better soon. It felt like a deep cut, a wound that might take a lifetime to heal.

Summer stared at her abandoned knitting project on the night stand—a pink and gray afghan. She'd learned the skill from her mother, and it had brought her pleasure in the past as a fun leisure pursuit, but now it felt useless and boring.

Had it always been so hard—just breathing and putting one foot in front of the other? She turned her attention to the glittery stars Granny had painted on the ceiling, which had been put there to entertain her when she was a child and spent the night for sleepovers. Oh, how that mini galaxy had enchanted her as a girl. Did Granny see those stars up close now?

Tears pooled in her eyes. She was happy for Granny—knowing where she was and that she was no longer suffering or struggling—but the sorrow from the loss was truly awful.

Granny had always been such a font of wisdom. When things went wrong with men or work or life in general, she always relied on her grandmother. Now who would she lean on, except for the Lord?

Summer fluffed her damp pillow and scooted up in bed. *Sorry, Lord. You are more than enough for this feeble soul.* She had indeed felt the Lord's tender mercies since Granny's home-going, and she was grateful. She picked up a glass of water from the nightstand and took a sip. But what had happened to Martin? Where had he gone off to? She hadn't seen him since the funeral. He hadn't come around even to check on her. He hadn't called. And more importantly, had he forgotten about her? Maybe he'd gotten busy with work again. Well, that was understandable. But still, his absence had left a hole in her heart. A big one right next to the one that Granny had left. In fact, it felt as if there wasn't much left of her but holes and remnants of the woman she used to be.

Summer downed the last of the water and burrowed back under the quilt. Drifting in and out of slumber day in and day out had at first felt foreign to her, since she was usually working at the bookshop. But with Amelia at the helm, her concerns in that arena had diminished. Amelia had proven herself to be quite the business-woman—organized, creative, and trustworthy. So much so, Summer wasn't sure if she ever needed to go back. Certainly not right away. But she did miss the stories and the children. She missed the shop, and if Granny hadn't banned her from her work for a short season of time, she would get up right now and drive over there.

Or maybe not. Sleep was becoming more than a luxury now—it felt like an escape, a sanctuary from grief. As that thought wandered its way through her head, she got all drifty with sleep again. In a half-waking, half-dreaming trance she imagined being in the balloon again, flying free above the earth. But just as soon as the vision captured her mind, it was replaced by another—the last breath of Granny and the smile she had on her lips as she passed into the arms of her Lord. Summer sighed, not knowing if it was a good sigh or one with traces of melancholy. Maybe it was both.

But what was that noise? Something tapped on the window. Summer raised her head to see what it might be. Martin? No one was there. Perhaps it was a little sparrow. She wished it were Martin tapping on her window. That thought brought a smile, even if it was a weak one.

Summer shoved her stringy hair out of her eyes as *why* rose on a wave of worry. *Why* hadn't Martin come around? He'd been so attentive, and then suddenly he was gone. Just like when they were children. She reached under her pillow for the carved birds—the treasured childhood gift—that Martin had made for her. The feathered creatures looked so contented in their little nest, so cozy and safe, as if nothing could harm them.

Summer kissed the keepsake and stuffed it back under the pillow.

While staring at the ceiling, she took her ruminations to a deeper level. In her grief, just after the funeral, had she told Martin that she needed some time alone? That day of the funeral had been such a blur, so surreal. But yes, now that she thought about it, she had said something to that effect. Maybe more. That she would call him when she was ready to see him again.

She rose up in bed. *Martin, I'm so sorry. What have I done to you?*

CHAPTER
twenty-six

Martin cruised down Bellaire Boulevard and then turned onto his street toward home. He saw the big house come into view—the Langtree mansion—but he had no intention of stopping by to say hello to his brothers. He'd head straight to the cottage. Ever since his brothers' outburst around the dining room table with Summer in attendance two weeks ago, he hadn't bothered to return to the main house. He'd taken their demands to "get out" seriously, so he stayed to himself in the cottage. He prayed that they would in time see him as their flesh-and-blood brother and also someone who was guiltless when it came to the choices of their parents. But he had no idea how long that would take—or if that day of reconciliation would ever be.

While Martin analyzed this matter he pulled into the Langtree driveway and then stepped on the brakes. *That's odd.* There were two vans parked in front of the house. Two vans—which appeared to be TV remote vehicles from some of the local stations in Houston. What in the world would that mean? Were they talking to Ivan and Desmond? But why? Had something terrible happened? Should he head inside to see what was going on?

Martin shut off the engine. But in that same moment, both of the vans opened and out poured news people, who'd apparently been hidden by the dark tinted windows. The reporters headed toward him with a determined gait and cameras ready. Martin slid out of the car but with some hesitancy.

One of the news people broke from the pack and greeted him—some guy with black-framed glasses and an ID tag that said he was Clark.

Are you kidding me? "How may I help you?"

"Is this the Langtree residence?" Clark asked.

"Yes, that's correct," Martin said. "What's happened?"

"From the descriptions we've been given you're not Desmond Langtree, are you?" Clark took a step closer to Martin.

"No, I'm his brother Martin."

The rest of the news people gathered around and all seemed to speak at once. Finally a woman's voice rose above the others. "I'd like to interview him, but no one is answering the door."

"I'm surprised, since someone is usually at home," Martin said. "But why do you want to interview him? What's this about?" What he really wanted to ask was, *What kind of trouble had Desmond gotten himself into?*

Clark spoke up, "Desmond Langtree saved a young boy's life this morning. He pulled the boy out of a car that had turned over in an accident. The car was on fire, and the moment he pulled the child out to safety, the car exploded. The boy, Peter Raines, is in the hospital recovering with some bruises and cuts. But it was because of your brother that little Peter is alive."

"Really?" *Truly?* Martin could barely find the words to continue. That was amazing. Miraculous, actually.

"Peter's mother told us the story," Clark went on to say, "but we'd like to have Mr. Langtree's response too, since he's the hero of this story."

"Do you think he's at home?" the female reporter asked as she pushed in a little closer.

A few cars driving along the street slowed, apparently to get a closer look at the scene.

Martin backed away from the small group of reporters. "Even if he's here, I can't guarantee Desmond will come out."

"Fine, but we'd appreciate the help if you don't mind. This will make a fine human interest story." Clark smiled widely, and with his brilliant white teeth and persuasive smile it was obvious he was used to getting his story and telling it in front of the camera.

"I'll see what I can do." Martin turned to head up to the house.

"Thank you. We'll be here."

The small assemblage of reporters stood on the lawn with their paraphernalia while Martin hurried to the house to let himself in. He hollered for Ivan and Desmond. No one answered. He then yoo-hooed for Miss Beetle. Nothing. The house appeared to be empty. Being ten thirty on a weekday, he doubted that Desmond would have gone back to bed, but he headed to his bedroom anyway. Maybe he'd been injured, and he wanted to rest. The door was open, so Martin stepped inside his room to take a quick look.

Desmond was indeed in bed, but he was facing away from Martin. Suddenly Desmond's body jerked and shuddered.

"Desmond?" Martin approached his bed. "Are you all right?"

He didn't respond.

Perhaps he had overdosed on one of his meds. Martin went around the other side of the bed to face him. His brother was curled up in a fetal position, and his eyes, bloodshot and swollen, were open, but he stared vacantly out one of the windows.

Martin pulled up a chair from a nearby table and sat across from Desmond. While he sat there quietly, waiting for his brother to speak, he took in his brother's sanctuary, a place he rarely entered. The bedroom, which was a large space, was full of antique furniture as well as accessories like a vintage chessboard, curios and figurines, and even a few antiquities displayed under a glass case. But on the other side of the room stood an old mirror that had a large crack in it, which ran from top to bottom. Perhaps Desmond had broken it on purpose in one of his rages. Not a good time to bring it up. "I'm worried about you. Please tell me if you need a doctor."

"No," was all Desmond said, but his voice seemed distant and raspy. He didn't appear to need a doctor, but it was obvious he was deeply troubled about something.

"Desmond, there are some reporters outside who want to interview you. I heard what you did. I'm really proud of you."

"Tell them to go away." His tone was hollow and without his usual passion.

"But why?" Martin leaned forward, his elbows resting on his knees. "People will be thrilled to hear about this story. You're a hero."

"They won't ever hear those words from me. I'm no hero." Desmond took on a blank stare and said just above a whisper, "I think I'm dying."

CHAPTER
twenty-seven

Martin quickly rose out of his chair. "Were you injured? I was told the car exploded."

"No. Except for a few scratches and bruises, I'm not hurt from the accident."

"Then what's wrong?" Desmond had always been a mystery to Martin, and his announcement was no exception. Perhaps he was experiencing post-traumatic stress disorder from the explosion. Or because his brother struggled with hypochondria from time to time, maybe he only thought he was dying. And yet his skin had an ashen quality to it. "Please tell me why you think you're dying."

Desmond took in a few long breaths, but it was some time before he said, "It's my—hatred."

"Hatred?"

"Well, it's killing me." Desmond seemed to be talking more to himself than to Martin.

Hatred. Martin sat back down. He was glad that his brother wasn't in any imminent danger of dying, and yet what a sad confession. "Who is it that you hate?" But did he really need to ask such a question? The hate in Desmond's eyes was no doubt directed at him. "Is it me?"

"Precisely. I've always hated you, and I encouraged Ivan to hate you too. He's just a copy of me, really, so it was pretty easy to convince him over the years."

Pain wound itself through Martin and tightened into a painful knot. Yet the admission was an odd relief to finally hear the truth out loud. "I thought that was the case. I want to understand why—"

"Please stop."

Martin gripped the arms of the chair. "Stop what?"

"Loving me so much." Desmond resumed his stare out the window. "That is yet another reason to hate you."

"But why?"

"Because I can't take it in as love," Desmond said. "It's like giving food to a starving man who's so sick he can't eat."

"I'm not sure I understand."

"You never did understand Ivan and me. Your love isn't a balm, Martin. It's the knife that reopens our wounds and keeps us from ever healing."

Exhaustion crept into Martin's spirit—from the years of turmoil and misunderstandings, of anger and resentments—and some part of him wanted to strike back at Desmond's accusations. Hadn't he also known what it was like to feel misplaced and unwanted? But more rage and unforgiveness piled on top of their unhappy past would be no way to live. The weight of it would surely be an anvil on all their souls. In spite of the tumult in his heart, Martin still wanted to acknowledge that familial bond, even if it was only a remnant. "I'm sorry you feel that way. But how can I stop loving you both? You're my brothers, my family."

"Your love is a power over us," Desmond said. "Your perfection. Your—"

"I am *not* perfect. Far from it. Why do you both think that? But I'm confused, since one minute you remind me how flawed I am, and then suddenly I'm too perfect. Which is it? I'm lost trying to understand you."

"I guess it all comes down to the way *Father* saw you." Desmond released a cheerless chuckle. "We have lived in your shadow since the day he brought you home, that day he introduced you to us and said you would be part of the family. He was so proud of you and set you up as the resident genius. The one we were to look up to as the oldest. The best. We were to emulate you in every way, but we couldn't. You were not only brilliant in our father's eyes, but you were a saint. So your goodness and love only made more trouble for us. There wasn't even a chance to compete for our father's love. And it's been impossible to exist in that world, the one you and father created for us."

God, what are the right words? "But I never saw either one of you as competition for—"

"Of course you didn't. It's hard to see specks of dust from the top of the tree house." Desmond spit his words out. "You're like this king who lives in the comfort of his castle. You're so high and away and above your subjects that, well, you can't know what it's like to be a peasant."

Martin let that comment sink in for a bit. He wasn't sure how to respond so he just let his brother go on.

Desmond pulled himself up in bed and fidgeted with his signet ring. "Ivan and I couldn't be as smart in Father's eyes or as good, so we just gave up." He reached over to a crystal knickknack of some kind and slowly let his finger push it onto the wooden floor. When he looked down at it, he seemed disappointed that it hadn't broken.

Martin knew a little of their trials, but apparently, he didn't know all of it.

Desmond picked up a family picture, one which he kept in an antique frame by his bed. It was impossible to miss that the photo had been taken before Martin's arrival into their family. "When Ivan and I were little, before you came, there was a lot of whispering around us. As you know, our parents were worried that Ivan and I were damaged from our nanny's 'special penances' for crying. I guess she thought that babies didn't have the right."

He placed the photo back on the night table. "Anyway, our parents—and the doctors—didn't know if we would live a normal life. Everyone was always staring, waiting for us to show signs of impairment. When we messed up on our multiplication table or we'd forget a line in the school play, they'd point their fingers at us. All mistakes, no matter how slight the infraction, were put under a microscope. The knowledge of what the nanny did, shaking us like that when we were infants, well, it was like they were afraid we'd turn into freaks. It never happened, not to the extent that they expected. But learning has never come easily to either Ivan or me. We think the nanny's actions did have a lasting effect, but our parents' methods of dealing with it made us all crazy."

Desmond raised his fist. "But even with this trouble growing up, we were working it out as a family. Ivan and I believed we would never have very high IQs, but it seemed we would have a good life in spite of everything. That is, until the day Father brought you home. Suddenly, the division between our parents widened, and we looked slow and damaged. Especially when compared to you. The day you walked through the door it was like Ivan and I suddenly morphed into the freaks of nature that our parents had always feared."

At first, Martin didn't respond, not knowing what to say. He had never once seen their plight—not from his brothers' perspective anyway. Perhaps this moment was a divine opportunity—one of his brothers was finally talking, really talking, and it was a time for his brother to be heard.

Desmond ran his fingers through his untidy hair and then squeezed the back of his neck. "But I need you to be someone I can hate, you see. Someone who is evil like the nanny. It would have made life so much easier for us. There is such a feeling of justice and rightness when you hate someone who deserves it. But my hate had nowhere to go. It sort of deflected off the good character of Martin Langtree, and it came back to haunt me." He stared at his hands as if looking for something. "And now it's trying to kill me." His hand twisted at the wrist as if deformed.

Such torment. God, help him. "Hate is never easy in the end," Martin said, wishing he didn't sound like a guidance counselor.

"Yeah, spoken like the true saint that you are." The sarcastic edge in Desmond's voice could have cut through the toughest hide.

But right now, Martin didn't feel all that tough. Any hope for understanding seemed to be slipping through his fingers again. He walked to the window, stuffed his hands in his pockets, and stared out at the cluster of trees just beyond the window. Before he could organize his thoughts, he blurted out, "I have memories too."

CHAPTER
twenty-eight

Desmond huffed a bit, but then said, "Oh?"

Martin watched the sparrows land on the trees outside the window, thinking how vulnerable they looked as they rested on the very tips of the branches. They were lucky, though—they had wings to fly away. But then that is what his father and stepmother had done, and it was no less than a disastrous move.

"Before I came to live here," Martin said, "my mother had just died, and I was alone. I was virtually a stranger to everyone in this house, but I was very grateful for a home and a family. Father showed me attention, yes, but I really did want to please my new mother as well. No matter how hard I tried, not once in all those years, did she hug me or tell me that she loved me. Well, she used to grasp me by the arms until they stung. That I do remember. But our relationship became distorted. Well, that's not quite the right word. But the colder she became, the more I tried to please her. One time I remember picking some wildflowers, and I held them out to her as a gift."

Martin stopped, remembering the look on his stepmother's disapproving scowl. "She slapped the flowers out of my hand and said that I should be ashamed of myself for gathering up flowers that didn't belong to me."

Desmond sighed. "I guess I'm supposed to feel sorry for you now."

Martin turned around to look at him. Was his brother void of all compassion?

"Look, I know what you want. You want us to be friends." Desmond took the end of the sheet and dabbed at his forehead. "But there's just so much history between us. And not much of it feels very good."

"But couldn't we make something new here?" Martin asked.

"I don't know," Desmond said blankly. "I keep trying, but this hate of mine has been with me for so long, I'm not sure how to live without it. We're old friends, you see."

"Maybe a loyal friend but not a very good one," Martin said.

Desmond laughed, but this time it had less of the sardonic sting to it.

"One step at a time?"

"Maybe."

Martin stared at his shoes. The strings were unraveled as usual. He leaned down and tied them both, wishing life could be tidied up as easily.

Desmond whispered something to himself as if remembering some of the past. "You're right. You really did work hard at being part of this family. I remember one time after our parents moved to Europe, you tried to keep us under a strict curfew, and we stayed out most of the night just to defy you. But Ivan and I got so tired that we snuck into somebody's backyard and fell asleep instead of going home. We didn't wake up until we heard the truck coming to dump their trash."

"I remember that night, but you never told me where you both went."

"I know." Desmond shook his head and grinned, and then after a long hesitation, he said, "Yeah, I guess we've been pretty strong-willed our whole lives."

Martin sat back down. "I know I got pushy as the oldest."

"Yes, that's right, you did."

"But it came from love not pride." He searched his heart to see if his statement was really the truth. Maybe not so much. "No, I guess that's not quite right. I was so used to being without a father growing up that when Father latched on to me and offered me that praise, well, it meant a great deal to me, especially since Mother showed none of that same attention. But maybe Father's applause did cloud my judgment. And then later when he wanted me to look out for you both because I was the eldest brother and all, well, that was pretty powerful stuff for me. Maybe those emotions gained momentum and eventually turned into pride. I think maybe it did, and that pride has only added to our discord. If I'm not mistaken, pride is considered one of the most grievous sins."

Desmond spread his hands in a sweeping gesture. "Not to worry. I'm sure God is more than willing to forgive Martin Langtree. But with me, I don't know. God and I haven't been on the best of terms."

"Well, God has had to forgive me countless times."

"Oh, yeah, for what? Name one misdeed when we were kids."

"Well, not long after I came to live here, I stole your compass, and when you couldn't find it, I blamed it on your carelessness."

Desmond looked incredulous. "You did that? I got into a lot of trouble, since that compass was expensive. It was a gift to Father from some dignitary, and then he gave it to me, which I have no idea why. It was the only thing he ever gave me that was of any value to him. So you stole it, eh? What did you do with it?"

"I lost the compass, and then later I was too embarrassed to confess; afraid that Father would no longer think I was the noble kid he imagined."

Desmond stared at him for some time. "Well. Maybe you *are* a sinner."

"I can show you my badge if it would help."

"That won't be necessary." Desmond leaned his head against the padded headboard. "What is it about children and their parents? We trip all over ourselves to make sure we're loved. We crave that parental love like drugs, and when we can't get it, well, we take drugs." He sighed. "I guess that news crew is probably still out there, but they can wait a minute or two more. If they get tired of waiting they'll go find a better story. Why don't you open the window? We need some fresh air in this place."

Martin went over to the window, opened the latches, and lifted the glass. Feeling a ray of encouragement from the positive turn of their conversation, he headed into a more encouraging topic. "You know, you and Ivan could have gone to college here in Houston like I did. You're both smarter than you give yourselves credit for. I know this might come off like it's not acknowledging your struggles with learning, but what if—"

"What if what?"

Martin sat back down. "What if all those years, everyone was seeing you through the eyes of what could happen from the nanny's abuse until they sort of made it come true? You know, like a self-fulfilled prophecy. It might have trapped you both in a life that wasn't a reality. It's just a thought. I know you struggled in school, but so did I, especially in areas like art and speech and sports. Not everyone can be good at everything. The subjects you both struggled with happened to be ones our father valued. But just because science and math were his personal preferences shouldn't be the final say in intelligence. There are many kinds of skills and talents, and even brilliance, that don't show up well on aptitude tests."

Desmond rubbed his chin. "I assume you're trying to say that our learning disabilities are in our heads?"

Martin knew he was heading out on thin ice, but an opportunity for this kind of up-close and personal talk with Desmond might never come again. And suddenly this line of thinking seemed like more than mere postulation. "You said yourself that the way they handled the situation was detrimental. And what about that chessboard? You play chess. Shouldn't that say something about your abilities?"

Desmond glanced over at the chessboard, which sat on a small table. "I don't play very well."

"Neither do I."

"Yes, but that's because you don't practice. You could have me locked in a checkmate in a handful of moves."

"I don't know. Sometime we should play. But don't you think my idea is something to think about. Pray about?"

"Prayer. Right. That's something I haven't done in a long time. As a kid you brought God into this house, but we didn't understand your brand of fervor. Our family was always the kind that pretended to know Him. We attended church on all the right days, but we didn't spend much time thinking about God Himself. In other words, we went through the motions, but our hearts weren't in it." Desmond picked up a book off his night table and held it up—it was a book on yoga. "I found this at the bookstore some months ago. I've been trying meditation, but it's . . ."

"It's what?" Martin asked as he sat back down.

"It's not helping. My issues seem to be getting worse. I get these violent thoughts that come out of nowhere. Sometimes I hear . . . voices . . . that tell me to . . ."

"Tell you to do what, Desmond? What were you going to say?"

CHAPTER
twenty-nine

Desmond's face twisted into what looked like torment. "Sometimes I hear voices that tell me to take my life. And lately I've had such thoughts . . . that seem truly evil, like they're from hell itself. Listen to me. It sounds strange. And yet I can't deny it. And this has happened with or without the meds, so I know it's not connected to the pills the doctor gave me." Desmond's voice drifted away.

"Maybe emptying your mind through meditation isn't the answer, but filling it with God is."

"I knew you'd say something like that," Desmond said. "I could have put money on it and won some of my inheritance back." He added with a grin that was almost friendly. "Sorry."

Martin let the topic rest while he gazed around his brother's room. The doors to Desmond's closet were wide open, and there on the floor by the doorframe sat a pile of painted canvases. "What's that in your closet? Paintings?"

"Yes." He held up his hand. "But I promise you I didn't spend any money on them."

"Are they from the attic?" Martin walked over to the closet and picked up one of the canvases to study it. The work of art was amazingly good—a still life using oils—but it had a black X scratched across the middle. What was that all about?

"No, but that's where the paintings are headed, to the attic. If I don't put them away in the attic, I'm afraid Ivan will destroy them completely."

"Why would Ivan want to do that? Are these *his* black markings?"

"Yes." Desmond paused. "I don't know if Ivan wants me to talk about it yet, but those paintings are his."

"What? Really? I had no idea. He's good." Martin examined the art again. Ivan's attention to detail, his unique style, and his mastery of the medium were astounding.

"Well, Ivan has been drawing for years, but he always tears them up and throws them away. That's why you never saw them. But now he's started to paint."

"But this is excellent work. It could hang in a gallery, it's so good. Surely he didn't destroy them all this way." Martin looked back in the closet, and the next one on the pile had the same markings.

"Yes, Ivan ruined them all."

"But why? Why would Ivan do that? He has a great talent I never even knew about."

Desmond sat on the edge of the bed and put on his robe. "This is what happens when a father doesn't encourage a son. Because Ivan wasn't acceptable to our father, he assumes his work must not be acceptable to anyone. So after he draws or paints, he ruins it in some way, so it can't be sold or even enjoyed."

"I still don't understand. That makes no sense."

"It does to Ivan. I guess it's because he's in control of something," Desmond said. "It's all he has. He can say the painting is not good enough before the rest of the world has a chance to say it's no good. That *he's* no good. Don't you see?" He turned his ring around and around on his finger. "Sometimes I've heard him cry out in the night."

Just like he did when he was a kid. Martin set the painting down. How long would the Langtree family continue to be trapped in time—in a desperate need for closure? For understanding? For forgiveness? For love? "I should have said something during those years. I should have taken up for you both. I was trying to be the brother who would watch over you, but I can see that I failed. What I really should have been doing was protect you both from Father's heartless behavior." Sorrow seeped into Martin's spirit. Moisture stung his eyes. No longer able to control his emotions, he turned his face away and wept.

After a few moments, Martin felt a hand on his shoulder.

Desmond said, "And I should have been watching out for you too. Mother didn't treat you right. You did nothing but want a home, like we did. I remember when I saw Mother treating you that way, I was glad. But I'm sorry for that now. For all of it."

Martin nodded.

After a moment, they turned and embraced.

When they released each other, Desmond said, "Maybe I did deserve to lose most of my inheritance. My just deserts as they say. I always was a—let's see—a prideful and pathetic and profligate prodigal." Desmond gave him a weak smile. "But no amount of alliteration or even goodness on my part will keep me from being a prodigal. Born that way I guess."

"To God, there's no one who hasn't been a prodigal child."

"Maybe."

After a thoughtful pause, Martin tried to lighten the moment by saying, "It's pretty warm and humid in here with the open window. We're getting too close to summer."

Desmond grinned. "Is that why you haven't spent any time with *her* lately? You're getting too close to Summer?" He sat down in a nearby chair and looked at Martin intently.

Martin got the connection, but he was certain it wasn't a Freudian slip on his part. "No. It's nothing like that."

"Then why?"

"Because she needed some space right now," Martin said, feeling more secure in allowing himself some candor with his brother. "She was pretty adamant about it, actually."

"What did you do?" Desmond puckered a brow, but his stern expression was tempered with a hint of a smile.

"I didn't do anything. It's just that life is being kind of hard on her right now, and so if she wanted to be alone, well, I wanted to honor that."

"It's her grandmother, isn't it?"

Since Desmond's expression seemed to reflect real concern now, Martin nodded. "Yes. Mrs. Snow died about two weeks ago. I should have told you, but I didn't feel like coming over here. I was wrong. I'm sorry."

"Oh. I see. Pretty heavy stuff." Desmond clawed his fingers over his hair.

Martin hated to make his brother feel worse than he did, since he seemed genuinely remorseful, so he closed the closet doors and replied, "She loved her granny deeply."

"Yes, I'm sure she did," Desmond said. "Will you ever be bringing Summer around again, so I can tell her that I'm sorry for her loss? And apologize for ordering her out of the house that day?"

"Yes, I hope so, someday." Martin went over to the window and closed it.

"Little Summer Snow. Such a pretty girl and such a loyal friend to you . . . at least from what you told me when you first came into the family. I envied you that friendship . . . more than you know." Desmond stirred in his chair. "That's the reason why I made up the lie when we were kids, when I told you that Summer didn't want to continue with the friendship after we moved. It felt like the perfect revenge. And it was the same reason I hated hearing about that adventure list of yours, the one you were doing with Summer. Envy. But I see how childish I've been."

Martin felt a surge in his spirit, so grateful for the changes in his brother. He felt as though he would burst if he didn't share what was on his mind. "Listen, I've got an idea." He sat down in a chair across from his brother. "I want to talk about college again. I know

Father didn't encourage either of you to go, but it was a mistake on his part. I really do believe it's not too late."

Desmond grinned. "So what brought on this college thing?"

"I don't know. It just seemed like the right thing to say. Well, and I have thought about it on and off through the years. I just never brought it up." *Like so many topics in their family*. He leaned forward, resting his arms on his legs. "I'll help you and Ivan with tuition if you'd both consider it."

Desmond looked away, his face strained with emotion. "You'd do that? Really?"

"Yes, I would."

"Even after all we've done and said?" Desmond asked.

"Yes."

Desmond looked straight at him then. "But why? For some reason I need to know."

"Because you two are my brothers. My family. And always will be. That's the way I see it. I'm afraid you're stuck with me."

"I see." Desmond relaxed his shoulders. "You're a pretty good brother to be stuck with. Anybody else might have wanted to shoot Ivan and me by now."

Martin snickered.

Desmond pulled off his socks and let them drop on the floor. "I'll think about your offer of helping me with college, but I doubt I'll take your money. And it *is* your money, Martin. In spite of Father's lack of interest in me, I know I've been given a lot over the years. That is, monetarily. But it's taught me nothing but idleness. Since Ivan and I went begging for our father's attention, we felt we deserved the money. Hey, if you can't have love, you might as well take the money, right? But that mindset wasn't healthy. It's kept us trapped into accepting everything and giving nothing back but bitterness. And now, thanks to my poor management of the money, even that is gone. Just as well. I need to find my own way now."

Desmond rubbed the back of his hand over his mouth as he stared at the floor. "Look at me. I don't even pick up after myself." He picked up his socks off the floor. "I'll bet Miss Beetle is pretty sick of us by now. Well, she was probably ready to leave a decade ago." He shook his head. "I don't know why she stays on, putting up with our inconsideration."

"I think she hated to be one more person to abandon us. She's a pretty loyal kind of woman."

"Right. I guess so. Somebody should give her a bonus, a big one. I would do it if I had any money," Desmond stated.

"I should have given her a bonus years ago. Maybe I will."

"No, please don't. Miss Beetle doesn't clean your cottage, so you shouldn't have to pay for that too. I'll find a way to reward her."

"Okay."

"Glad that's settled." Desmond fingered an antique music box on the table. "Maybe I could sell some of my antiques. There are a few pieces that would sell for quite a lot. That way I can help."

Martin wanted to speak up with some words of encouragement, but Desmond didn't seem to be finished.

"If you knew, really knew the truth of what happened today with the boy in the car accident, you wouldn't want to be so . . ."

What did Desmond mean? "You mean saving that boy's life? But that was heroic. I am so proud of the way—"

"No. Please." Desmond held up his hand. "I'm going to tell you why I didn't want to be interviewed by the reporters." He rubbed the back of his neck. "Do you think they've finally gone away?"

"No. They're probably still out there. They were pretty adamant about talking to you."

"I want them to go away."

"But why?" Martin asked. "What you did was selfless and courageous. There's no reason you shouldn't talk to them. Right?"

Desmond's expression withered some. "But the story isn't what you think it is."

"Do you want to tell me?"

"Not really, but I must, for my own sanity." Desmond ran his fingers along the arms of the chair. "I was on one of the country roads near the city when I saw a car that had turned over. It appeared that the accident had just happened. I saw a woman outside her car, waving for me to help her. She was red-haired and beautiful. I was mesmerized by her, and I found myself parking the car and running to help her. I only thought she needed me to phone someone."

Desmond shifted in his seat. "But when I got closer I saw that she was trying to tell me that her son was still inside the car, and that there was smoke. She had injured her arm and was having trouble pulling him out. I hesitated, knowing the car might explode at any moment. But wanting to be a hero, I burrowed inside the car, undid the boy's safety belt, and pulled him out. His mother was ecstatic, of course. Then we backed away from the vehicle just in time, because moments later, the car did indeed explode. The boy would have no doubt died."

"Now that's an amazing story."

"But I wonder. Had the woman not been so beautiful and had I not wanted to be her hero, would I have stopped to help? We would have had a very different story to tell today." Desmond pressed his finger against his forehead. "The thing is, I don't know for sure, and it will be that question that will haunt me the rest of my life."

"I believe you would have saved the boy no matter what," Martin said.

"I wish I could believe you. Only God knows the truth." Desmond looked toward the door and frowned. "What's that noise in the hallway? Ivan? He was supposed to have come home by now. He's been hunting for a job again."

"I'm right here." Ivan stepped inside the bedroom and leaned against the doorframe sporting a sheepish expression. "I heard it all, and I guess it's been a long time in coming—this forgiveness thing.

And Martin, on that college tuition offer, I say, 'sure, why not?' That is, if the offer is still open."

Martin smiled. "It is. But only if you help with the expenses."

"I can, and I will." He pressed his hand over his chest. "You'll be happy to know I do have a job. As of today, I'm officially an assistant to the director at the Manchester Art Gallery downtown."

"Good, Ivan. Excellent," Desmond said as his voice gained momentum.

"That is very good news," Martin said, feeling genuinely proud of his brother for following through.

"Thanks."

"We need to celebrate," Desmond said. "But maybe we can find a way to do it without spending the last cent of our inheritance."

"We can try." Ivan said. "But for now, what are we going do to with those reporters on our lawn?"

"You mean they're still there?" Desmond groaned.

"Yep."

"Tell them no," Desmond said. "I just can't."

"Are you sure?" Ivan asked. "Look, I know your reasoning, but it still might be fun to be on the evening news, looking like a superhero and all that. You'd have everything but the cape." He grinned.

"You may tell the reporters this: I'm not a hero of any kind," Desmond said. "If they want to interview a real hero they can go to any police or fire station. Those men and women save lives like this all the time."

"May I quote you on that?" Ivan asked.

"Yes." Desmond waved him on. "Now go tell them, before they pitch a tent out on our front lawn."

"I'm proud of you," Ivan said.

"I don't know why," Desmond replied, "but thank you."

"We're not going to hold hands now and sing campfire songs, are we?" Ivan asked.

"No," Martin said.

"Good. By the way, Desmond," Ivan went on to say, "we are a lot alike, yes, but we're not copies. Okay?"

Desmond nodded. "Okay."

Then Ivan slapped the doorframe and headed down the hallway.

When he'd gone, Desmond walked over to the night table, picked up his book on mediation, and after gazing at the cover, he let it slip from his hand into a waste bin. "I need some time alone now. I might have a few things to say to God."

Martin walked to the bedroom door. "I'll come back and check on you later, if you want me to."

"No. You should go and check on Summer. What she said . . . well, that sounds like grief talking. There's no way she'd give you the boot." Desmond picked up his jeans and shirt off the floor.

"Maybe you're right," Martin asked. "By the way, how did you know I hadn't been seeing Summer lately? I've stayed to myself in the cottage."

"Because when you walked into the room earlier, the light was gone from your eyes. The same light I've seen since Summer returned."

"Oh."

"Something's been going on between you two."

"That's true." Martin shuffled his feet and thought how juvenile that looked. "But I wasn't sure what Summer felt."

"You know, for someone as smart as you are, I'm surprised you can't see it."

"See what?"

"Martin." Desmond held open his hands in an *isn't-it-obvious?* gesture. "Summer is falling in love with you."

CHAPTER
thirty

"Really?" Martin asked. *Can it be true?*

"I've seen the way Summer looks at you." Desmond grinned. "And it sure isn't the way she looked at you when you two were kids. There's something else going on behind those blue eyes. I mean, I can't know for sure. Who can know the heart of a woman? But you'd be a fool not to try to find out how she feels."

Martin gazed at his hand, which had a death grip on the door handle, like his hand had been fused to the metal. He was overwrought. Was that the word? He'd never felt such turmoil and joy in his life. But then why not? This was no ordinary woman. His feelings had already become so intense and private that he was afraid to tell his brother all of it. But to him, his precious Summer was as memorable as Beethoven's Fifth. As brilliant as the theory of relativity. And what else? As beautiful as a work by Michelangelo. Yes, to him, this was Summer Snow. But Martin kept these deeper feelings to himself and simply replied, "It's just that, well, I was so grateful for Summer's friendship, I wasn't sure if I should hope for more. I mean, what if she didn't feel the same way? I could—"

"You could drive her away? You can't play it safe, man. Not when it comes to love." Desmond rolled his eyes and laughed. "Listen to me. What do I know about it, really? I've never been in love. But still, if I were you, I'd get going."

"All right."

"And considering what just happened with her grandmother, Summer might need someone around to share her grief, in spite of what she said."

"Yes. Good call. I can't believe I've left her alone so long." Martin turned to go and then looked back at his brother. "Are you going to be all right now? I'm mean really?"

"I think so." Desmond nodded. "Thanks."

"You're welcome."

"Now go," Desmond said, shooing him out the door. "The season of Summer has arrived."

Martin waved, hurried down the back staircase, and out the door to his car. As he pulled out the driveway, he took note that the TV vans had all gone. Guess Ivan had done a good job in sending them away. Desmond's courageous act would have no doubt been a good human interest story. But then if he'd told the news crew that he thought the real reason for the good deed was to impress the boy's attractive mother, well, that would have taken a bit of the shine off the report.

And yet, how many heroic deeds through the ages could be considered completely free of "self"? Even in his youth when his father had lifted him up as a noble specimen of boyhood, had he not been the opposite when he failed to foster goodwill between his brothers and their father? There was only one clear answer to that question. He had taken his elder brother status seriously, but not in the ways that really mattered. *Lord, help me. I allowed pride to get in the way of love.*

As he sped across Houston on 610 and then 290, he wondered if he'd allowed the same thing to happen with Summer. After attending the funeral with her, he'd stayed away, not just to give her the space she'd asked for, but also because her words had bruised his pride. A better man would have set his feelings aside and put the needs of another first. Perhaps he wasn't even worthy of Summer's affections. Since he knew Summer was staying at her grandmother's house, he headed toward the Snow residence, hoping that he'd find Summer doing well.

A half an hour later, he rang the bell. Growing more and more impatient to see if Summer was all right, he knocked on the door for good measure. He tapped his foot. And then he leaned on the door, drumming his fingers.

Just when he considered pounding on the door, it opened.

Before him stood Summer, but not the girl he'd always known. Grief had ravaged her sunny countenance. Her sparkling blue eyes were shadowed with dark circles, and she appeared thin in her long night dress. "Aiya," he said.

"Aiya," she repeated. "But where have you been, Martin?" she asked whisper soft.

"Can you ever forgive me? When you said you didn't want to see anyone for a while, that you wanted to be alone, I should have checked on you anyway." *Even if you'd said, "get out." Even then.*

"I'm sorry I hurt you by saying that. It's just that I couldn't stand for you or anyone from church to see me this way, even when they offered to bring me food. I know God doesn't want us to grieve as the world does, and I knew that was exactly what I would be doing. I was ashamed for anyone to see me like this. Oh Martin, I've been such a—" Summer teetered as if she would fall over.

Martin didn't give her another second to falter. He was next to her in a moment and lifted her up into his arms. "Do you need to lie back down?"

"Yes. I think so." Summer circled her arms around his neck. "The guest bedroom at the end of the hallway."

Martin carried Summer to the room that she specified and gently laid her down on the bed. He slipped her house shoes off and tucked her in with the quilt. *Oh my.* There were those auburn tendrils here and there around her face. His hand almost reached out to touch them, to move them from her dampened face, but he held back. No matter how much he wanted to share his new feelings,

Summer might not appreciate him coming over with amorous intentions when what she needed was food and friendship.

"Thank, you. I'm being so silly." She smoothed her hands along the bed cover. "I'm weak because I haven't eaten, and that's my own fault."

"You are looking kind of wispy."

"Wispy?" A faintest smile lighted on her lips. "Did you really say that?"

"I've never said that word in my life, so I don't know where it came from. But you do look wispy."

"You sure you don't mean wonky?"

"I'm sure." He grinned. "You should eat. I could make something or go out and pick up whatever you like." He stepped toward the bedroom doorway.

"No. Now that you're here, well, no need to go right away." She blushed. "Please."

"No need to go." *None at all.* "Okay, how about some chicken soup? Is there any of that in the pantry?"

Summer paused. "Yes, there might be. That does sound good. Something easy to make and easy to go down."

"All right, chicken soup it is. Good comfort food." He smacked his hands together. "Be right back."

"Martin?"

"Yes?"

She opened her mouth as if to speak, but then shook her head. "Nothing."

"Are you sure?" He took a step closer to her, hoping she would say more. Maybe she would speak of the affections that Desmond had mentioned.

"It's that . . ." Summer faltered. "I so appreciate your friendship. It means so much to me. The older I get the more I realize how precious a good friendship can be."

Martin smiled, but he knew his expression wasn't all that animated. "I appreciate your friendship too." Then he walked out of the room, wanting to pound his head against the wall for not speaking first, to say what was on his mind.

CHAPTER
thirty-one

Summer stared at the doorway where Martin had been. His stride was unmistakably heavier than when he'd first arrived. His expression, which had previously been lifted in hope, seemed to sag at the mention of friendship. Had he expected her to say something different? Something more? Perhaps. It grieved her not to speak up, to know for sure what was on his mind, but telling him what was really brewing in her heart didn't seem wise at the moment.

If Martin didn't feel those first stirrings of love, it might hurt their friendship, perhaps even destroy it. She couldn't bear to lose him as a friend. And certainly not after losing dear Granny. And then there was the Elliot factor. Pursuing a new romantic relationship so soon after her breakup wasn't using common sense. And yet Martin wouldn't run away if things got too uncomfortable emotionally. It wasn't in his nature.

On the other hand—and why did there always have to be another hand?—a romantic revelation would no doubt change everything between them. Like a bucket of paint dropped on white carpet. The fibers would be forever colored. Nothing would ever be the same. Nor could it be.

It was official—she was at an impasse. Perhaps time would work it out.

Or not.

Summer slapped the bed. Why was falling in love so vexingly complicated? So impossibly dreadful? And surprisingly wonderful all at the same time? Strange that those feelings were almost foreign to her. Had she really not loved Elliot at all? Then what had she felt? Admiration? An affectionate attachment without the real thing? What if she'd married without love? *God, thank You for protecting me from myself. I have been the queen of fools.*

But what was that smell? She lifted her night garments and gave them a whiff. *Oh. It's me.* That's what happens with no shower and no clean clothes. Guess that was one of the reasons she'd told Martin that she might need some space after the funeral. She knew he'd see her like this—a mess—not to mention an immature, emotional disaster.

She shoved her hair out of her face. So how bad could it be? Summer opened the drawer on the night table, yanked out a mirror, and with a shaky hand, gazed at her reflection. *Oh, great day in the morning,* as her granny always said. To call herself disheveled would have been an understatement. Added to her lack of recent showering and grooming, her hair's propensity to frizz made her head look like it had been plugged into a live outlet. None of that had ever mattered before when she and Martin were only friends.

Now everything felt different.

She grabbed a brush from another drawer and gave her defiant hair a good thrashing, which made it frizzle even more. Then she smoothed it back severely and tied it with a scrunchie. There, not good. But better. Then Summer reached up to a shelf above the bed, removed a favorite teddy bear, and hugged it to her.

Martin popped back in the doorway with a tea towel thrown over his shoulder. "I want to know why you haven't been eating. You look too thin."

"What?" Martin's abruptness took Summer by surprise. "I don't know." She scooted up in bed against the pillow. "I suppose I let sorrow get the upper hand." She sighed.

"I'm heating your soup right now, and I'm brewing some very strong black tea."

"That sounds pretty good."

"And from looking around in the kitchen," Martin said, coming toward her with concern, "I see the little bit that you have been eating and it makes me think you're trying to do yourself in."

"What?" Once Summer recovered from the shock of Martin's blunt comment, she asked, "Why would you think such a thing?"

"Because there is a half-eaten can of cat food in the kitchen, and I remember your grandmother saying that her cat died almost a year ago."

"Cat food. What?" Summer searched through the fog in her head for answers. "Oh, no. So that's why that tuna tasted off. Good thing I didn't eat the whole can." Summer shivered inside and swiped at her mouth. "This is disgusting." *I'm disgusting*. She plucked a few tissues from a box on the nightstand, and not caring that Martin saw it, scrubbed off her tongue with the tissues. "Eewww. I hope I'm not going to be sick. "I can't believe I let things get this bad."

Martin shook his head and stuffed his hands into his pockets.

"It's not your fault, Martin. I was just so bleary-eyed with sleep and grief that I wasn't paying any attention to what I was doing." She thought more about her deed. "I can't believe I ate cat food. That can't be too healthy."

"I think it'll be okay this once, but if you start feeling funny I'm taking you to the emergency room, okay?"

"Okay." Summer fiddled with the corner of the sheet, flicking in between her fingers and feeling like a kid. "You sound angry."

"I am. I'm angry at myself for allowing you to go so long by yourself when I should have been checking up on you. Here you are, barely able to get out of bed and you're eating pet food."

"Look, I promise it's not your fault. Granny would be ashamed of me, the way I'm carrying on. This isn't what she would want. She's happily tucked into heaven now with family and friends as well as her Savior. I know this, so what you see is a woman who is feeling sorry for herself. I am anguishing over *my* loss."

"You should feel some anguish. It's okay, Summer. Don't be too hard on yourself. I knew your grandmother well enough to know she will be terribly missed by many people I'm sure, including me."

"Thanks. Truly, Martin. I do feel better."

"And something else you're wrong about."

"Oh? What's that?"

"Your granny wouldn't be ashamed of you. If she could see you, she'd know how much you loved her and miss her. Most people would give anything to be loved like that. But eventually, yes, she would want you to fulfill your destiny just as she did."

"My destiny. I guess I've always been a little short on that one."

"Isn't that what the list was for?" Martin sat down on the bed.

"Oh, the list. I guess there are still of couple of things to do on that thing."

"That *thing*?" He tilted his head at her. "Are you sure you don't want to finish it?"

"I'm not sure about a whole lot right now, but yes, I guess so." She gestured to the waste bin by her bed. "In a moment of misery, thinking that the list meant nothing without the woman who created it, well, I crumpled it and tossed it into that trash basket."

"Really? But you made a promise to your grandmother that you'd finish it."

"I was hoping you wouldn't remember that."

"I do remember. So what's left on the list?"

"Two things." Since the last item on the list was *Kiss Someone You Love*, Summer felt that would be too uncomfortable to bring up at this point. "The next thing is for me to sing in public. I'm really not up for it. I'd just freak out or have a meltdown or do something equally embarrassing."

"You're not going to have a meltdown. You did have a beautiful singing voice," Martin said. "I remember when you sang a few times at the bookstore. You know, when we put on our little made-up plays on her stage?"

"You remember that?" Summer covered her face with the sheet. "I was such a little show-off."

"No, you weren't. You were good. Did your grandmother secretly hope you'd go into music?"

"Not necessarily. She just wanted me to try if I wanted to. She thought I never got a chance, you know, taking care of my parents and all. I used to love to sing in high school, but that was so long ago. Feels like a lifetime ago. I can't imagine pursuing anything like that now. It's too late anyway."

"It's never too late," Martin said.

"Yeah, I've heard that old expression. Well, at least I will finish the list for Granny. Okay?"

"Good."

"Of course I'll be terrified singing in public, wherever it is."

"Maybe you could practice while you're singing in the shower," Martin said.

Shower. Oh dear, he said shower. The ripe smell. It was a hint. "I guess you noticed I have stopped showering."

"Hard not to notice. The off-gassing is pretty bad. Toxic levels and all. I'm thinking about hosing you down with disinfectant." He grinned.

"Disinfectant." Summer grabbed a loose pillow and gave him a solid whack, hoping it would hit him dead-on. It did, even though he tried to duck.

"Hey. I'd forgotten how lethal you are with a pillow."

Summer wanted to laugh. "You're getting kind of pushy in your old age."

"I'll rather be too pushy than not show up."

She almost walloped him again with another blow of her pillow but then lowered it. "You're never going to forgive yourself for this, are you?"

"Probably not."

Summer smiled.

"It's good to see you smile again. By the way, I did get some work done while I was away, so I'm caught up enough to go with you to that bohemian café you mentioned."

"Let's do it." Summer felt an overwhelming desire to hug Martin then, but she instead grabbed her teddy bear and hugged it to her. "This is the room I always stayed in when I had sleepovers with Granny, ever since I was little. Lots of stories were told in this room, and there was lots of cocoa and lots of love."

He looked down at the fuzzy companion resting in her arms. "So is this your bear from childhood? I assume you had a unique name for him."

"His name is Hercules." She held up her bear proudly, but one of the arms dangled loosely by some threads.

"I think Hercules has been trying to fight one too many monsters. His arm is falling off."

"Yes, he's been that way for years." Summer planted a smoochy kiss on her little bear, wishing it were Martin's cheek.

"I'll bet it just needs a needle and thread and a little loving attention, and it'll be good as new." Martin stared at her, and then he leaned toward her slowly, almost as if he were going to kiss her. "You might find it interesting to know that there are Egyptian paintings of stuffed animals around their tombs, so some believe the concept of having a stuffed animal to hold and to kiss has been popular for a very long time." He hovered even closer to her face.

"To hold and kiss. Is that so?" Summer leaned toward him, wanting to bridge the gap between them. "Tell me more."

Suddenly the teakettle let go with a shrill whistle, interrupting them and making her startle.

"I'd better get that," he said.

When Martin left the room, Summer slid back down under the covers with a lamenting mutter, just shy of a serious pout. Then in spite of his bum arm, she flung Hercules across the room. *And I'd like to throw that teakettle across the room too!*

So close. Or maybe she'd only imagined Martin had wanted to kiss her. Could a woman want a kiss so badly that she could conjure up things that weren't there? Oh well, maybe it was best—she hadn't had a shower and so the kiss would have been more malodorous than melodious. She smiled at the corny thought.

Poor Hercules. She got up and retrieved her teddy bear, gave him a kiss, and then before climbing back into bed, she reached over to the waste bin and pulled out Granny's list. The crumpled mess made her sad all over again. "I'm sorry, Granny." She laid the paper against her knee and tried to smooth out the wrinkles. "I can't make it right." Maybe she'd crumpled the list because she was mad at God for taking the last of her family. *Oh dear.* She pressed the parchment against her face and breathed in. The scent of her granny's perfume was still on the page. No, it wasn't really on the page, but she could imagine it. "Oh, how I miss you." Tears squeezed from her eyes and ran onto the paper.

Summer pulled the page back and stared at it—the wetness from her tears smeared the lovely penmanship and a few of the pretty swirls. "I'm sorry, Granny. I just got lost in my grief for a while, and I didn't see the point in going on since you were in heaven. And God, if I'm upset with You, which I probably am, show me how to let that go. I know it's not a good way to live."

She held up the paper toward heaven. "Please God, take good care of Granny. Of course You will. And if You would, please tell her that I will finish the list. I will. And tell her I'll be all right now. Thanks for watching over me and all my foolishness, Lord." The rest of the prayer, she said silently. *I'm glad You sent Martin. Thank You for that. I just wish he were more than my best friend. If You don't mind, maybe You could help me with that too. It's getting complicated. I love You.* She folded the paper gingerly and set it on the night stand.

Martin arrived in the doorway, but he wasn't smiling.

"What happened?"

"I burned the soup. I think we're down to cat food or eating out."

Summer frowned. "Did you do that just to get me out of the house?"

"Yes."

"Okay." Oh, how she loved Martin's honesty.

"But first I have a surprise on the other side of this wall." He grinned.

"Surprise? What is it?"

Martin reached around on the other side of the doorway and brought out a small dog carrier.

"You brought Laney?" She clapped. "Oh, thank you, Martin."

He opened the crate door, took Laney out, and placed the small dog into the waiting arms of Summer. The dog licked her cheek and it felt like tiny kisses. "You little sweetie." She set her down on the bed, and Laney circled around happily. Then Summer let the dog cuddle down into the curve of her arm. "I missed you, Laney." She rocked her gently like a baby.

Martin smiled, but his shoulders sagged a bit.

"I missed you too, Martin," Summer added.

CHAPTER
thirty-two

Two days later when Summer felt revived from the food and the prayer and the loving attention from Martin, she let him drive her to the Scrapheap Café—the beatnik-style eatery in the Heights that she'd told him about.

When he parked in front of the café, which was a hodgepodge of shanties nailed together and painted an interesting array of non-coordinating colors and topped with a tin roof, she asked, "So what do you think of the place?"

Martin shrugged. "Looks like a dump."

Summer smirked. "It *is* a dump. That's why the name of the place is the Scrapheap Café." She fluttered her eyelashes, pretending to be a snob. "It's supposed to be chic and cater to an eclectic crowd." Summer rubbed her arms. "I think I'm coming down with a cold. I feel chilled."

Martin turned off the car's air conditioner. "I think you're scared, but you have no reason to be."

"I guess that's why I've been running off at the mouth. Look, Martin, they don't want to hear my song. I know they don't."

"You can't know that." Martin took her by the shoulders and turned her to him. "Remember when your grandmother told you that the list was more than just a list? She had prayed over it a great deal while she was creating it. I believe God is in this day whether you ever pursue music professionally or not."

"Okay. Yes. I do think that. It's just that I'm not used to singing in public."

"Just sing to God, not me, not anyone in the room. Just to God, and you'll be okay."

"Okay." *Sing to God, not anyone else.* Summer repeated his words, hoping they would sink in.

Martin opened the car door for Summer and helped her out. The moment felt like a date, and she relished the thought, wishing it was that very thing. But she wasn't sure if that knowledge would make singing any easier. Probably not.

They stepped inside the eatery, and Summer looked around, trying to concentrate on the surroundings and not what she was about to do. The décor reeked of cold metal and scrap wood and all things cast-off. Maybe the owners were trying to make a statement about belonging—especially if that person was misunderstood in a world that didn't always get those with artistic dreams.

Summer glanced upward. A corkscrew-like staircase led up to a rustic balcony, and a pop art portrait of Andy Warhol painted in primary colors dangled on chains from the second story. Yes, it was indeed an artsy place, and the crowd appeared to fit in well with the surroundings. There was an assorted array of piercings and ink and mohawks and goth attire.

I am in so much trouble just singing a hymn. Would they boo her off the stage? Toss wadded napkins at her?

No matter what, though, she would follow through. *Just sing to God.* She kept close to Martin's words, running them through her head as a pep talk.

Martin pressed his hand on her back and led her to an empty table. He made no comment about the café or its customers. Maybe he was afraid to say anything that might make her bolt.

When the server showed up at their table—a woman wearing steampunk attire and cologne that smelled a lot like weed—Martin ordered for them. Two root beers straight up. Sounded good, but when the drinks came, Summer couldn't move. Life became one of those slow-motion blurs where everything was dreamlike. Summer considered fleeing for her life, since it wouldn't matter then, if it was really all a dream. Right? But instead of fleeing, she sat still like a rock.

The young woman up on stage—whose face had drained of most of her lifeblood and whose skin tone had taken on the hue of wax paper—was reading a poem called "Hemlock." None of the words made sense to Summer, though. Something about doom and men and marriages gone toxic. In the meantime, Martin slurped on his soda, looking cheerful. Guess he was trying to keep her at ease so she wouldn't run out the back door. Which was becoming more tempting by the second.

Then the poem lady curtsied slightly and walked off the stage to scattered applause.

Martin said nothing, but she knew—it was time. *Now or never.*

Summer rose from her chair, which made the silly thing scrape across the wooden floor with an ireful sound and made all heads turn her way. She walked on wobbly legs to the small stage area and took her place behind the mike. Suddenly she realized that she should say something before she sang her song. The hymn would have infinitely more meaning with some background, some history about how the song was in memory of the precious woman she called Granny. Why hadn't she practiced something to say? *Lord, please help me. I'm out on a long, thin limb. I can't go back, but I'm about to fall.* Then a voice came—a still small voice.

I've got you, Summer.

Martin looked at her and smiled, but he also nodded, giving her the encouragement to begin.

"Hi. I'm Summer Snow. I'm going to sing, but first I want to tell you why. My granny passed away very recently, and boy, do I miss her. She wasn't the kind of grandmother who baked gingerbread cookies or planted a garden of roses, but she loved a good story.

Granny Snow owned a small children's bookshop in northwest Houston called Once Upon a Time. Maybe some of you have heard of it, since it's still there. Granny never made a lot of money, but she always felt her life was rich in other ways, like by having the opportunity to love all the children who came through her bookshop."

Summer shifted her feet and gripped the mike more tightly. "Years later when those same children grew up, some of them came back to tell her what she'd meant to them. They said it wasn't just the books she read to them or the stories she told but the way she treated them, like they were the most wonderful creatures that God ever made and that they could accomplish great things with His help. And they believed her, of course, because it was true. This song is dedicated to that woman—to Granny Snow. It was her favorite hymn, and we sang it together just before she left for heaven." Summer cleared her throat and began the lyrics that she'd memorized as a little girl.

> Softly and tenderly Jesus is calling,
> Calling for you and for me;
> See, on the portals He's waiting and watching,
> Watching for you and for me.
> Come home, come home,
> Ye who are weary, come home;
> Earnestly, tenderly, Jesus is calling,
> Calling, O sinner, come home!

Summer suddenly choked on *home* and stopped. She put her finger over her lips to control her tears but they came in spite of her internal demand that she get her act together, that she not fall to pieces in front of a roomful of strangers. But it was no use.

She looked at Martin, who was still smiling, but as she looked around the audience, they too were smiling.

And then Martin stood, alone at first, but soon, one by one, everyone in the café stood. They seemed to be waiting for her, wanting her to take her time to get control again so she could finish. So she could share this celebration of Granny's life with them.

Yes, I will finish for Granny. Summer started in again, and sang the lyrics as sweetly and clearly as she could. She sang for the Lord. She sang for Granny. And she sang for all the people in the room who needed to know these hope-infused lyrics. When the last of the song was finished, the café—which had previously been littered with noise—was now as quiet as falling snow.

Then came something Summer had not expected.

Applause.

CHAPTER
thirty-three

Two days later, Martin still felt the warmth of that moment in the café when the audience rallied around Summer and the song she sang for her grandmother. Her voice had been so lovely. Why had she ever given up singing? It was obviously a gift from heaven. The only downside to the day was that he still hadn't asked her out on a real date. The timing always seemed off. But soon, very soon, he would make his intentions known.

Desmond hollered from the kitchen that lunch was almost ready.

"Thanks. I'll be there in a minute," Martin yelled back from his room at the top of the stairs. Since their day of epiphany, Desmond had continued to explore the past and heal as well as move forward with the choice of forgiveness. And because Ivan couldn't do anything without his brother—no matter how much they argued and pretended to hate each other—he too had embarked down that same redemptive road. So much so, the three of them had begun the process of becoming friends. It was awkward at first, but the first seeds of brotherhood were indeed taking root. Now if Martin could only figure out how to stay at the big house without having to eat Desmond's cooking.

Martin trotted down the long, winding staircase as the doorbell rang insistently. Whoever was on the other end couldn't seem to stop pushing the button.

"Hey, can somebody get that?" Desmond called out, still in the kitchen.

"Got it." Martin opened the door, not bothering to look through the peephole, thinking it might be a neighbor in need. It didn't appear to be, though, since two strangers stood on the porch—two well-dressed professionals to be more exact—who'd taken grooming to a new and painful looking level.

The taller of the two strangers said, "My name is Elliot Whitfield. Are you Martin Langtree?"

"Yes, I am." Martin shook his finger. "You know, you look a little familiar. Are you the Whitfield who's running for office?"

The man smiled, splaying his hand over his heart. "Yes. And this is my campaign manager, Kent Robertson."

They both reached out their hands, and Martin completed the pleasantries, thinking they were doing some canvassing for votes.

Elliot Whitfield tapped his thumbs against his now folded hands, looking as if patience was not his strongest virtue.

"I'm sorry we don't have any babies here to kiss," Martin said, trying his best at a political joke.

Both men displayed practiced smiles. When Mr. Whitfield changed his expression abruptly, so did his sidekick. Solemnly, he said, "But you *do* have something I want."

"Oh?"

Elliot Whitfield cleared his throat. "I'm here because I found out that Summer Snow is going out with you."

Martin had some trouble finding his speech again. "Well, we've not had an official date yet. But may I ask why you'd need this information?" *Or how you'd even know this kind of information?*

"That's very diplomatic of you to word it that way since I'm sure you think this is none of my business."

"That thought had crossed my mind." Martin grinned but he knew it wasn't as congenial as before.

Whitfield smoothed his tie. "Well, I'll get right to the point."

I wish you would. Whitfield was starting to annoy him—a real Mr. Smooth. He had glossy hair, skillful speech, and an impeccable suit. Martin wondered if those polished qualities came from continuous perfecting, or if a man could be born that way.

The other man, Kent, took one step back and clasped his hands in a way that looked more like a bodyguard than a campaign manager—especially since he'd still not removed his sunglasses.

Mr. Whitfield raised his chin and said, "Summer Snow is my fiancée."

"What?" Martin's heart lurched. Perhaps he'd heard the man wrong. "Could you repeat that? I don't think I heard you right."

"I said, 'Summer Snow *is* my fiancée.'"

"Is? Did you say is and not *was*?"

"I said *is*, yes."

"Oh." Martin searched for the right words. So Summer *was* engaged to Whitfield. What a staggering blow—that is, if what he says was true. "Summer did mention she'd been engaged, but she'd only said your first name. I didn't want to press her for more information since it seemed painful for her to talk about it. But she did make it clear that you two were no longer engaged. That she'd broken it off."

Whitfield gave a flourish with his hand. "Yes, well, that is a minor technicality. A temporary problem that merely needs some, er, massaging."

Martin frowned. Did Whitfield really say that? He always hated to judge a man before really knowing him, but this guy was shaping up to be a real stooge. And he had this annoying way of talking out of the side of his mouth. Summer was still actually engaged to this guy?

"But how can it be a minor thing? Did Summer come to you and tell you she'd changed her mind? That she wanted to marry you after all?" He prayed it wasn't so.

"No, she did not."

"By the way, how did you find out about me?" Martin asked, knowing Summer wouldn't have said anything. And yet how could Whitfield know? Was he being followed?

"Oh, you know. The usual." Whitfield shrugged.

"I have no idea—"

"I will be clear. You are the 'other man' who's keeping this wedding from going forward. Without you in the picture, I know I can convince Summer to marry me just as we had planned. I'm sure you see how amazing Summer is, how special." Whitfield slowly moved his hands with gestures that befitted someone who was used to being in command. "She has a great capacity to love young people. I intend to give Summer every possible opportunity to fulfill her destiny. She will be able to change the world. Will you be able to give her that chance, Langtree?"

"No." Martin crossed his arms. "But I can give her love."

"Well, of course, that's a given." Whitfield glanced at his watch. "Look, I love Summer too. I have since the day I met her. But I'm willing to give her so much more than other men can offer. The bottom line is, I want to win Summer back, and you can help me do that."

Whitfield's manner seemed more befitting of a strategy meeting than the wooing of his beloved. "But so far, we haven't even had a date," Martin said, "so I'm not sure you have any reason to bother with me."

"So are you two just friends? It appears that way, but I wondered if your intention is to ask her out for a real date."

"I don't know where you got that information, but yes, I intend to ask her out," Martin said, "but I was waiting."

"Waiting for what? Actions speak louder than words, Langtree."

Martin bristled. How much should he tell this fellow? "I was waiting for an appropriate period of time for Summer to grieve."

"Grieve? You mean from the breakup? Over me?" Whitfield's smile glimmered with elation. Was he revving up for a victory speech? "I knew it," he said. "I did. Summer just couldn't live without me."

The audacity of his comment would have amused Martin had the subject not been so serious. "No. Summer is grieving, Mr. Whitfield, because her grandmother died."

It was the first time Martin had seen Whitfield break from his all-powerful posturing. "Oh, I see. I didn't know that Mrs. Snow had died."

"Yes. Mrs. Snow was very dear to Summer as I'm sure you know. It's been a very hard time, especially since she was the last remaining member of Summer's family."

"I'm sure it is hard. Very hard." He pursed his lips as one who was straining to keep his emotions in check. "She must be suffering. I've got to call her." He glanced over at his manager. "Kent, make a note of that. Remind me to call Summer. Work it into my schedule. Okay?"

"Got it, sir."

"Good." Whitfield turned back to Martin. "I wish you no ill. We just happen to love the same woman. But as the old saying goes, 'May the best man win.'" Then Elliot Whitfield backed away, so did the man named Kent, who seemed to be not much more than an echo of his employer.

Before Martin could think of an appropriate reply, the two men moved as one down the steps and onto the long sidewalk to their waiting limo.

Still paralyzed, Martin didn't shut the door. Whitfield couldn't have known that the words he'd said were the very ones that worked like a knife through his heart. The man had been right, though—actions did speak louder than words—and his words weren't without truth. Even though Martin had tried to make up for it, he had indeed failed Summer in her time of need.

So he stood there at the door—stunned, questioning himself again, and deep in his spirit, bleeding.

CHAPTER
thirty-four

Summer glanced around, searching the parking lot for Martin and wondering if he still intended to meet her at Granny's gravesite. He was twenty minutes late. Had he forgotten? Maybe he'd gotten busy with his work.

She tightened her fingers around the bouquet of yellow roses she was holding until one of the thorns dug into her skin. Summer winced, and loosened her grip.

Summer took a whiff of the roses. Nice fragrance, but the blooms were already wilting. Thinking that Martin might catch up with her later, she took the walking trail past an ornamental pond and over to an old oak tree where her granny was laid to rest. Or at least where her body was buried. Summer knew well that Granny was long gone, gladly occupied in heaven.

She placed the flowers on top of the gravesite and then sat down on a bench that was situated close by. The words engraved in the headstone read, "Here lies Emily Mae Snow—a woman who laughed, loved, and lived for Christ—and who now resides most happily in heaven." Ah yes, how she loved that epitaph. Says it all. "But Granny, how I miss you so," she murmured. "But I wouldn't have you back in this fallen mess, not even for me. I wouldn't ask it of you or of God, now that I know you're happily settled in the home you belong, your real home. My home too, come to think of it."

Summer sighed. In spite of that fact that it was a lovely day in May, the earth would surely darken without Granny's special shine.

Her creative spark. Her precious love. *But even in the midst of my grief, Lord, I'm finally ready to pray the last part of Your prayer, and truly mean it this time. The hardest part of all.* She bowed her head and spoke aloud quietly. "Thy will be done on earth as it is in heaven."

She glanced around the cemetery. Such a peaceful place to be but a lonely place too. She considered the sea of headstones and their epitaphs. Maybe people should think about it more—those final carved words—and what they want them to be. Or more importantly, how they will live out their days. And hours.

From a good distance, she could see a family making their way across the lawn. Each person held a single rose and one at a time, placed it on what appeared to be a new gravesite. Who were they mourning over? A parent? A child? A friend? What was their story? She would never know.

The sound of someone approaching, crunching on the gravel walkway behind her, made Summer turn around. "Martin." She looked more closely. His usual happy expression appeared altered. "I'm so glad you came, but are you okay?"

"I had an accident, but it was only a fender bender."

"Only a fender bender. I'm so sorry."

"It'll be fine. No one was hurt. But that's why I'm late." He sat down next to her. "I'm sorry for that."

She smiled. "Well, it wasn't your fault. I'm just grateful you're okay."

"Maybe it was my fault. I was drifting in my thoughts, thinking about all sorts of things."

"And was one of the things . . . me?"

"Of course." He smiled at her and then stared toward Granny's gravesite. "A fresh grave always looks forlorn, doesn't it? Fresh grief."

"Yes. I miss her more than words can say."

Martin was quiet for a bit, making Summer wonder what he was thinking. He seemed dejected. She knew he was also grieving over Granny's passing, but there was something else going on with him. Perhaps he was about to tell her something—final—which was not a good word.

"I had a visitor today." Martin gazed over at her.

"You did? And who was that?"

"It was Elliot. *Your* Elliot," he said quietly.

"He's not *my* Elliot, I assure you. Well, not anymore." Summer rested her fists on her waist. "And why in the world did he come to visit you?" *Oh, dear.* Elliot was on a campaign again, and it had nothing to do with politics.

"You never told me your fiancé was Elliot Whitfield. *The* Elliot Whitfield." Martin didn't seem upset, really, but perhaps bemused and disappointed.

"I'm sorry if it bothers you, that I didn't tell you everything. Well, that I didn't say *who* it was." Oh, why hadn't she told Martin all of the story? It would have been so easy, and he would have understood. But Martin was certainly being a bit intense about Elliot's visit. Why?

"It's okay, but . . ."

"But you think that it was dishonest of me." Summer touched his arm.

"Not dishonest, but it came as quite a surprise having Elliot Whitfield come to my door." Martin tried to laugh. "Whitfield is pretty well-known, and I just wouldn't have put you two together. At all. You two are like classical physics and quantum physics. They don't mesh."

Somebody's jealous, Summer singsonged in her head, enjoying every second of the scene. Or at least she hoped Martin was a little jealous. She swallowed her grin and said, "You're so right. And now that I've had more time to think on it, I wouldn't have put us together either."

Martin took her hands in his.

Wanting to encourage Martin, Summer scooted closer to him.

"Just so you know . . . Elliot wanted to renew your relationship. He wants you back."

Oh, no. If she could have dissolved into the bench, she would have. "I can't believe it. Well, maybe I can." Summer stared into a puddle of water next to her feet. She could see her lost and lonely reflection, the one that Elliot had put there—again. "That is *so* like Elliot. How many times have I told him it was over? He thinks he can sweet-talk his way back into my life."

"Oh?"

"Yes, that is his way. Elliot is like a planet, and he expects all the people who frequent his life to be like these little moons that do nothing but circle his sphere. I know eventually that kind of life would have been wearing if not destructive to a marriage. I should never have allowed it to go as far as I did."

Summer clung to the bench, wishing it could absorb her angst. "But I guess I thought when I broke it off this time, well, that it was for good. He called me an incurable romantic, and he didn't mean it as a compliment. If he believes that about me, being hopelessly starry-eyed and all, I don't see why he would continue to be interested in me." She shrugged. "Maybe I am what Elliot says I am, and these whimsical notions of mine are childish."

"No," Martin said. "God made you endearing and fanciful, and I wouldn't change a thing about you."

"Ah. That kind of talk could warm a girl's heart."

Martin placed his arm behind her on the back of the bench. "I'm glad, but just to be fair, in his defense, when I told Elliot about your grandmother's death, it upset him. I think he meant to call you right away."

"He didn't call. He probably won't. And I can tell you why that is."

"Oh?"

"Because something else must have come up," Summer said. "His campaign manager, Kent, will find something else for him to do. Something urgent. And that's best. Because the last thing I want to do is to renew my relationship with Elliot."

Martin didn't comment but gazed up at the darkening sky. "I think we're going to have a storm."

"We've been having a lot of those lately, but it's expected."

Martin leaned his elbows on his knees and looked back at her. "By the way, Elliot brought Kent with him."

"You're kidding? No, you're not kidding. It doesn't surprise me." Summer huffed. "Kent may stand back like he's out of the picture, but he's a very controlling force in the Whitfield universe. And Elliot doesn't seem to mind. But *I* did."

"That's quite a circle Elliot has."

"Circus is more like it," Summer said and tried to laugh, but couldn't quite do it.

"Beyond Kent's control, you seem to be saying that Elliot was no longer attentive when he should have been? Was that one of the reasons you broke things off?"

"That was only a small part of it."

"Sometimes I feel that I've done the same thing to you. That I wasn't there for you when I should have been." When he looked at her, his eyes seemed heavy with concern.

"I guess you're still referring to that time after the funeral. But we have that all settled. I promise. It wasn't your fault. It was mine." Feeling fidgety, Summer rose. "Listen, I don't know what Elliot said to you, but I wish you wouldn't let him get under your skin. He has a way of doing that. What did he say? Did he try to break up our, uh, friendship?" She wasn't sure what to call what they had.

Martin touched the sleeve of her dress with such a light caress, she thought maybe it was only in her imagination.

"Elliot told me that with his connections, he could help you fulfill your destiny."

Summer laughed.

"That's funny?"

"It is when we're talking about Elliot. He's mostly interested in his own destiny and collecting all the warm bodies necessary to fulfill it. He won't stop until he's in the White House."

"And that doesn't appeal to you?"

"No." She stared at Martin, trying to figure him out. "Am I missing something here, Mr. Langtree? Are you trying to talk me into going back to Elliot Whitfield?"

"No," he said loudly and then grinned. "Not at all." Martin rose and stood next to her. "The things he said, well . . ."

"Remember, he knows how to manipulate words to get his way. He's been doing it for a long time. A trained professional at it. Just wipe away that whole conversation with him. I could never be Mrs. Elliot Whitfield. Look, I wish Elliot well, but if I don't even know what's been going on in his political life or any other part of his life, then one can safely say that I've moved on. No turning back and apparently not even peeking." She gave his arm a squeeze.

His shoulders relaxed. "I'm glad for that. More than you know."

"Elliot tends to mow people down to the ground, but you must have good roots to have survived one of his talks."

Martin picked up a stone from the ground. "I don't know what kind of roots I have."

"You have deep roots, the kind that make for a steady man."

"And you like that?"

"I like that a lot. Now can you please tell me the real reason that Elliot Whitfield has you so upset? We're dancing round something here, and I—"

"There is more, and I'm about to tell you what it is, my darling girl, but first . . ." Martin held the stone in front of her. "Do you know what this is?"

Summer smiled, trying to keep herself from bouncing on her toes, excited about the new direction of their chat. And the words "darling girl" had such a lovely ring to it. What Martin held was a rock, of course, but she felt a bout of playful banter coming on, so she said, "Okay, so is that a miniature planet you're holding, doused by the magical shrinking potion from *Alice in Wonderland*?"

"No," he said, with a twinkle in his eyes, "it's a matrix. These are common, but full of intrigue. Did you know in South Africa sometimes they find diamonds in matrix?"

"Nope. Didn't know that." Summer didn't know what rabbit trail Martin was on, but she knew that wherever he took her, it would be worth the chase.

"You are so like that to me, Summer. The rest of the world is the matrix, and you're that rare diamond found in a mountain of rock."

Oh, she really liked this rabbit trail. "What a charming thing to say."

"Good. I've never considered myself smooth. It's hard for me to know what to say sometimes. It's in my heart, but it doesn't always come out of my mouth right."

"Martin, there is more appeal in that guileless heart of yours and in that endearing look in your eyes than in a million smooth words by other men."

"Thank you." He grinned. "By the way, I've wondered about something."

"What's that?" Summer asked.

"Your grandmother's list."

"Yes?"

"You haven't finished it, and I know your granny would want you to."

She gave him an emphatic nod. "Yes, she would."

"I read the last thing mentioned on her list." Martin gave her a tender look. "I've been thinking about it for a long time."

Summer flushed, thinking about that very thing—the last item on the list—which was to *kiss someone you love*. Yes, she had dreamed about it too. And she'd hoped and prayed that man would be Martin.

He took hold of her shoulders. "I was thinking about the person who should help you with that particular item. And it has to be just right, since it's the very last one on the list."

"Absolutely. And so who might be the right man for the job, Mr. Langtree?" Summer batted her eyelashes, trying on the look of innocence but gladly failing.

Martin leaned over and whispered near her, "I'm thinking it should be me."

Summer touched his cheek. "I've been thinking the same thing since you opened your hobbit door to me."

He rested his hand over hers—the one that caressed his cheek—and said, "I can feel the pulse in your wrist. Your heart is speeding up."

Summer grinned. "It is?" Of course it was. The silly thing had been boom-banging since Martin moved in closer to her.

"That beat is here, of course." He placed her hand over his heart. "But even before your heart is racing, the medulla must be engaged." He touched the back of her head and massaged the area ever so gently. "Right there."

"Oh? The medulla? I didn't know that. Odd name. Well, I'm glad the old noodle is good for something," she said, her voice disintegrating into soft, breathy words as he continued to massage her neck. Martin was officially making her tipsy with his romantic teasing.

"I wonder if it would be appropriate for us to fulfill the last item on the list right now," he suggested.

Summer gazed over at her grandmother's gravesite. "Yes, it's a very fine place, especially since all of this joy started with Granny and her list."

Then Martin grinned, and oh, it was one of those grins riddled with meaning—one of those grins with romantic connotations that made her toes tingle and her spirit swoon.

Then Martin cradled Summer's face in his hands, and they in-dulged in some of those delicious connotations he alluded to. The kiss—which was warm and stirring and sweeter than her granny's pecan pie—well, it made Summer forget all the kisses she'd ever known. None of them could compare.

When they came up for air, Summer grinned. "Friends do kiss, but not like that."

"I think we can officially say that we are more than just friends."

Yes, and she wished she could say more. Something like, *You might find it interesting to know, Mr. Langtree, that I'm falling in love with you.* But someday when the time was right, she would.

"So does this mean you'll go out with me on an official date?"

"Yes. I would love to."

"Seems like we're doing things kind of backwards."

"Even when we were kids we never did things like everyone else. We were little renegades."

"Yes, and you always were the prettiest renegade I'd ever seen. Still are."

"Thank you." Summer tugged on the lapels of his shirt. "It wasn't easy for us, was it? It was such a gamble. This moment. The kiss. If one of us hadn't felt the same way, this romantic affection would have destroyed a friendship. The best. But God saw things differently as He usually does. And Granny had an inkling that this would be the case, that there was meant to be more between us."

"That doesn't surprise me. Your grandmother was always very intuitive about people, and she walked closely to the Lord, didn't she?"

"Yes, and now she's walking with Him arm in arm along some lovely beach. I just wish Granny could see us start a new phase of our relationship. I'm not sure how God has that set up; you know, if He were to allow that sort of thing. But if Granny could somehow watch us through that veil, even for a brief moment, I know she'd be smiling."

"I'm sure she would be too." Martin touched her chin.

She suddenly remembered Martin's carved birds in her pocket and, wanting him to see them after all these years, she pulled out the tiny memento and handed it to him. "Do you remember this carving you made for me when we were kids?"

"I do." He studied it for a long time, turning it this way and that. "It was supposed to be a pair of birds in a nest, but it's kind of crudely made, isn't it?"

"Not at all. I think it's a masterpiece considering how young you were when you made it."

"I did work on it a long time, that I do remember. But I can't believe you kept it all this time."

"I did. You'd said the birds were really two friends that could never be parted, for their wings were carved as one." Summer smiled.

"I carved it that way, so the birds would always fly together." He placed the keepsake in her palm and closed her fingers around it. "Maybe instead of merely asking you on some routine date, I should say, come fly with me."

"Maybe in a way, I never stopped flying with you." Summer hoped he could sense all the meaning in her words.

"You don't know how glad that makes me, since I'm not very good with goodbyes either," Martin said, "not when it comes to Summer Snow anyway."

Thunder rumbled around them, which made them look over at the clouds.

"Now how about that date of ours," he said. "I was thinking we could go to this—"

Martin's cellphone buzzed to life.

CHAPTER
thirty-five

Martin ignored his noisy phone. In fact, he had a sudden urge to give it the heave-ho into one of those nearby ponds.

Summer said, "Please, go ahead and answer it if you want to."

"That's okay. I should have turned it off."

"But what if it's important?"

Martin glanced at his phone. "It's a text from Desmond." He looked at it more closely. "Desmond says he's gotten some new information about our parents. He says it's so important that he's calling a family meeting. He's says it's an emergency."

"A *family* meeting, and he's included you." Summer gave him a gentle pat on the shoulder. "You guys really *are* making progress."

"Yes. I've never seen them like this. I think it's been a miracle."

"No more Hotel California at your house then?" Summer asked.

Martin grinned. "I think those days are gone. At least I hope so."

"Good. So when is the family meeting?"

"Right now. And he's invited you too."

"Me? Really?" A pleasant kind of surprise lit Summer's face.

"How about it?" Martin asked. "But I'm certainly willing to stay here with you a while longer."

"We'd better go now. This meeting sounds important." She looked over at the billowing storm. "And besides, the rumbling growl over there makes me think that those clouds want to eat us alive."

At that moment, a flashing blade of lightning cut through the sky, startling them both.

Martin agreed. "I think you're right. Let's go."

They took one more look back at Granny's gravesite, and then Martin offered her his arm. "Shall we?"

"We shall." She circled her arm through his and gave him a squeeze.

Having Summer on his arm felt right and good—like she was always meant to be there.

Thirty minutes later when they were all seated in the Langtree library and after a few friendly greetings all around—friendlier than Martin ever imagined possible—Ivan stood before them.

He clasped his hands together. "I wanted Desmond to announce what we've discovered," Ivan said, "but he thought I should do it. Desmond says I've been living in his shadow for too long, and that I needed to be my own man. As hard as that was to hear, and as angry as I got when he said it; well, in the end, I had to admit there was some truth in it." Ivan looked at Summer. "Before we begin, first, I want to tell you how sorry we were to hear about your grandmother passing away. We know it was a great loss."

"Thank you, Ivan." Summer smiled at him.

Martin gave his brother an approving nod, grateful for their remembrance of Summer's grandmother and also still deeply grateful for the attitude change in his brothers.

"You're welcome." Ivan shuffled his feet. "Anyway, I'm here to say that when Desmond fired the detective who was hired to look for clues about our parents as well find their current whereabouts and phone numbers, well, the man decided to throw us a bone. I think he was afraid we were about to turn him into the Better Business Bureau for robbing us blind. Which isn't a bad idea, really."

Desmond chuckled.

"Anyway, Mother and Father did move around a lot it seems, so they were hard to locate. But we know where they are now, and the phone numbers are current."

"Did you call them?" Martin moved a little closer to the edge of his seat.

"We did." Ivan fiddled with a notebook in his hands. "Desmond called Father, and I called Mother. We should have waited for you, Martin. I'm sorry about that."

"That's okay. No problem. Please go on."

"I guess we thought the chances of those phone numbers being in use were slim," Ivan went on to say. "We'd had old numbers before, which obviously didn't work. But this time—"

"You mean you really did get through to them?" Martin crossed his arms and then uncrossed them.

"Yes, we did." Ivan tore out a page from the notebook and handed it to Martin. "That's the current info."

"Thank you. What did they say?" Martin asked abruptly.

Desmond rubbed his hands along his slacks. "Not much, I'm sorry to say." The mantel clock chimed. "For the little bit that I talked to Father, he said they were ashamed of what they did to our family." He rubbed the back of his neck. "They felt that their grievous sins and lies forced them to forfeit their right to be our parents. They assumed we would eventually find out about Father's affair, and about the lie that you were adopted, Martin, and that you were really his son. And Mother still blames herself for the nanny's behavior toward Ivan and me, as well as the way she tried to injure you emotionally, Martin, as a way to punish Father for his adultery."

"But we've *all* sinned," Martin said. "And there are countless families in worse shape, but they keep trying to make it work." He stared down at his shoes. They were tied neatly, but this time his spirit felt like it was coming undone. "I wish they could have found a way to at least try."

"I guess they felt their sins kept multiplying until they were un-forgiveable," Ivan said. "Years ago I know we talked about going to Europe in an effort to find them and convince them to come home, but I don't think it would have worked. Not then anyway."

Martin looked over at Summer, whose hands were folded tightly on her lap. Perhaps she was praying. But she must be thinking once again how his parents' behavior contrasted to the affectionate spirit within her own family.

"But there's more, Martin," Ivan said. "Mother and Father both find it more difficult to live abroad as they age. Neither one of them is in good health. They need to come home to Houston, where they can get the best medical care."

Their return home sounded incredible, but it was a shame that it would be ill health that would finally bring them back. "What's wrong with them? Do you know?"

"No," Ivan replied. "They've both been unwell for some time now, so they feel it's time to come home for some tests and some medical help."

"I'm sorry to hear that, but it will be wonderful to see them. What else did they say?" Martin looked back and forth at Desmond and Ivan.

"Father didn't say much," Desmond said. "I think he seemed glad that I'd called, but in general, he sounded quiet, older, and unhappy."

"And I'm sorry to say that Mother sounded similar," Ivan said. "Although I would add that she seemed more nervous than I re-member and perhaps more hesitant than Father. If either one of them were to back out, I think it might be Mother."

"Oh?" Martin lowered his gaze. "I'm sure you told them how much we love them and miss them. How much forgiveness we have here when they come home."

"We both said something like that. Basically, we begged," Ivan said. "If they do come home, which we believe they will, it will be in a couple of months, more or less. As soon as Father can get out of his furnished apartment and Mother can sell her furniture from her rental house. For some reason they do have each other's phone numbers, so that's good. But I have no idea if they've been communicating with each other over the years. Maybe they connected recently because of their ill health. I don't know. We weren't able to talk that long with either of them. But then we expected that."

"Still, it could be a miracle," Martin said.

"Yes," Desmond said. "But there's one more thing."

"Oh?"

Desmond touched his forehead, which appeared to be perspiring. "Their health issues did help with their decision to return. But in an effort to make that commitment a little more certain, we did mention one other thing. But now that we've had some time to think about what we said—what we promised—Ivan and I might have gone a bit too far in our desperate attempt to bring them home."

When Desmond didn't say any more, Martin shrugged. "Well? What did you say to them exactly? What did you promise?"

"We told our parents that if they didn't come home, they would miss the wedding." Desmond's smile appeared jittery.

"A wedding?" Martin raised his eyebrows. "Whose wedding?"

"Your wedding, Martin." Desmond coughed a little. "We told our parents that you were marrying Summer Snow."

CHAPTER
thirty-six

What a funny and outrageous and very pleasant shock. Martin looked at Summer, and they both exploded with laughter.

And then Ivan and Desmond exploded with laughter right along with them.

When the merriment settled down, Desmond grinned nervously. "So why are we laughing? Were we way off? You mean, you two aren't getting serious? But we thought that . . ."

"Yes, just so you know," Martin said, "Summer and I are more than friends now. But we haven't had a date yet. I appreciate the fact that you both succeeded in getting our parents to come back to Houston, but Summer and I might need a little more time before we—"

"But you two have spent a lot of time together recently. Right?" Ivan said. "And if you haven't had a real date with Summer, whose fault is that, Martin, old brother of mine?" He raised an eyebrow and grinned.

"Well, for your information, I have asked Summer out, and she has agreed, but just as we were considering the next phase, my phone buzzed with *your* message." Martin smiled, enjoying the camaraderie. "When you two leave the library, I think I will rectify that problem of being without a location and time for our first actual date."

Ivan slapped Desmond on the arm. "Hey, we get the hint." They both rose, said a jovial goodbye, and walked out the library door.

Summer sat down next to Martin on the loveseat. "I'm excited about your parents coming home. What an incredible turn of events. Really."

"It is incredible. So much so that it's hard to believe it's happening." He shook his head. "But my brothers and their creative antics about the wedding, though. They were out of line on that one." Martin waved his finger. "I'm sorry if it was too much of a shock or—"

She took hold of his finger and gave it a playful shake. "Please don't be too upset with your brothers for what they did. I know it wasn't right to tell your parents that we were getting married. It was wrong of them to do it, yes. But I'm not angry. I promise."

Actually, it's a lie that I wished were true—someday.

"I'm happy, actually, that your brothers did it with such a good motivation," Summer said. "It's kind of heartwarming, don't you think?"

"It is. I'm not that upset with them, but I'm mostly concerned about you. It must have been a jolt to say the least." Martin rested his arm across the back of the loveseat, leaned toward her, and whispered, "If the Langtree brothers three get too awkward and demanding, I'm worried you'll want to make a run for it."

"Martin, please, know this. I'm not going anywhere." She touched his arm. "We're like two pieces of Velcro stuck together, you and I."

"I've always loved Velcro." He smiled. Maybe that was what he needed for his perpetually untied shoes. And his life.

"By the way, I have an idea about our first real date, if you don't mind." The words came spilling out of Summer's mouth with what Martin would call effervescent amusement.

"I don't mind at all," he said, hoping to reflect her lively mood.

"First, there's something I haven't told you. Granny's list worked in a number of different ways. When I sang in the café, I had an epiphany of sorts."

"You've been kind of silent on that topic, so I wondered."

"Well, I put a lot of thought into it—and prayer—and I've come to the conclusion that while singing is satisfying, it's not what I want to do with my life. I might like to serve on the worship team at church, but I don't feel compelled to make it my life."

"What do you want to do?" Martin asked.

"Exactly what I've been doing. During these couple of weeks away from the bookshop, I missed it. I missed the kids coming in after school. I missed the parents coming in to choose just the right book for their children. Perhaps a special story that will change their lives. Or help them see the gifts God has given them. So even if Granny had pushed me into taking over the bookshop all those years ago, it was the right way for me to go. I'm glad Granny gave me the chance to take some time off to explore, to have a little adventure. But I was away plenty long enough to know what I was meant to do. Now that I've made my decision, I can hardly wait to get back."

"I am so glad for you. Lots of people, too many, go through their lives and they're clueless when it comes to their calling. I'm glad for you. And maybe I'm a bit selfish to say it, but the best part of Granny's list was that it brought you back into my life."

"So could our first date be story time at the shop? We can take turns reading just like we did when we were kids."

"We can, and we will." Martin lifted her hands to his lips and kissed them. "What a good idea."

❧❧❧

Martin had followed through with his promise, and their first date had indeed been at the bookshop for story time. It had gone so well that Martin came as often as he could when he wasn't working. Soon Summer was happily ensconced in her bookshop, working full-time again and doing what she loved best. And Elliot, well, he did call her not long after Martin had mentioned his visit. He offered his condolences concerning the loss of her grandmother, but he had not tried to win her back as he'd told Martin he would. As it turned out, Elliot had found someone else, this time a young woman more suited to political life. All in all, it had been a good time of closure for them both, and for that Summer would forever be grateful.

Then on one sunny afternoon toward the end of May came a lovely delight—Martin showed up unexpectedly at the shop with a smile on his lips and a storybook in hand.

He gave her a wave. "Aiya," he said.

"Aiya," she repeated, grinning. She put down her duster. "I'm surprised to see you on a Monday." The best part of Summer's week—when her dear Martin strolled through the front door.

"I got caught up with my work again, and so they gave me some time off. I couldn't think of anyplace I'd rather be than here."

Summer smiled. "Good. The kids will be glad to see you. They've already started to gather for story time. But be ready for some squirming, since it's getting close to the last day of school. I see you brought a book. What is it?" She reached out to have a peek.

"Not yet." Martin lifted the book away from her grasp. "It's a surprise."

"And are you going to read us this surprise today?"

He leaned against the oak counter, leisurely and gave her a rascally grin. "It'll be more fun if one of the kids reads it."

"All righty." What was he up to? Summer rang the silver bell, which she always hoped made the children think of Tinker Bell, and summoned the last of the children for story time. With Amelia's help, the children all gathered around—a dozen or so boys and girls of various ages—and seated themselves on the rows of benches in front of the small stage. A few of the parents hovered around behind the benches and chatted quietly.

Summer said to the children, "Mr. Martin brought us a new picture book today. Who wants to read it?"

A few hands shot in the air. Summer picked Julie, one of the older girls, since she raised her hand the highest and her fingers seemed to wiggle the most.

Martin handed the book to Julie, and she marched up onto the stage with her usual endearing flamboyance and situated herself on the bright red chair, which was the throne—the storyteller's place of honor. Summer sat behind her on the stage in case she wanted help with her words.

Julie stared down at the book as her eyes widened. "The title. It's your name, Miss Summer. The title is *The Legend of Summer Snow*." She turned the book around and showed all the children, who then made little oohing sounds.

Summer sent Martin a curious look, but he merely responded with a few fluttering blinks and an innocent smile.

Julie crossed her legs at her ankles. She opened the picture book with some pomp and began, "Once upon a time, there was a princess named Summer Snow."

What is my dear Martin up to?

Julie tilted her head and then went on with the story, "The princess enchanted everyone who met her, not just because she was beautiful, but because she had a heart of gold." Julie's pert little nose scrunched up a bit. "How can a person have a heart made of gold? I don't get it."

Martin grinned. "It means that the young woman was kind to everyone she met."

Julie beamed. "Okay. I like that."

Summer's face flushed as Martin's face lit with mischief.

Julie seemed to miss the silent exchange between them and breezed on with her reading. "But Princess Snow was all by herself in her castle, and lonely, and since the kingdom loved their princess so much, they didn't want her to be alone. They invited her to dwell among them for a while, and if it pleased her, she could choose a husband to share her life with. Princess Snow knocked on every door of every commoner in the land, but none of them touched her heart, until she arrived at the cottage of a peasant whose name was Martin Langtree." Julie looked up again with a petite frown. "Isn't that your name, Mr. Martin?"

Martin agreed. "It is."

"Oh." Julie held the book up closer. "My mom would call that curious. She likes that word, curious."

Summer saw Julie's mother smiling.

"Yes, well, I would call it curious too," Summer said. "You may read on. The story is getting *really* interesting, don't you think?"

Julie cleared her throat dramatically and turned the page. "The cottage where Martin Langtree lived had a door that was round and the color of green, green grass." She looked at her audience. "'That sounds like a hobbit door, doesn't it?"

"It does indeed," Martin said.

Julie looked at the picture book again and read on. "And when Martin opened his round green door to Princess Snow, he was utterly enchanted with everything about her." She said this last part with dramatic flair as she lifted her fingers in the air like a ballerina. "First, the princess and the peasant became good friends, but then as time went on, something wonderful happened. The couple fell in love."

Some of the boys fidgeted in their seats. One boy moaned, "Kinda mushy."

Yes, it is wonderfully mushy. Summer placed her finger over her lips, encouraging the boys to quiet down a bit.

"I'm not finished yet." Julie glared at the boys until they shushed their whines. "And even though the humble peasant offered to slay dragons in her majesty's name, Princess Snow assured Martin that his love was all that she'd hoped for. As a token of his love, Martin carved two birds in a nest and gave it to her as a gift. The wings of the birds were made as one, so that if they ever were to fly, they would always be together."

Julie sighed and turned the page. "Even the summer season bowed to their love, so that on the day when Martin got down on his knee to propose marriage to Princess Snow, huge flakes came floating down as delicate as lace and as light as air. Everyone in the land rejoiced at the news of their betrothal, and the day of their wedding was a great celebration with a feast and music and gifts for everyone in the village. As years went by, everyone in the kingdom kept the tale in their hearts like a treasure, and with each telling, the story became more and more beguiling, until it came to be known as the Legend of Summer Snow."

Julie looked at Martin on the front row and asked, "Did they live happily ever after?" Her big brown eyes were bright and expectant.

"I'm sure they did," Martin said.

Summer's heart pounded so hard she thought the kids might hear it. *What is this, Lord? A proposal?* She could hardly breathe.

At that moment, Martin stepped up on the stage and knelt down on one knee in front of Summer.

One of the parents gasped.

Amelia winked at Summer.

Little Julie turned around and looked at Summer and Martin with a surprised stare.

Then the rest of the children went as quiet as mice.

Oh, Martin. My Martin. The answer is already yes.

Martin took her hands in his. "Summer Snow, just as the story said, I am utterly enchanted with you. Not just because of your beauty, but because of your heart of gold. I started to fall in love with you on this very stage, twenty years ago, and now it's more than right that I ask you to be my wife where it all began. Miss Snow, would you do the honor of becoming my wife?"

Julie said to Summer in a loud whisper, "Say yes."

Some of the children wriggled and others giggled.

All of the shop—including the rows and shelves of beloved stories, and the twinkling eyes of all those who looked on—faded in an instant. Summer was perfectly alone in the moment, and that moment was all about her Martin and the one word that would change her life—their lives. "Yes. Oh, yes, I will marry you, Martin Langtree, because just as the story said, I have been lonely, waiting for you. I love you, and there can be nothing better than to be your wife." Summer leaned down and dropped a soft kiss on Martin's cheek. Later when they were alone, she promised herself, she would thank him thoroughly for his wonderful surprise and give him a proper kiss that showed him just how much she really did care for him. But for now, she hoped her misty-eyed look of love would please him.

One of the boys let out a groan. But some of the children as well as the parents clapped with some serious zeal. There were also a few sniffles here and there while Amelia gave her the thumbs-up.

Then one of the newer children, Danielle, ran over to a window. "Danielle?" Summer asked. "Where are you going?"

"I'm looking outside," she said. "I want to see if it's snowing."

Martin and Summer burst into laughter.

Whether all the children knew if the marriage proposal was playacting or real, it was hard to know for sure. But smiles circled around their little troupe as sweetly and as welcome as a dip of ice cream on a hot summer day.

CHAPTER
thirty-seven

Summer eyed the Langtree front door for the hundredth time. With her gaze still glued to the door, she asked Martin. "Are you sure my hair hasn't gone too frizzy?"

"No. You look like an auburn version of Grace Kelly."

"Really? Thanks. And you're my Jimmy Stewart."

Martin stood a little straighter. "Jimmy Stewart is one of the greatest actors of all time. One of my favorites."

Summer grinned at him as she tried to snap off a loose thread on her sleeve. The thread came off, but so did a button, and it went tumbling and spun itself right underneath the buffet table. *Good grief. I have got to calm down.* It wasn't a vital button that was holding up her dress or anything, so she let it go on its merry rolling way. The last thing she wanted to do was to be caught scrambling like a goose on ice under the buffet table just as his Dad arrived. Martin seemed to have missed the whole button mini drama. *Good.* No sense in having him scrambling either.

She glanced at her engagement ring, which was also a bit loose. Still there. Whew. That was the last thing she wanted to have sailing off her finger. Funny how that detail made her think of her breakup with Elliot—when she'd desperately wanted to remove the ring, but it had gotten stuck. *Oh, Elliot. I wish you as much happiness as I have now.*

Summer paused again to admire the treasure on her left hand. Such a lovely thing, spectacular really—a single marquise emerald on a band of meteorite. Only her Martin could have envisioned such a unique ring, such a fantastical surprise. "Have I told you how much I love my ring?"

"You told me an hour ago, but you may tell me as many times as you want." He grinned. "Feels good, since I wasn't sure if you'd want to wear something that had come from outer space."

"Well, since outer space is limitless, then that's how I'll always think of your love for me."

"And you'd be right." Martin gave her cheek a playful stroke.

Summer smiled up at him and said, "Martin, you haven't said much about it, but I know it's bothering you, you know, that your mother changed her mind about coming back."

"It does bother me, but because she did say she would return one day, I can live with that."

"You're a very forgiving man, Martin." Shooting another glance at that infernal front door again, Summer quickly changed gears. "So my dress is okay, right? I'm not used to buying expensive clothes. Your Dad won't think it's too frothy or too close to the color of undercooked meat?"

Martin laughed. "You look like a pretty flamingo, except you're standing on both legs."

"That's not exactly the look I was going for." Summer gave Martin a droll expression. "It's just that this is such an important night for all of us. I don't want anything to go wrong. You know how I get sometimes when I'm nervous. I would be mortified if one of my cherry tomatoes went flying."

"All is well," Martin said. "I don't think there are any cherry tomatoes being served tonight."

She grinned.

Martin rubbed little circles on her back. "No need to fret. You are loved everywhere you go." He straightened his bow tie.

Summer rose up on her tiptoes and gave Martin a peck on the cheek. He grinned and kissed her back on the lips. What a new and fun occupation—kissing Martin Langtree.

The pianist—who'd just arrived with a flourish—sat down at the grand piano in the entry hall and began to play something light and classical. Summer took another sweeping glance at the long buffet table covered with gourmet treats of every kind and the elaborate decoration, which included an ice sculpture, no less. "I still can't believe that Ivan and Desmond paid for this engagement party."

"They insisted, so I let them. And don't feel too bad. They have jobs now, and they can afford it." He leaned toward her and said softly, "But also, I think it's a redemption kind of thing. Good for the soul."

Summer nodded. "I understand."

Martin straightened his bow tie—for the umpteenth time.

Now look who's nervous? She could see right through that Mr. Calm routine of his. He too was concerned that at this engagement party his Dad would feel at home. Martin and his brothers wanted to make sure that he no longer felt like he was living under a cloud of shame for what had happened in the past. Surely God would honor their prayer. Summer said, "I'm surprised that your Dad didn't want to stay here instead of paying for a hotel."

"My father has always been independently minded. And maybe there're too many memories in this house. Right now I think his priority is to find a condo near the medical center area."

Summer chose to remain silent on the health of Martin's dad, since she didn't want to give him any unnecessary worries. But when she met with him the week before, right after his homecoming to Houston, he had indeed looked ill. And he had not aged well, but looked like someone who had absorbed too much sorrow, too much regret through too many years. *Lord, help me to make him feel welcome. Let him feel loved. Please let the past fall away from us all like chaff in the wind.*

Miss Beetle sashayed in from a backroom, sparkling in an evening gown and smiling all over the place. Tonight the Langtree brothers insisted she attend not as a maid but as an honored guest— a reward long overdue for her faithful service in the Langtree family.

"My, don't you look gorgeous." Summer gave Miss Beetle a hug.

"You do indeed. Azure blue suits you," Martin said, taking the hand of Miss Beetle and twirling her around.

Miss Beetle moved gracefully with Martin in a few waltz steps. Then she curtseyed and pretended to fan her face.

Summer chuckled.

Miss Beetle grinned. "Now isn't this a great day?" She patted her hands together. "I've been praying for this since the day they left. Tonight isn't just a party, it's a miracle. And as of this moment, it's official. I'm putting in my resignation."

"What?" Martin asked. "Why would you do that? You know you can stay as long as you like."

"Well, I only meant to stay as long as I was needed, and now with this miracle of your dad's return I no longer see the need. And I believe your momma won't be far behind. You'll see."

"What can I say to make you change your mind?"

"Not a thing, but it makes me happy that you'd like me to stay on. And I do appreciate that large bonus." Miss Beetle raised her dress a mite, and a pair of shimmery spike heels peeked out from under the hem. "That's how I bought these Cinderella slippers."

"Wow," Summer said. "Lots of style."

"But I didn't give you that bonus." Martin smiled. "You can thank Ivan and Desmond."

Miss Beetle gave Martin a slow, knowing nod. "I'll be sure and do that."

"But where will you go? Do you have another job set up?" Martin asked. "You know you'll get an excellent reference from us."

Miss Beetle put a hand on her hip. "Well, here's the deal. I've been housekeeping for so long, and I have enough good business sense, that I thought I might start up my own little company. Maybe I'll call it Spitspot Housekeeping Services." She wiggled her eyebrows. "Got a nice ring to it, eh?"

Martin pulled Miss Beetle into a hug. "You sure will be missed more than you know." He eased back. "I know you'll do well with your business, but if you ever need anything, please let me know. The Langtrees owe you a great deal, so we want to make sure your company succeeds."

"Thank you, Mr. Martin."

"You're welcome. But I'm no longer your employer, so now you'll have to call me Martin." He smiled.

Miss Beetle patted him on the arm. "Martin. Thank you. I know—"

At that moment, the doorbell rang.

Summer's stomach lurched. Must be Martin's dad, since he was to arrive early.

Ivan and Desmond rushed out of the kitchen, and with light feet and a quick step, they made their way toward the front door.

Ivan straightened his jacket and opened the door to Edward Langtree. The older man was dressed in celebratory finery and he seemed more contented than when she'd met him the week before.

If Martin's dad had worried that there would be angry words hurled at him or condemning looks—he could have put his weary heart to rest. The brothers had decided that all queries would be answered in the proper time, but first should come mercy—a season of open arms. So the moment the elder Langtree stepped over the threshold—he was surrounded only by love. Summer saw it was surely a thing of beauty the way God had prepared all of them for that special moment.

Summer took a step or two back from the family huddle, long enough to breathe a prayer of thanksgiving. What unexpected wonder had come from the stirring hand of providence as well as from that divinely appointed list. There had been a homecoming of grand proportion, there had been the gift of forgiveness given all around, and there would be, come midsummer, a wedding between two very old friends.

CHAPTER
thirty-eight

Martin waited at the bottom of the grand staircase in the Langtree home for his bride to appear at the top of the stairs. If he was nervous, it was only because he was awestruck by the thought of marrying Summer Snow. He smoothed his tux and took a whiff of his boutonniere to calm himself.

Martin exchanged smiles with Summer's pastor, who was officiating the ceremony, then with Ivan and Desmond, his two groomsmen, and Summer's attendants, Amelia and Miss Beetle. Martin was glad Summer had wanted a more intimate wedding, since it seemed appropriate to use the occasion to allow for more healing and bonding.

While he waited for the imminent arrival of his beloved, Martin took one more look at the nook just below the staircase. There on a marble-topped pedestal, and on constant display, was the infamous vase that had fallen and broken into pieces. Ivan had restored the heirloom using his artistic talents, by mending it back together using a special resin that was mixed with real gold. The gilded veins throughout the vase made it even more beautiful. The heirloom was no longer worth anything monetarily, and yet it had become a family treasure, because of what it represented. What was hidden had now become known. What was broken was now—by the grace of God—made whole again.

And then it happened—the moment he'd waited for—Summer appeared at the top of the stairs. Martin became transfixed. Yes, there she stood, shimmering like the sun sparkling on a silver sea. He was more than happy to be captivated by the splendor of Summer Snow. The thought that such a golden-hearted woman actually loved him and wanted to spend the rest of her life with him was incomprehensible. But it was something he was willing to embrace in spite of its great mystery.

Edward Langtree stood next to Summer at the top of the stairs. He'd said he would be honored to stand in as her father and be the one to escort the bride. Much of his father's gaunt and ailing appearance from the previous weeks had improved, and his look of despair had lessened considerably. In fact, today he seemed eager and filled with joy.

When the pianist began to play, Summer and his father made their slow descent down the staircase. She wore a long flowing gown with an even longer train. Something she called a cathedral veil. All Martin knew was that the wedding dress made her look like royalty. A princess.

Summer smiled down at him, and in that moment, well, all the rest of the world fell away.

EPILOGUE

Summer tossed her North Face jacket on the bed and pulled back the curtains to their sumptuous honeymoon suite at the Grand Hotel. The picture window overlooked a turquoise lake at the foot of the snow-capped Rockies. *Spectacular.* "I can't get over this, Martin. You must have paid a fortune for this room."

"Doesn't matter." Martin stepped over to the window and gazed out at the view with her. "I wanted us to do something very different. I'm glad you like it."

Summer took in more of the view as she tugged on her earlobe.

"I know you've got something special on your mind when I see you doing that."

"I was just thinking how happy I am. But maybe I should show you instead." She took hold of Martin's lapels, eased him down to her lips, and gave him a hearty kiss he wouldn't soon forget.

"I'll endeavor to always make you that happy," he promised.

Summer smiled. "I wouldn't have imagined that hiking the Canadian Rockies up to a glacier would be such fun. But with you it's been the most incredible adventure of a lifetime. Thank you."

"You're so welcome."

"I'm not used to seeing snow, but experiencing it in the summertime, well, it's magical."

"That's the reason I brought you here," Martin said. "I wanted you to see snow in summer."

"Are you the most amazing guy, or what?"

Martin nodded as if giving the matter serious study. "Maybe I am."

Summer chuckled as he took her into his arms. Then she closed her eyes—and on each lid, he kissed her softly.

He looked at her then—with such love—that it made Summer's heart speed up and her eyes mist over. *Goodness gracious.* How that man could make her giddy.

"I have prepared a speech, my love," he whispered in her hair.

"I can't wait to hear it."

Martin released her, and she sat down on the bed. She slapped her legs in a drum roll. "Okay, I'm ready."

Martin threw his shoulders back. "You are like the most unique phenomenon of nature."

"Tell me more." Ever since Martin had gotten the hang of compliments, it had become a favorite pastime to come up with little tributes to her.

"You, Summer, are mysterious and beautiful, like the nighttime ocean beach when it lights up with electric blue."

"Electric blue?" Summer smiled playfully. "Come on. You're making that one up."

"No. I promise I'm not. It really can light up from the glowing plankton."

"Now how did I not know that?" Summer grinned. "Okay. Go on. This is even better than the truffles you bought me."

"You are wonderful and rare," Martin went on to say, "like the frost flowers that float on the icy waters of the Arctic. Like the moon-bow that arches across the sky. And well, you're as rare as . . . summer snow."